Diversion Books
A Division of Diversion Publishing Corp.
443 Park Avenue South, Suite 1008
New York, New York 10016
www.DiversionBooks.com

This is a work of fiction. Names, characters, places and incidents either are the
product of the author's imagination or are used fictitiously. Any resemblance to
actual persons, living or dead, events or locales is entirely coincidental.

For more information, email info@diversionbooks.com

First Diversion Books edition June 2015.
Print ISBN: 978-1-62681-701-2
eBook ISBN: 978-1-62681-700-5

both sides now

a novel

BARBARA FERRER

DIVERSIONBOOKS

To Lewis, who never lets me stop believing.

To my twinling, who kicks me
whenever it seems as if I might need it.
Which is a lot of the time.

You love me for no other end
Than to become my confidant and friend;
As such I keep no secret from your sight.

—Dryden

Author's Note

References to treatments and medications were kept deliberately vague not out of laziness or a lack of research, but rather, from a deep respect for the fact that each individual's experience is profoundly unique and different. With treatments and methods of diagnosis constantly evolving, what's commonplace now could well be archaic in less than five years' time. If this book is ever to become obsolete, I want it to be because cancer, itself, has been conquered and no longer exists.

Prelude

I'd love to say the knock was completely unexpected—but I'd be lying. Opening the door, I stood aside so he could walk past me into the hotel room.

"You should be resting." Even though I knew he'd been sleeping most of the day, his eyes still maintained that sunken, ill look, and I could feel the mild heat of his lingering fever as he brushed past me. His red-rimmed eyes flickered over toward the turned-down bed and back at me. Silently, I nodded and disappeared into the bathroom. After I was done, I left the light on but pulled the door almost completely closed, allowing a thin sliver to shine through as illumination. He was in bed, already half asleep, by the looks of it, his lids appearing heavier with each slow blink. Drowsy though it was, his gaze still followed my progress around the room as I closed my laptop, turned off the television and the various lights, and finally, when I didn't have anything else I *could* do, untied my robe, revealing an oversized and decidedly unsexy sleep shirt.

It was almost as if he was staying awake to make certain I really was going to slip into bed next to him—the answer to his unspoken question.

He'd lost the sweatshirt he'd been wearing when he entered the room, although he still wore a thin T-shirt. I knew, too, even though the sheets and blanket were pulled to his chest, that he'd also lost the sweatpants. My hand resting on the bedside lamp, we studied each other. A hollow feeling took over my stomach as I realized that, unlike last night—when I'd slept on top of the covers—tonight, I'd be feeling all of him against me—no barriers.

Somehow, that seemed so much more intimate than sex itself.

Turning off that final light, I swung my legs into bed, not surprised to feel the sheets and blanket being smoothed over my body as I settled against the pillows.

"I thought I was supposed to be taking care of you."

He curved himself around me, chest to back, fronts of his thighs solid and warm against the backs of mine as his arm settled over my stomach. "You are."

His lips only barely brushed against the sensitive skin of my ear, his voice little more than a hoarse whisper, but both vibrated through my body in a gentle, comforting hum.

Settling myself more closely into the cradle of his body, learning the contours, the textures, even the smells, I sighed. "I've missed this the most, you know."

"Me too." Seconds later, his breathing settled into a steady, deep rhythm, with only an occasional, lingering rattle vibrating through his chest. Waiting only long enough to reassure myself he really was asleep, I let myself go, falling into the best sleep I'd enjoyed in…I don't know, months, years, maybe?

I should've felt appalled. Maybe ashamed.

Neither.

All I felt was relief.

Libby
AUGUST 29

"Look, Libby—fresh meat."

At Nan's offhand comment, I glanced up from the magazine I was thumbing through.

"Ten bucks says he passes out," Marilyn offered, her thin face lighting up.

"Doesn't look like a fainter," Nan replied. "But twenty says his breakfast goes."

I sighed. "Honestly, you are *such* a pair of ghouls."

Not like I should have been surprised, though. Nan and Marilyn spent most of their waiting room time placing bets against each other. Sporting events, the outcome of soap opera story lines, political debates, which doctor was most likely to divorce next, which colleague they were likely to romance in a broom closet—you name it, they bet on it.

But, *really*. Even if gallows humor was what got us through most days, it rarely came at the expense of a newcomer. We'd all been there. And we'd all suffered. Each of us in our own ways, some more obviously than others, but no question, we'd *all* suffered. Tossing the magazine aside, I crossed to the waiting room's water dispenser, grabbed a paper cup, and pressed the lever until it was full.

"Come on now, bebe, you know we mean no harm." Nan dropped into one of the surprisingly comfortable easy chairs, curiosity having given way to her normal placid expression.

"That's right, Libby," Marilyn added, looking apologetic. "Guess we just got carried away—someone new coming in, especially now with Ben gone."

It got quiet there for a minute, except for the soft click of the beads as Marilyn automatically began a rosary. Ben was gone because his wife had finally given up, succumbing to the pancreatic cancer that was as aggressive and mean as my *abuela* on a bad day. Poor Ben. Viv had only been in her early fifties and otherwise healthy, not to mention stubborn as hell. That iron will of hers had allowed him to believe she had a good shot at recovery. And because he'd believed, she'd fought even harder, until the reserves were drained and she just couldn't anymore.

He'd looked so damn lost at the funeral last month.

Not all that different from the expression on our newcomer's face down the hall. Lost and bewildered, like he couldn't quite wrap his brain around what he was hearing. The fact that he was even here meant he'd already heard a lot, but it was a whole different ballgame when you were standing in the sterile hallway of an oncology unit as opposed to the more personal—and private—environs of a doctor's office. And as he stood there listening to the doctor, lost and bewildered gave way to a grief that seemed to visibly age him. Boy, did I know that expression. Intimately.

"Give the guy a chance—let him settle in."

"God, I hope he doesn't," Nan sighed, the softening of her voice intensifying the French-Canadian lilt that thirty-odd years in South Florida hadn't managed to completely eradicate.

"That'd be nice." I studied the exchange between Dr. Aguirre and our new arrival, waiting for a good moment. "Maybe he'll be one of the lucky ones."

I tried to paste on a smile as I approached, but it was hard. I didn't come naturally by Nan's gift of being able to switch emotional gears, and it'd already been a rough morning with Ethan. This was probably the last thing I needed to be doing, edgy as I was, but with the way the Ghoul Squad was carrying on, I was the safest bet as today's welcome wagon.

"Libby, ¿*qué tal, mi vida?*"

"*Hola,* Marco." I offered my cheek for his kiss, feeling my smile relax into something more genuine as I caught sight of the startled expression on our newcomer's face. It came as a shock to most people, the level of informality they encountered here, even with the doctors. A lot of it came from this tangible sense of being comrades in arms, the lines between the hierarchies blurred into near-nonexistence—a sense aided by the casual atmosphere. There were potted palms scattered throughout the various waiting areas, a radio at the nurse's station tuned to a salsa station, and at any given hour of the day, a *cafetera* of aromatic Cuban coffee brewed and waiting for anyone who needed the caffeine jolt. The vibe was loose and relaxed and completely different from any hospital I'd ever been in.

But when the shit hit the fan, the staff was kick ass—efficient, tremendously gifted, and completely focused on the cutting-edge treatments that had landed Miami-Flagler Cancer Center on several national "Best Of" lists.

"How'd Ethan do today?"

I shrugged. "Okay." Kept it light—no need to scare our newbie any more than he clearly was. Besides, right now wasn't about me or my husband. Marco's nod let me know he realized I was downplaying and that he'd get the details soon enough. I turned from him and held out the paper cup.

"Hi, I'm Libby. Forgive me if I'm being forward, but it looked like you could use this."

"Thanks." Poor guy's hand trembled as he accepted the cup and drained it in one long swallow.

Marco watched also, his gaze concerned behind half-moon glasses. "Nick, I need to get going, unless you have any other questions?"

"Uh no, I, uh…don't think so. No…*no.*"

Honestly, I wasn't so sure about Nan's assertion that this Nick guy didn't look like a fainter. Even as he spoke, his skin was fading to the sick yellow that passed as pale for people with olive complexions, and his pupils dilated, almost obliterating dark brown irises.

"*Mira, m'ijo,* if you have any questions at all, don't hesitate to ask. If I'm not around, then ask one of the nurses. If they don't have the answer, they can page me." Marco's voice softened. "We're going to do our best for Katharine. *Te lo prometo.*"

"Yeah, thanks."

As Marco walked away, I touched Nick's forearm. The blank expression he turned my way made it clear he'd totally forgotten I was there—if he'd ever even registered my presence at all. Eyes widening, his hand convulsed around the paper cup he still held, crushing it, a few drops spurting out to land on his fist. I watched as a single drop trickled down taut, white-knuckled skin before catching on the edges of a simple gold ring. Katharine was the wife, then. And despite the grief and fright aging him, it was obvious he was even closer to my age than I'd originally imagined and just as shell-shocked as I'd once been, what felt like forever ago. *El pobre.* It was easier then to push aside my rough morning and raw emotions—to focus on the kinship that had already made a tentative appearance, at least on my part.

"Do you need anything else? More water?"

He shook his head, glancing over his shoulder toward the closed door a few feet away. "I need to get back."

"Okay." I patted his arm again. Sometimes, little things like that were what kept you in the here and now. Eventually, he'd get that. "Someone's usually hanging out in the waiting area," I pointed over my shoulder with my free hand, "if you need a break."

Even as he nodded, he began backing away, saying, "Look, I *really* need to get back."

I sighed as I watched him disappear into the room.

"He's going to be tough, isn't he?" Nan's voice came from just behind me.

Studying the closed door I replied, "Yeah. Looks like he'll hole up until he just can't take it anymore."

"Sounds familiar."

"Even I reformed."

"Not until you'd nearly given yourself a nervous breakdown, bebe."

"Yeah, well, nearly doesn't count now, does it."

"No, I suppose it doesn't." Nan tucked her arm through mine, and led me away from the closed door. "So, where shall we go for lunch today?"

• • •

"Get *out*!"

Pain rocketed up my spine as I stared up at Ethan from the floor. Grabbing onto the bedrail, I tried to pull myself back up, but somehow he was able to summon enough strength to shove my hand off before I got completely upright, making me lose my balance and collapse to the floor once more. Fresh bolts of pain shot up my spine and radiated sharp, icy tingles out through both legs and arms.

"Get the fuck out, Libby. Get *out*!" His voice cracked under the strain of his fury—or was it pain? Who could tell the difference anymore?

I dropped my head to my knees, tears hot against my eyelids, but damned if I'd let them fall. Wouldn't do either of us any good. Taking a deep breath, I reached instead for a nearby chair, hauling myself to my feet.

"It's bad today," Corrine observed, as she pulled the covers back over Ethan's chest.

I nodded at the nurse, not trusting myself to speak.

"Stop talking like I'm not here. I just want to be alone, dammit. Didn't you hear me, Libby? Alone."

I didn't move. Not because I was ignoring him, but because I was simply watching as Corrine went about her duties, taking care of my husband. Kept my gaze fixed on him, even though his painful thinness, obvious even beneath the loose T-shirt he wore, twisted through me like a knife digging a sharp path between my ribs, right through to my heart.

Always did. Never mind that Ethan had always veered more toward rangy and lean than broad-chested. Never mind that it had been long enough since he'd been himself physically that I should've been more than used to seeing him like this. Or at the very least, numb to it. I wasn't. Didn't want to be. Even though the alternative—constantly acknowledging all those changes—hurt so damn much.

No sooner than the covers were up over his chest than he was flinging them off again, tubes flailing. "Don't want the goddamn covers, don't want water, don't want anything. Get out." His bright blue eyes were wild and unfocused, lips pulled back from his teeth, his entire demeanor that of a cornered animal.

"Honey, you're probably better off going," Corrine said, leading me toward the door. "I'll look over his chart and page Dr. Aguirre— see what might've set him off."

"We tried a new cocktail this morning—he seemed fine before I went to lunch."

"Sometimes it takes a while before the side effects kick in. We'll get some extra Ativan in him—try to settle him down."

Again I nodded. What else was I going to do? Stay? Not as if I was exactly helping Ethan right now. When the anxiety grabbed hold like this—when it exacerbated the agony and the fear—there wasn't a damn thing I could do. A final glance over my shoulder revealed him staring after me.

"Go, Libby." Said much softer—pleading really. And another piece broke off my heart. Even after all this time, after all we'd been through, he still hated my seeing him like this.

Outside the room I rubbed the back of my neck and breathed deep. "Call if he wants me?" I said to Corrine who'd followed me out.

"You know we will, honey. But why don't you go on and get some rest? You look like you need it."

Yeah. Rest. Right. But what else was I going to do? The theme of my life for the past couple years—doing what others felt would be best for Ethan or best for me. Best for both of us. It was possible some day I'd be able to reclaim the right to decide these things for myself. At the moment, however, it seemed like an unattainable luxury.

I nodded again, punched the elevator button, stepped in, rode down to the second floor, and took the walkway across the street to the parking garage. I climbed into the Volvo station wagon we'd bought only because it was low to the ground and had room for Ethan's walker or wheelchair—whichever he might need on any given day—exited the garage then drove the short distance along Alton Road to the hotel I stayed at every time Ethan had overnights at the hospital.

Thank God for that drive. Thank God for Las Palmas, the hotel with which the hospital had an arrangement. I'd learned early on that I *needed* the distance from the hospital—needed the time to myself. And, even though I was ashamed to admit it, needed some time and distance from Ethan.

This time though, the drive that was usually just long enough for me to pull myself together after a bad day wasn't anywhere near long enough. So I pulled into a secluded parking space, sat in the car, and blasted the stereo loud enough that I couldn't hear myself crying and screaming into my arms, which were crossed over the steering wheel. Finally, I took a final, shaky breath, wiped my face, blew my nose, and headed into the hotel.

"*¿Señora Walker, comó estás?*"

So tempting to reply, "Like shit, and you?" but I didn't. Carlos was being nice and didn't deserve my snarly mood. So I just murmured some inanity as I signed the registration slip and accepted my key card.

"Would you like me to have some tea sent up? *¿Alomejor un tacito de café?*"

I glanced up from returning the credit card to my wallet. "*No, gracias*, Carlos."

"*Bueno*, just let us know if there's anything you need."

A smile—I could manage a small one. "Thanks." Could go now. Could escape.

I gathered my things, turned—and stopped. This morning's newcomer stood just inside the lobby doors with a bewildered expression on his face like he had some faint idea of where he was, but no clue how he'd gotten there.

A sense of déjà vu swept over me.

Leave it be, Libby. Just... leave it. The day's been crap enough.

Right. As if I could.

My sneakers made only the faintest noise on the blue-veined marble tiles—an awareness that had me ever-so-cautiously reaching out to touch his forearm. Just like back at the hospital.

"Hi—Nick, right?"

Blank. Those eyes were two dark, blank holes in an equally blank face. I sighed and wondered why the hell I even tried.

Because the others tried with you. And kept trying. And it saved your ass.

"I'm sorry, do I—"

"No." I cut him off before he could finish. Making an effort to gentle my tone, I added, "I'm sorry I bothered you." It was only a little white lie. He didn't know me. From experience, I knew he wouldn't remember much at all about this day—much less two brief encounters. Lifting my backpack to my shoulder, I turned to resume my path to the elevators.

"Wait. The hospital. This morning—"

I stopped, turned my head a fraction, just far enough to catch a glimpse of him from the corner of my eye.

"You gave me water."

I turned more fully. "Yeah, that was me."

"I...I'm sorry." He stood there, looking miserable and defeated and thoroughly lost.

"First days are hell." I shrugged and shifted my backpack higher onto my shoulder. "Anything outside of your doctor and your wife is bound to fade to decorative wallpaper status."

His eyes widened, black brows rising. "How'd you—"

"Educated guess."

Dammit, there he went, going that sort of sick sort of yellow as he realized what I meant by "educated."

Smooth move, Libby. Give the man more to stress over. He's just trying to get through one wretched day and now you've got him fixating on just how long this might take. How much more miserable shit he might learn.

"I'm sorry, that was insensitive of me."

"No. It's okay." His head dropped as he shoved a hand through his hair, making it stick up in wild spikes and cowlicks. "There's just so much…it's all so…"

Overwhelming. Horrible. Nightmarish on a level that couldn't be comprehended unless you'd been there. Yeah, I knew. And he didn't want a damn bit of it. Been there, done that, had the free bumper sticker that came with the initiation package. But I was tired, and as much as I owed the newest member of our involuntary club a little of the same pay-it-forward I'd been granted when I'd stood quaking in his shoes, I simply couldn't. Not today.

"Well, I guess I'd better let you get checked in." I managed one more nice, noncommittal smile.

"Wait—um…dinner? What do you do?"

He remained frozen in that same spot, cloaked in an almost palpable misery.

"You're not having dinner at the hospital?"

His eyes closed, and I could see the muscles of his throat working as if swallowing around something hard. Opening them, he said, "Katharine's been really sick today. And when she hasn't, she's been asleep. They told me I'd do her more good by getting some rest. Come back later and maybe by then she'd be up for a short visit."

They'd told me the same thing my first day. Did I leave? Hell, no. I'd been stubborn and stayed. When I hadn't held vigil over Ethan's bed, I'd parked myself against the vending machines, eating bag after bag of Fritos and stale Hostess cupcakes, washing them down with Diet Dr. Pepper until I finally got good and sick myself, barely making it to a bathroom to throw all of it back up before collapsing in a defeated heap on the waiting area sofa. Just by being here, Nick was already proving to be brighter than I'd been. Good for him. Even if he didn't know quite what to do with himself. *I* was planning on a shower, room service, and sitting and just being quiet.

Wasn't going to happen, was it?

I sighed and took him in again. Despite the grays peppering jet-black hair and the fact that he was this big, athletic looking guy, there was something about his overall demeanor that suggested a lost child. A very tired, very frightened child. And once again, I felt that subtle, tentative thread of kinship. One I couldn't ignore. Not and be able to live with myself afterward. Damned karma.

"Would you like to grab something to eat?"

There was an audible rattle as he took in a shaky breath. "I...I thought I wanted to be alone."

I'd already let him off the hook—just in the asking—but as Nan had observed earlier, he was going to be tough. "Honestly, it's better if you're not." I offered the advice gently, not certain how he'd take additional evidence of long experience. "But at the same time, you should get some rest. Couple hours? Then we can meet back down here?"

Admittedly, not an altogether altruistic suggestion on my part, not with the crying jag I could feel hovering around the edges. This Nick's dilemma was scraping against some genuinely exposed nerves today, his misery rubbing against mine with the coarse, gritty rasp of sandpaper. But I couldn't take my offer back. Not with the way he was smiling—or trying to, at least.

"Okay, couple hours, then, uh—" He stopped, his mouth slightly open as if hoping what was missing would somehow magically jump off his tongue. And while he didn't blush, not even the faintest hint of pink, the skin around his eyes visibly tightened, like the muscles were cringing in shame.

I released the handle of my rolling overnighter, feeling the blood rush toward my fingertips as the muscles relaxed. Offering my hand I said, "Libby. Libby Walker."

A short breath escaped him as I said my name. "You told me that at the hospital, didn't you?"

"Well, not the Walker part."

"Still...I'm sorry."

"You can stop saying that. I promise, I understand."

He still appeared to be doing a little mental berating as he said,

"Nick Azarias."

The lilt and roll he put on his surname clued me in on how to respond as his hand closed around mine. "*Un placer*, Nick."

"Thank you." His fingers tightened and he released a deep breath. "*Y el placer es mío.*"

Nick

"I thought I wanted to be alone."

"It's better if you're not..."

I kept curling and uncurling my fingers around the room's door handle. The metal, which had started out icy from the air conditioner, was warm and slick beneath my palm. How long *had* I been standing here, like some indecisive jackass?

She didn't want to go. There wasn't a lot I was seeing today outside of Katharine and her pain, but I'd seen that this Libby—and what the hell kind of name was that anyhow?—didn't really want to get something to eat with me. But she was nice. She'd brought me water. Had offered reassurance that it was okay. That I was allowed to be blank and thick and fucking stupid.

Hell, she knew I could barely remember meeting her at the hospital. Didn't stop her from coming over and talking to me downstairs. From offering to go to dinner with me, and I wasn't sure why. All she wanted was to hide out in her room, order food she wasn't going to eat—

Cry until she was sick.

Scared the shit right out of me—that I recognized that—because, clearly, she was a vet. Who knows for how long, but she definitely knew what it was all about and still, she felt like that. There was no way—I couldn't take it.

Jesus. Listen to me. *I* couldn't take it. I wasn't taking shit, unless you considered watching my wife having poison blasted into her body to cure another poison as taking anything.

How did she do it?

This Libby woman—how *did* she take it?

That's what finally prompted me to turn the handle, step out into the hall, and head for the elevator. What had me pushing the button and compelled me to cross the lobby floor to the palm-lined sitting area.

She wasn't there.

At least, I didn't think so. I was having a hard time remembering what she looked like—as a whole picture, at any rate. Only out of sheer habit and years of training in noticing details could I recall at least a few little things. Like her touch on my arm. Her hand had been warm and firm, but gentle too, as if she were afraid to scare me.

She had a nice smile, and as she'd turned away, I'd noticed that her hair was pulled back in a long, dark braid that made me feel sick to my stomach because Kath's hair was long and thick and beautiful and was going to start falling out any time now. She was being so brave and amazing about it, saying it was just hair and now she could try all those tacky wigs she saw in magazines. But I'd heard the forced cheer that only just masked the pain. It wasn't just her hair. It was everything.

Madre de Dios, why Kath? Why now?

I needed to get back to the hospital. No matter what they said. What if Katharine needed me? What if she—

"Hey."

I closed my eyes at the disappointment—and relief.

Turning, I found Libby standing a few feet behind me. She looked fresher. Another detail—she'd changed clothes. But come to think of it—oh man, I didn't want to make it obvious.

"You're wearing a clean shirt."

I glanced down. A T-shirt instead of the wrinkled polo I vaguely remembered. "I…uh…wasn't sure, actually."

"I know." One corner of her mouth eased up. "I never pack anything that's too similar. Makes it too easy to mistake yesterday's shirt for today's. Next thing you know, you smell like stale coffee and the cafeteria's Tuna Noodle Special."

"Right." I made a mental note of the advice.

The faint smile disappeared, but her demeanor seemed a little… looser, I guess. "I also don't ever bring anything terribly dressy," she said, gesturing vaguely at her khaki shorts and T-shirt. "There's no real reason, you know?"

I nodded but couldn't think of anything to say.

"Most everything around here's casual, too."

I nodded again, kind of feeling like one of those stupid bobblehead dolls we'd give away on fan appreciation nights.

"Casual's my favorite kind." Hell, I wasn't hungry. Just didn't want to be alone. I may have thought it's what I wanted, but honestly, the last thing I wanted was solitude. I did, however, want a stiff drink.

"Great place a few blocks away." Her eyes narrowed as she continued to study me. "Good bar selection. Close enough to walk."

And not have to drive. She was starting to scare me. "Lead on."

It wasn't until we were standing on a corner, waiting for the light to change, that she spoke again. "Was Harbor House full?"

Harbor House…Harbor House…. It *sounded* familiar, but so much of today was a blur. *Harbor House….* Finally, it clicked into place—the facility adjacent to the hospital for families.

"No, they had room. I just didn't—I couldn't…"

Jesus, how could I say I had to get away from the hospital without sounding like a total dick?

I was saved from saying anything by the tricked-out vintage Impala that pulled up to the intersection, bass thumping. I could swear, though, that beneath the throbbing bass, I heard a quiet, "smart guy."

We headed down a long, partially blocked-off thoroughfare that seemed to be just one unbroken line of shops and restaurants.

"What is this?"

"Lincoln Road Mall." She glanced up as she maneuvered us around gawking tourists and kids on skateboards. "I take it you're not familiar?"

I shook my head slowly. "We—" My throat closed around the word like a vise. Taking a deep breath, I tried again. "We live up in

Boca—near Kath's job. Since I work in Coral Springs, it's convenient for both of us." That was better. I'd at least recovered enough to make it past her name without tripping.

If Libby noticed my verbal slip, she didn't say anything. Leading us down a side street, she paused in front of a bright red door that stood propped open despite temps that had to be ninety plus, even this late in the day. As we crossed the threshold, though, we were slammed with the icy chill common to every South Florida interior in August.

"Only down here," I observed as we followed the hostess's vague wave to seat ourselves anywhere. Libby glanced away from the chalkboard with the day's specials scrawled on it in English, Spanish, and… Chinese. *Coño*, there was something I hadn't seen in a long, long time.

"What? The arctic air conditioner/open door combo or," she waved at the chalkboard, "that?"

"The first."

"So Cuban-Chinese doesn't throw you but air-conditioning and open doors does?"

I grinned at the flood of memories. "There were some fantastic restaurants in the city back in the day. Unfortunately, I think a lot of them are gone now."

"The city? Where exactly are you from, then, Nick Azarias? Since I'm getting the distinct vibe it's not from around here."

Shifting my study from the chalkboard to the bar, I replied, "Jersey. Close enough to New York that I saw more than a few of those." I gestured at the trilingual menu. "Although I've lived in Florida for over ten years. " I turned back to look at her. "You?"

"Born and bred in the Keys—still live down there." She smiled; an instant later, her expression turned serious. "So what's your poison?"

No question there—it was a tequila sort of night. "Patrón Silver, double straight up," I said to the waiter who'd appeared with glasses of water and a basket with a long row of saltines and a plastic tub of dip.

"Forget the double. Just bring the bottle, a lot of lime, and two glasses." Her tone was so casual, the words took a second to register. She cocked her head and smiled again, but it still retained a trace of serious. Grim, even. "What? You didn't think I was going to let you get ripped by yourself, did you?" She calmly spread some dip over a cracker and held it out. "Put something in your stomach. Not too much though, because they pretty much frown on those who hurl all over the floors. Seeing as it's one of my favorite restaurants, I'd kind of like to not be banned."

My fingers grazed hers, the cracker suspended between us as our gazes met. "I know how to drink."

Her gaze never leaving mine, she released the cracker and reached into the basket for another, spreading dip across the surface. "Do you know how to drink after a day like today?" Her eyebrows rose as she eyed the cracker I held.

"Not a fucking clue," I said with a long sigh before biting into the cracker. What do you want to bet she also knew I didn't have squat in my stomach? Tequila against bare stomach lining? Not such a good idea. Again and again, she was right—this Libby.

"What kind of name is Libby?"

Man, that came out belligerent. Not at all what I'd intended, but like every other goddamn thing, I couldn't seem to control what I was saying or how it came out sounding. But either she didn't hear it that way, or, more likely, chose to ignore it. All she did was smile at our waiter as he deposited a bottle, glasses, and a bowl of cut limes. Pouring us each a shot, she licked the top of her hand, shook salt, licked again, swallowed the tequila, and bit down on a wedge of lime in a rapid, sequence that was so graceful, all I could do was sit there and stare.

"I wasn't named after canned corn, if that's what you're asking." She pushed my shot glass closer, watching as I echoed her movements.

God*damn*, but the burn felt good. Felt unbelievable sliding down my throat and landing in my stomach, all liquid heat. Grabbing the bottle, I poured our second round.

"Well, can you blame me for wondering?" I swallowed my second shot, closing my eyes against the sting. Opening them, I said, "You're the only person I've ever met with that name."

Pausing in the midst of shaking salt on her hand, she looked up. "At one time it was a pretty common derivation of Elizabeth."

She held my gaze as she swallowed her shot and, for the first time, I noticed her eyes. Not so much the color as the condition. Red-rimmed, maybe a little puffy—and all of a sudden I was hit with a stark, vivid recollection of standing in front of the bathroom mirror, dispassionately studying my reflection. I'd stood there for I don't know how long, taking in the bloodshot puffiness of my eyes, the dark angry circles beneath, until finally, I'd leaned down into the sink and splashed water on my face until my shirt was soaked through.

That's why I'd changed.

"Nick?"

I blinked, losing the image in the mirror and coming back to the restaurant, to this table, where Libby was sitting across from me, looking concerned. "Uh…sorry."

"It's okay."

She poured us each a third shot, filling the glasses to the brim. I wondered about the wisdom of a third shot so quickly, but…fuck it. Reaching for the saltshaker, I tried to pick up the thread of our conversation. "So, why not go with Liz or Beth or one of the more common nicknames?"

The corner of her mouth eased up in that small half smile. "All I said was that it was once a common derivation of Elizabeth."

I lowered the saltshaker to the table and waited.

Gaze fixed on the table, she said, "Liberty," in a quiet voice. Lifting her head, she met my gaze head on. "My full name is Liberty Estrella Santos Walker. I am the spawn of the only Cuban hippies known to mankind. Or at least, known to me." She sighed and reached for her third shot, tossing it back, no salt, no lime, *nada*.

Damn, but I was glad I'd decided against that third shot. Because it would've been genuinely rude to spew tequila all over the one person keeping me from coming completely unhinged.

Just then, our waiter made a reappearance. I found myself pushing my still full shot glass and the bottle toward the waiter— I'd had enough. I did order a Corona, though. Hated to waste all the lime.

After Libby echoed my request for a Corona and we both placed our orders, silence fell. It wasn't particularly uncomfortable or anything, but at the same time, I felt this itch to keep the conversation going, to keep talking—anything to keep my brain from going into overdrive. Seconds stretched into minutes until I finally couldn't take it anymore and blurted the first thing that came to mind.

"So—Cuban hippies?"

She sighed and reached for another cracker. "Yep."

"That's…different."

"You have *no* idea." And while she smiled, she didn't elaborate any further, instead staring out the restaurant's wide window. Well, so much for that. At least there was one of those triangle-shaped golf peg games on the table I could fidget with. And after the waiter brought our beers, I had the bottle to hold. A label to pick at, even though it was normally a habit that drove me batshit.

"You know, we really don't have to talk if you don't want."

I glanced up from shredding paper to find her studying me. "I want." I took a sip of beer—forced a small smile. "Seriously, this is too good to pass up."

"All right then." She smiled again—knew I was grasping at anything that would keep me hanging on.

"My mother was—is—the Cuban hippy." She shook her head and rolled her beer bottle between her palms. "My father is your garden variety gringo hippy tinged with Jack Kerouac beatnik aspirations, which means he spends most of his time wandering the country on a beat up Indian motorcycle that he keeps put together with some combination of baling wire, chewing gum, and spit, and working in an ever-expanding variety of indie-slash-organic-slash-Fair Trade coffee shops where he can shoot the shit over the latest draft of his Great American Novel with other aspiring Great American novelists. From time to time, he makes his way back down to Marathon so he can stop in and visit the old lady, and, yeah, they're still utterly, irrevocably together."

God—my upbringing was so goddamn boring by comparison. "Come on, you can't stop there," I urged as the waiter reappeared with our meals.

Lifting the lid on a covered dish of *maduros*, she said, "You honestly can't want to know more about this, can you?"

"Are you kidding? Come on, I come from your basic, straightforward Cuban family—living *la vida* American Dream complete with mortgage, two cars, and just enough assimilation. This is completely beyond the realm of my experience."

"Oh, how often I've wished it was beyond the realm of my experience." She spooned black beans over her rice. "What I wouldn't have given to be living *la vida* American Dream rather than reliving the Age of Aquarius well beyond its expiration date. Can you imagine how mightily it sucked to be me the first day of school? The one day where the teachers read, and, in my case, mangled, your entire name out loud, in front of the whole class?"

I could imagine. Suddenly, Nicolas Miguel Azarias didn't seem so bad.

"There I was, stuck with Liberty Estrella in classrooms teeming with Jennifers and Tammys and Lisas having to explain, *again*, about my name."

Mouth full, I simply raised my eyebrows in question.

She sighed again. "The easy explanation is that my birthday's July fourth."

I swallowed. "And the real explanation?" Because clearly, "easy" did not translate to factual.

"Because it's the day after the anniversary of Jim Morrison's liberation from the earthly chains that bound him or some such bullshit. Estrella to honor his rightful place dancing amongst the stars."

"What does Jim Morrison have to do with you?"

"He's my spiritual father."

"Beg your pardon?"

"This is according to my mother who attended some music festival/memorial orgy *thing* where the plan was to summon the spirits of all those gone too soon in order to keep their gifts alive. Obviously, various psychotropics and herbal—" she paused for an air quote—unnecessary by now "—*remedies* were involved."

"Uh-huh."

"Yeah, I know." She grinned and rolled her eyes good-naturedly. "At any rate, also in attendance during that momentous occasion was—"

"Your dad?"

"Score one for the smart man." She raised her bottle in toast. "In her stoned, sixteen-year-old hippy idiocy, she saw shining within him the spirit of old Jim, climbed on the back of his bike, and took off on an adventure that lasted two years, until she got too big to comfortably ride on the back of the Indian. That's when she came back to Florida and when my nice, middle-class Cuban grandfather had a fit for the ages. Can you imagine what it must have been like for the man? Seeing his former Catholic schoolgirl daughter pregnant out to there and not married, even though Nora kept insisting they'd been married beneath the stars and the heavens and that nature recognized their union, blah, blah, *blah*."

"You call your mother by her first name?" Out of all of that, *that's* what stood out.

"She's barely eighteen years older than I am. Besides, she has this crackpot theory where she sees us as equals." Libby shrugged, although it seemed kind of tight. "Anyhow, after Abuelo had his fit, she took off for a commune of friends down in Marathon. That's where I was born and grew up with Nora and the occasional flyby visits from Stan. My father," she clarified, although by now, I could've guessed.

"And eventually, Nora grew up—as much as she's capable of, at any rate—gave up the communal living when I was about six, for a house where she still lives and makes custom jewelry." She touched one of her ears, nudging the silver hoop with beads forward. "All very natural stuff, of course. Very organic and in tune with a Florida vibe, as she likes to say. Sells her stuff to one of the local boutiques and does pretty good with web-based mail orders. She's got an amazing site."

A full out grin crossed her face. "Now see, there's irony for you—the organic, down-to-earth hippy benefiting from the most modern of technology."

I found myself grinning back. "Hey, if it works for Ben and Jerry—"

"Good point."

"So you've lived there your whole life, then?"

"No." She looked down at her plate, wiping at a stray blob of *mojo* with her finger. "Spent some time in Chicago." And with those words, her whole face transformed. Just…lit up and softened all at the same time.

But before I could ask anything about Chicago, a raucous cheer erupted from the bar area, drawing both of our attention. From the looks of the action on the wall-mounted television, it appeared the Marlins were getting something going.

Glancing from the screen to Libby's rapt expression, I asked, "Do you like sports?"

"I am the most unathletic human on the planet." The edge of her mouth curled up in that half smile as she forked up a bite of pecan pie. "But I'm a *great* fan."

I dug into a slice of Key lime pie I didn't remember ordering, but hell, I wasn't complaining. "Any favorites?"

"Well, baseball," she said with a nod toward the screen, "and figure skating."

"Oh hell no, Libby, not figure skating. That's not a real sport."

"Oh, and *you* can balance on a blade an eighth of an inch wide and not fall on your ass?"

"As a matter of fact, I can, and I don't have to wear sequins to do it," I shot back.

"Ah." Comprehension dawned, lighting up her face.

"Hockey player."

Man, I could feel how cocky my grin was, but it couldn't be helped. "Guilty. At least once upon a time. You know someone who plays?"

She shook her head. "No. But my husband's a lifelong Blackhawks fan." And there went that wistful expression again. Chicago had something to do with her husband. Maybe everything.

After settling our bill, we headed out into the still-stifling heat to make our way back toward the hotel. Night had fallen completely, bringing a whole different vibe to the street, neon and bright lights illuminating the people wandering in and out of art galleries, shops, and restaurants with a cheery pastel glow.

"Feels kind of surreal, doesn't it? The way things just…go on."

"Yeah." Again, I was unnerved as hell by that eerie way she knew things. However, when I glanced down at her, about to finally say something about how cool it was to be able to talk to someone without having to really talk, it became my turn to recognize something without her having to say a word. "Hey, Libby, are you okay?"

"It's nothing." But her body—her expression—said different even as she tried to shrug it off. "I fell earlier today," she confessed. "Smacked the shit out of my tailbone. But it's no big. I'll just force myself to swallow some ibuprofen when we get back and hope to hell I don't lose dinner."

"Ibuprofen shouldn't affect you on a full stomach."

She shook her head. "Not the medicine, the pills. I don't do well taking a lot of pills." She hesitated, then quietly added, "It's kind of a mental thing."

"Can you swallow one big pill?"

"I don't know…maybe."

"I should have eight hundred milligram tabs." Or maybe not. Who knew what the hell I had with me? I hadn't even been sure about clean shirts.

"Really, Nick, it's okay. I'll deal."

"Why should you have to when I've got something that

can help?"

Another ten or so obviously pained steps, and she finally sighed and gave in with a quiet, "Okay, thanks."

Good. Because in those ten steps it had become monumentally important that I help her. I wasn't going to question why it was important—I just knew I needed to.

At my room, I swiped the key card and pushed it open, saying, "Should only take a sec—"

That's when it fell apart. Collapsed, like a house of cards.

Sitting open on the huge king-size bed was my small case, a few precisely folded shirts and my favorite pair of jeans still neatly packed inside. On the bed beside the case was my toiletry kit, filled with all the essentials, including the bottle of ibuprofen I never traveled without and a brand-new toothbrush, still in its pristine, sealed packaging.

It was the last that did me in. That had me dropping into a chair and tilting my head back, staring up at the ceiling and wondering *again*, how the hell were we going to get through this.

A light touch on my forearm had me snapping my head down and meeting Libby's worried gaze. "She packed for me." I barely recognized that hoarse, choked sound as my own voice. "She packed it, even though I told her not to bother, because she always packs for my trips. And like any other trip, I must've opened my bag—changed my shirt. I went out and ate fucking grilled shrimp and Key lime pie."

God, what was I doing? It's not as if I'd forgotten, not really, but at the same time, I had. I'd at least pushed it to the back of my mind. Going out…eating, having what amounted to a good time while Katharine…my wife…my God, she was in the *hospital*, probably puking her guts out.

"Here." Lurching from the chair, I grabbed the bottle of pills and blindly shoved it into Libby's hands as I urged her toward the door. "You have to go, Libby. I'm sorry. You have to—I have to…I need to go back."

"Nick, it's okay—"

"No, goddammit, it's *not* okay." For the first time, something she said wasn't right. Pissed me off to a point where I saw red. "It's not okay and you should know that, Libby. Just go, *please*. Go." I shoved her past the threshold and pushed the door closed behind her, unable to hear whether or not it clicked shut over my heaving and gasping into the toilet I barely made it to in time.

Nick

I never made it back to the hospital that night. Had every intention of going—but I couldn't. I was so afraid of what Kath might see. Of what I might see. All I could do was haul myself off the floor and stagger to the chair beside the window where I sat staring out into the night until my eyes felt gritty, and my throat felt clogged and raw with the tears I couldn't release. At some point, I yanked off my damp shirt and fell across the bed in my shorts, not bothering to deal with the covers or even make certain I landed with my head on the pillows. Just let the exhaustion take over and swallow me whole.

As a result, the next morning, I had cotton mouth the likes of which I hadn't had since college, accompanied by the mother of all headaches that even all the hot water at my disposal couldn't alleviate. But it wasn't until I went to reach for one of my pain pills that it really hit me.

No doubt about it, I was an insensitive prick for forgetting about Kath's agony for a couple of hours, but the way I'd treated Libby? That was complete asshole territory. The woman had been nothing but good to me, and I'd repaid her kindness by losing my shit and kicking her out.

Complete and total asshole.

"Front desk, how may I help you, Mr. Azarias?"

My hand fisted in the bedspread. "Yes, uh, can I be connected to Mrs. Walker's room? Libby Walker?"

"I'm sorry sir, she checked out this morning."

"Shit," I muttered under my breath.

"Excuse me?"

"Nothing—sorry. Thanks." I shoved my hand through my hair.

The receiver was halfway to the cradle before I realized the clerk was still talking—"Excuse me, what?"

"I said, sir, that she left a message for you."

"Yeah?" Well, why hadn't the *cabrón* said so from the start?

"It will be waiting for you down here, Mr. Azarias."

Oh, a real message. Right. Hanging up, I finished getting ready, feeling another stab as I unwrapped the toothbrush and pulled my favorite toothpaste from the bag. Kath hadn't forgotten anything. She never did; she was so unbelievably efficient. Part of what had made her so successful—Not *had*, dammit. Just, made. Makes.

Downstairs at the desk, Carlos, the concierge, gave me a small manila envelope with a bulge in it. A suspiciously pill bottle-shaped bulge. Sighing, I ripped it open and upended it over the counter. Yep. Just as expected, my bottle of ibuprofen. Unexpected was the note that slid out behind the bottle.

> *I wanted to make certain you got these back. Thank you so much—it really helped. I hope you don't mind, but I took one more to have for the drive home today.*
>
> *Thanks again,*
> *Libby*
>
> *P.S. If you need anything, don't hesitate to ask any of the gang hanging around in the waiting area. Nan, she'll be the lady with the blonde hair and slight French accent (except do not refer to her as French—she's Canadian and crazy-proud of it), she's got it more together than I ever could. She was my saving grace those first couple months.*
>
> *Please take care*
> *—L.*

You'd think I'd have been relieved not to see her again. To have an excuse to not see her again. And maybe I was, for about five seconds. But while I've never had a problem being an asshole to other guys, with a woman... *Mira*, it's different. I'm just Cuban enough that that kind of behavior really bugs me. Not to mention, made me feel like my mother and my *abuelitas* and my three sisters were all hovering over me, each of them taking turns smacking me upside the head.

I read the note over once again. *"Please take care."* Even from a distance she was offering reassurance.

"How long ago did she check out?"

Dude's gaze flickered down to the bottle of pills still on the counter, then back to me. I knew that look—assessing, checking out, top to bottom to see if there's something of worth beneath the surface. I knew *that* look like I knew my own name. Just wasn't something I was used to being on the receiving end of. However, this wasn't my usual turf, and I couldn't count on an automatic answer. Finally, though, he said, "Less than an hour ago."

It took longer than that to check someone out of the hospital. Even if it was a regular thing. At least, that's what I was betting on as I drove toward the hospital, anxiety leaving my hands sweating and slipping on the steering wheel. Anxiety that stemmed from more than just wanting to make things right with Libby. Because if I was completely honest, I'd admit that I was scared to see Kath. Was I focusing on the Libby situation so I could avoid dealing with Kath for just a few minutes more?

Who the hell knew? But it was sort of a moot point, since when I got to the hospital, Libby was nowhere to be found. But there was a blonde lady. I pulled the note from my pocket, skimming it again as I stood in the waiting area.

"Excuse me—Nan?"

The woman turned to face me, her blue gaze friendly and curious. "Hello…Nick, yes?"

"Uh—yeah." Guess she'd already spoken to Libby. Great.

"Marilyn, this is the young man Libby was telling us about. Nick, this is Marilyn Ramirez."

I exchanged nods with the woman seated over by a window, a rosary twisted in her hands.

"Have you seen Libby this morning?"

"As a matter of fact,—" Nan's chin lifted, as she looked past my shoulder. Following her gaze, I turned and there she was, standing outside a room with Dr. Aguirre. I watched as he took her chin in one hand, tilting her head to meet his gaze. As he spoke, she smiled, nodded, even reached up to give him a kiss on the cheek in parting. The second he was gone, however, her entire demeanor changed. Head down, shoulders slumping, not unlike the air slowly being let out of a balloon. A hollow pit sensation clawed at my stomach. *Dios mío*. Was that what I'd looked like? What she'd seen?

With that in mind, I was careful as I approached, reaching out to touch her forearm. Like she'd done with me, I tried my best to keep it gentle, doing my best not to startle her.

"Libby?"

With a sharp breath she straightened, her shoulders squaring as she turned to meet my gaze with the same smile she'd used with Dr. Aguirre. "Hey, Nick. Wasn't sure I was going to see you before we left. How are you doing?"

Good God, that was fast—that transformation. "I—all right, I guess. Are you okay?"

Another smile—a wave of her hand. "Oh, I'm fine. A little tired. A lot sore," she said with a small laugh as she reached around to rub her back. "But good, otherwise. Thanks again for the pills, by the way."

"No problem."

"Have you seen your wife this morning? Is she doing okay?"

"Uh…no. I'm on my way, but I wanted to see if I could catch you first."

She cocked her head.

"I just…" I looked down to where I still held her note. "I had to say I'm sorry."

Libby

"I had to say I'm sorry."

God love him, he really was a newbie, thinking he had to apologize to *me* for a minor freak out.

"What's got you smiling, gorgeous?"

I glanced away from the deep turquoise expanse of water, the last long stretch of bridge that signaled we were getting near Marathon. Home. Thank God. Even though we only tended to stay away for two, maybe three, days at a time, it was still too long.

And to think—once upon a time, I'd wanted nothing more than to get the hell out of this subtropical burg and the craziness it represented. Now I couldn't imagine living anywhere else. With anyone else.

"Oh, nothing much. We've just got a rookie, and he and I had..." What to call it? "An encounter. Poor guy felt like he had to apologize."

"Must've been a hell of an encounter."

"Only to him."

And ignored the little inside voice that was whispering "*Liar.*" I'd worried about Nick last night. Almost as much as I'd worried about Ethan. To say that it caught me by surprise—well, that would be understating it a bit.

I leaned into Ethan's touch as he reached beneath my braid to stroke my neck. "Everyone had to be a rookie at some point, sweetheart. Cut the poor son of a bitch some slack."

"I did. Like I said, not a big deal. Certainly not to me."

"Libby, come on. This is me you're talking to." His long fingers massaged gently—he didn't have the strength for more than gentle, but it felt good, nevertheless, loosening muscles that were perpetually frozen. I sighed and leaned farther back into the seat. Into his touch.

"Did you…?" His fingers stilled on my neck as his voice trailed off. Not a common occurrence for Ethan who was one of the most verbally decisive people I'd ever met. Pissed me off monumentally when we first met. Almost as much as it turned me on.

"What?"

His voice remained soft, his trace accent deepening. "Did you and this new guy get into it because of what happened with us? Because of me?"

"Oh no, Ethan, no." I reached back and grabbed his hand in mine, bringing it around and pressing a kiss to the thin fragile skin. "No, *mi vida*, I promise that wasn't it at all."

"You were pretty upset when you left."

"You noticed." Oh God. I *hated* that. I tried so hard not to let him see, and he'd already seemed so out of it.

"Some. I know I hurt you."

Afraid of hurting him, I tightened the hand not holding his around the steering wheel, blinking away the suddenly blurry vista in front of me. "Ethan…"

"I know you're not pissed about that, Libby. We both know it wasn't necessarily *me*, who did that. But I hurt you. Physically, emotionally…and if this guy—"

"Nick," I filled in.

"If this Nick had the bad luck to catch you after that…"

I shook my head, pressing another kiss against his hand before lowering it to rest on my thigh. "It was his first day, Ethan, and he's having a hard time dealing. He let himself push worry for his wife to the back burner for a couple of hours and freaked. I tried to tell him it was okay, but like I said…rookie, with all the issues and emotions that come with."

"Oh, Jesus, guilt complex."

"Big time—and he's Cuban."

"Oh, Jesus, Cuban guilt complex."

"He seems like a smart guy in spite of that," I joked, trying to lighten the mood. Ethan did *not* need to be stressing over this.

"Smart, huh? I'll bet he's good-looking too."

God, I loved this man. "I guess. Nan and Marilyn referred to him as fresh meat."

"Did they, now?"

"They did."

"Beyond that, what's Nan think of him?"

My tales of the waiting room brigade had helped us pass more than a few hours in the hospital. I'd tell Ethan about our dinners and lunches, Nan and Marilyn's running bets—describe the occasional movie we managed to take in. When I didn't have a choice, because I'd have to be away for a few hours, I'd have to mention the funerals, even though we never spoke of those in anything more than passing. But being Ethan, he probably knew more than I could or would tell him. How I hated going to them, hated anything that took me away from him, *especially* the funerals, but I had to go. Had to offer support to the people who helped and supported me.

I had learned, and it had been through painfully hard experience, that you had to form some sort of camaraderie or run the risk of going out of your mind. I'd tried the independent, don't-need-anyone-to-lean-on route, and as Nan had pointed out, I had nearly driven myself to a nervous breakdown.

Maybe that's what I was trying to save Nick from. If he was anything like me, he was going to need saving from himself more than anything else.

Okay, not *if* he was like me. Again, I recalled that lost expression I'd seen in his dark eyes—the haunted look I recognized so readily because I'd faced it all too often in my own mirror.

"I think she likes him."

"Good. Maybe you'll get to be friends, gorgeous. That'd be nice for you."

Ethan's voice was sleepy; the words slurred. I resisted the temptation to remind him that we were only a few miles from home—that even now I could see the palm trees and sandy borders of the island drawing closer. Any sleep he could get was sleep he needed. Even if it was only a few minutes' worth, it would help give him that little bit more strength he needed to keep fighting. To get better. So all I said was, "Yeah, I guess it would."

Nick

SEPTEMBER 12

Carefully, I eased the door to her room open, then stood there, staring.

"Kath, what the hell are you doing?"

"What does it look like I'm doing, Nicky?"

"But…" She'd felt like shit after her treatment yesterday. She was getting another one as we spoke, the I.V. taped to her hand. Yet—

"I can't believe you're working. Now?"

In a reassuringly familiar habit, she reached up and twisted a strand of hair around her finger as she continued staring at her laptop's screen. "Come on, Nick. Dr. Aguirre said the best therapy would be for me to keep life as normal as possible."

"Within reason, babe." And the first round of treatments a couple weeks ago had left her so miserable, so completely drained, even though she toughed it out and tried to play it cool. I didn't *want* her playing it cool. I was all for having her taking it as easy as possible. I even beat her to packing my bag before this trip— didn't want her doing so much as that little bit. She'd bitched— told me I was being silly. Didn't much care. She wasn't infallible, for God's sake.

"I'm in bed," she countered. "With my laptop. I'm not even on the phone or texting, for Christ's sake. And I need to get this proposal done. Events don't plan themselves, you know."

"You have assistants, Kath. As in, they're supposed to assist."

"And they will. As soon as I give them directions as to how I expect things to be done."

I leaned a hip against the mattress, curling my fingers into the blanket, then uncurling them, one by one, forcing myself to keep them flat, trying for relaxed. Details were her forte—even more so than mine. She'd notice if I was too tense. "How long have they worked with you?"

She finally looked up, but not at me—more off into the distance as she thought. "Karin's been with me for five years, Jorge for three." She returned her attention to the screen.

"And you don't think they know enough of what you expect by now that they couldn't handle this on their own?"

"If it was something minor, yes, but this is slated to be one of the biggest charity events of the Palm Beach social season. If we get it right, the foundation this benefits could earn upward of half a million dollars from this one party. Could you even imagine? The kind of events we'd get hired to plan in the wake of something like that?"

Okay, I got that it was important and a lot of professional cred was on the line, but this was her health we were talking about here. The stress of planning a major league event was exhausting on a good day. "What about one of the other senior planners? Can't they help out, work with Karin and Jorge on your behalf?"

"It was given to me."

"That was before you got—" I bit the word off before it could escape.

"Being sick shouldn't matter." She glanced up from the screen again, red splotches marring her otherwise pale face. "If you had a top prospect to check out, would you trust it to one of the more junior guys?"

"Yes." Because I'd done just that this week, passing a trip on to one of the more junior guys in the organization because Kath needed me here.

A short, hard sound that was somewhere between a snort and a laugh escaped her as she shook her head. "No you wouldn't. I know you and—"

All of a sudden, the bed was drenched as Kath lurched forward, streams of vomit covering the blankets and her computer, hot drops splattering across my arm and the front of my shirt.

"Oh shit!" I scrambled for the call button, jabbing at it as I tried to reach for Kath with my other hand, trying to support her head as she kept choking and spluttering. But as I leaned in, I stepped in some vomit and slipped, my hand landing square on her chest. A split second later, I staggered back, her scream reverberating in my ears.

"Don't touch me!"

Vaguely I registered a crash, then a pair of nurses were there, one of them supporting Kath, easing her up while the other demanded, "What's going on?"

I stared helplessly at Kath, hunched, arms crossed over her chest, still heaving but at least not throwing up anymore, thank God. I was a different story, fighting to maintain control while sucking down air and trying not to choke at the sour acid smell. My eyes watered as I watched her swaying back and forth, the ends of her hair wet and sticking to her cheeks.

"She got sick."

I swallowed even harder, bitter bile flooding my mouth as I noticed how much hair was left behind on the pillow, the long, dark red strands swirling against the white pillowcase, like some fucked up modern art painting.

Her head lifted, dark blue eyes wild and slightly unfocused. "Because you made me!" She shook her head again, then picked up the puke-spattered computer and threw it at me. Instinctively, I reached out to try to save it, but my hands were wet, the machine was wet, my reflexes were fucked—it slid right through my grasp and landed on the floor by my feet where it split nearly in half, spluttering and hissing. "You wouldn't leave me alone. All that work ruined because of *you*, Nick. Get out! Get out! Just leave me alone. Leave me alone…"

Oh God… she was crying. I hadn't seen her cry since… I couldn't remember when. She hadn't cried when I asked her to marry me or at our wedding. Not when she got the diagnosis, or when they'd told her how bad it was, or what her options were, or what it might mean for our future. She hadn't cried before or after the surgery.

The last time I think I saw Kath cry—

Shit, I couldn't remember.

I extended a hand, reaching for her. "Kath—"

"Go *away!*"

"Mr. Azarias, you'd better leave. We've got to get her calmed down and cleaned up and..." The nurse's touch was gentle as she turned me away, her voice just as gentle. "I think it might go easier if you're not here. Sometimes it's like that. It's not you—it's the meds. They provoke different reactions in different people. We'll page Dr. Aguirre and let him know."

She kept talking, her voice soft, the words soothing and calming, and before I knew it, we were in the hallway. Dazed, I looked around the brightly lit corridor, at the pale green walls and white tile floors— at the people walking back and forth. Vaguely, I registered the sounds of conversation, and the crackle from speakers as a disembodied voice made an announcement calling for a doctor. I was standing there with the distinct sensation of having been full-body checked into the ice; the kind of thing where one second you were staring up at the overhead lights, trainers and teammates hovering over you— next thing you knew, you were sitting on the bench with no clue how you'd gotten there. And wanting nothing more than to go back into the game—no matter how much you hurt, because you had to help the team. Couldn't let them down.

I *had* to help Kath. Had to be with her, didn't I? But as I reached for the door handle, the nurse's hand grasped my wrist, her hold soft, but as effective as a pair of handcuffs.

"No."

"But..." I stared from her to the door and back, focusing on the name tag pinned to her pale blue scrub jacket. "Cory... I need—"

"No you don't, Nick." That use of my first name made me stop cold. Made me drop my hand to my side as she patted my arm, knowing she'd won this round.

"It's not you, honey," she repeated. "A lot of the patients...they feel like they've got to keep control of something. And we've got to do our best to let them have that—or at the very least, the illusion."

My mouth opened and closed, like I wanted to say something—to ask, what about the rest of us? The ones who weren't patients? What were we supposed to do?

Far as I could tell, we were supposed to nod and mumble some sort of inanity and turn and walk away because it was for the best. What I was supposed to do after that, I had no idea.

What was I supposed to do now?

Jesus, but I *hated* this feeling. The aimlessness...the inescapable sensation of being lost. Not in some deep, metaphorical sort of way, just...lost. In the traditional geographical way. Because I was so fucking angry—at myself, at what had happened, and yeah, even at Kath—that I hadn't paid a damn bit of attention to which way I turned out of the parking garage. Hadn't paid attention to the streets or what direction I was going until I found myself across the bay, with downtown looming ahead.

What the hell. I just went with the flow of traffic, chuckling as I picked one car, then another to follow; shifting lanes at the last second if another car caught my eye. Neglecting to signal and laughing out loud as horns blared.

Finally, tiring of playing follow the leader, I eased off on the next exit ramp, blinking as I finally began registering my surroundings. Followed by an eerie sense of recognition. For once I was grateful that traffic was heavy, so I was able to just slowly cruise, taking in the gaudy billboards, the advertisements splashed across the backs of the bus stop benches, the storefronts with small knots of people gathered around open, bar-style windows. Didn't have to look any closer to know they were likely drinking small cups of that hot, caffeine jolt known as Cuban coffee and chasing it down with glasses of ice water. Maybe ordering a *media noche* or *sandwich cubano* to go.

I rolled down my windows and just took it all in. The shouted Spanish, the salsa competing with the reggaetón from other passing cars—the windows displaying big gaudy-ass *quinceañera* dresses next to *mercados* that probably had everything from frozen *croquetas* to thick candles in glass pillars with some saint printed on the side to Compay Segundo CDs.

Go figure. Totally lost, and I had up and found myself in Little Havana.

All of a sudden, I was overwhelmed by this urge to get out of the car and out of an environment that seemed every bit as sterile as that green hospital corridor. I wanted to breathe real air and hear the sounds and feel the September sun soak into my skin and make me sweat. I wanted to feel it all. Spotting a space along the street, I pulled in and parked.

I walked along the brick paved sidewalks, pausing to look in the occasional window and read the Spanish-language flyers taped to many of them advertising some festival or new restaurant, until shouts, followed by an unmistakable clicking and rattling sound, drew me toward a corner park. The closer I got, however, the more the smells overrode the sounds, slamming me right in the gut with visceral recognition. As I found myself enveloped in the rich aroma of fresh Cuban coffee combined with the deep, smoky scent of a good cigar I was once again five years old, sitting on my father's lap as he played dominoes with his brothers and cousins, just passing the time on a Sunday afternoon.

"Makes you wish you were a kid again, doesn't it?"

Looking over my shoulder, I saw a guy, probably a good ten years older than me, sitting on a bench and watching the action. For a second I was pissed at having had the memory yanked away before I was ready to let it go, but another deep breath, another glance back into the park, and it was back—that feeling of...I don't know. Something reassuring, maybe? So I was able to look back over my shoulder with a half smile and a nod.

"Yeah, actually."

"In there it's simpler." He nodded toward the tables filled with old men in snowy white undershirts and pastel-hued *guayaberas*, shuffling the tiled domino pieces while they chewed on cigars, occasionally pulling them from their mouths and using them to emphasize whatever point they were arguing. Loudly.

God, it was so...home.

"It's all so uncomplicated," he continued in a slightly accented voice. "Even if the circumstances that brought them here are beyond complicated." Then he shook his head and laughed. "*Perdoname*. I'm waxing poetic again. Must be the heat."

"No, it's okay, really. Kind of feeling that waxing poetic thing myself."

Standing, he leaned forward, extending his hand. "You're very kind, Mr.—?"

"Nick. Nick Azarias." I shook his hand.

"*Mucho gusto*, Nick. I'm Tico Martinez." He nodded at the bench. "You look hot. Sit for a moment?"

Oh yeah it was hot—in the way that only South Florida in the middle of September could be—shirt sticking to my back, head feeling like it was on fire. Sitting, especially on a tree-shaded bench, sounded damned good. While I settled onto the bench, still bemused at having found myself in what seemed like a bizarre parallel universe, Tico walked a few feet to one of the open-windowed storefronts, returning with a pair of Cokes, straws sticking out of the open cans.

"The women in there, they all think we're still children finding joy in sucking the carbonation through the straws. I let them believe it—they pretend not to see me throw the straws away." Which he did, while past his shoulder I saw a scary *viejita* briefly scowl at his back before turning away to deal with another customer.

I laughed long and hard as I accepted one of the cans of soda, then drained half of it in one long swallow. "*Gracias*," I said as I rubbed my chest to subdue a huge burp.

"You looked like you could use it." He sat on the opposite end of the bench and took a fairly long drink of his own before saying, "And if you'll forgive me for saying so, you look like you could use a new shirt too."

As I glanced down at my stained and seriously ripe T-shirt, the morning came rushing back, the carbonation from the Coke rumbling in my gut, hard and uncomfortable. Releasing a deep breath, I dropped my head back and stared up through the leafy branches of the trees.

"*Disculpa, m'ijo.* I didn't mean to make you feel badly."

"No...you didn't. I just..." Had managed to forget, *again*, what was going on in my life. God, I was getting good at that. Too good.

"*Perdoname.*" I stood from the bench and retraced my steps to a store I'd noticed before the domino players had caught my attention—one of those mercados that carried a little bit of everything. Five minutes later, I resettled myself on the bench, wearing a vintage-style Cienfuegos baseball club T-shirt. With a practiced flick my wrist, I tossed my old one into the nearby trashcan.

"I'm sure it can be washed."

"Of the stains, probably."

"I see."

"I doubt it." I picked up my soda, the outside slick with condensation, and drained the already warm remainder in a couple of quick gulps.

"It doesn't take a genius to see that you have something troubling you. Something difficult going on."

"You a priest or something?"

"Yes, as a matter of fact."

He laughed as I stared at him sitting there in jeans and a polo, his Marlins ball cap turned backward. "A priest named Tico?" was all I could come up with.

"My given name is Alberto, but because I was a Junior, I was always called Albertico, which, by the time I was a teenager, was just plain ridiculous and didn't do a thing for the girls, so I shortened it to Tico. Luckily, that stuck."

"A priest named Tico who dated girls?"

His eyebrows went up. "Wasn't always a priest, *tú sabes*?"

Visions of ancient, wrinkled Father José who'd been my parish priest growing up crowded my memory. I tried to envision him dating. Or human.

I couldn't. This cat, however...

Tilting my head until it rested against the back of the bench, I closed my eyes and said, "My wife's got cancer." It was easier to say it with my eyes closed.

"*Ay m'ijo*, I'm sorry."

I opened my eyes and slid a sideways look at him. "And please don't spout some pious crap about God's will and how He works in mysterious ways and there's a blessing in disguise, blah, blah, blah."

He kept his stare fixed on the domino players. "My father had cancer. I was so damn angry at God that He would allow this to happen to a man—a good man—who had never done anything other than work his ass off to provide for his family. I was angry to the point where I nearly left the priesthood. Cancer sucks, Nick. It turns your world inside out and makes you seriously examine everything you ever thought was important. Made me really question my faith, you know?"

Somewhere in the middle of what he was telling me, I had turned my head back and closed my eyes again. "Not my faith I've been questioning. No offense, Tico, but it's pretty far down the list." As in, not even on the list. Kath and I hadn't even been married in church—we'd gone the fancy hotel wedding route.

"I said everything *you* ever thought was important." His voice was mild with only a hint of "you fool" in it. "For you, I'm guessing it's your wife who's first and foremost."

"That's just it." I kept my eyes closed, praying that it would continue to make this easier. "Thing is…I find myself forgetting what she's going through, even if it's for a couple of hours. Because when I do think about it, I'm pissed as hell. I'm mad at the world, and I'm mad at myself. I'm even mad at her. Isn't that fucked up?"

The skin around my eyes felt tight and itchy as I realized how profane I was being with a man of the cloth. Any minute now, Sister María Ignacia was liable to swoop down, metal ruler in hand, and rap me a good one. Tico, however, didn't seem to notice—or if he did, didn't seem to mind.

"Are you feeling guilty, because you let yourself forget?"

Was I? I thought about that as I opened my eyes and pushed myself to a more upright position. Rubbing my lip with my thumb,

I finally said, "Yeah. I mean, ninety-nine percent of the time, it consumes me, then boom—it's like it doesn't even exist. Then, I remember. And it's even worse."

Surprisingly, Tico laughed at that while I stared at him, confused—and getting ticked.

"Man, if I had any doubts you were Cuban—or Catholic—they've just been dispelled. Martyrs, the bunch of us."

Okay, he had me there. Couldn't count the times my sisters and I had referred to our mother as Joan of Arc—never when she could hear, of course.

"However, I'm getting that it's more than just guilt-fueled anger, Nick." His voice was gentle, but insistent, and if I'd had *any* doubts that he was a priest...

"It is. She's...I'm..." I couldn't believe I was telling all of this to a stranger. But he wasn't just a stranger. He was a priest. And maybe it wasn't the quiet, wooden booth in the back of Our Lady, but a bench in Little Havana served as a pretty decent substitute.

"I don't *know*." A short, harsh breath escaped as I shoved my hands through my hair. Guess I couldn't tell even a priest. At least, not yet.

Tico must've been a really good priest, because he didn't push anymore after that. The two of us just sat there for a few minutes more, letting the scene around us ebb and flow, the surrounding noise more than serving to fill the silence.

Finally, he said, "I need to be going."

Nodding, I stood with him, offered him my hand. "Sorry I laid all of that on you."

He shrugged and smiled as he shook my hand. "I asked. It's what I do. And I enjoyed meeting you."

"Me too." And was more than a little surprised that it felt genuine.

Still holding my hand, Tico studied me.

"How long has it been since you said a Rosary?"

"Couldn't begin to tell you."

"You remember it though?"

Now I found myself laughing. "Twelve years of Catholic school, man, what do you think?"

"I'll take that as a yes." He smiled, then his expression went thoughtful. "You know, it's not just about penance or obligation. I've actually found it's a great tool for meditation and just finding a quiet place to go in your head."

Once again, I felt the muscles around my eyes twitch. "Honestly, I don't even have a clue where my rosary is."

With his free hand, Tico reached into the pocket of his jeans then turned my hand over, dropping the string of ebony beads with its silver cross into my palm. "I know you can find a rosary in any one of the *mercados* around here, but let me save you the trouble. At least until you can find yours or take the time to buy the right one."

"Tico, I can't." Not like I was a rosary specialist, but even I could tell the one I was holding wasn't just some supermarket special. The beads were smooth yet irregular, sign of a lot of years of use.

He shrugged, closing my fist over the rosary. "Sure you can. Because I expect you to return it to me. I hang out here every Wednesday—watching the *viejitos* and doing that waxing poetic thing. Or you can drop it by the office." He pulled his wallet from his pocket and extracted a card. I took it in my free hand, looking down at it.

Gésu Church, Rev. Alberto "Tico" Martinez, S.J.

"A Jesuit." I looked up, shaking my head. "Should've known."

He raised his eyebrows to which I answered, "High school."

"Which one?"

"Saint Peter's Prep. Jersey City."

"I've heard it's a good school."

My turn to raise my eyebrows. "You know it?"

A sad smile crossed his face. "I was a teacher, *m'ijo*. It was my first calling, and I loved it like nothing else, working with kids, encouraging them to think and to dream beyond boundaries, real or imagined. But remember what I said about questioning everything I thought was important?"

"Yeah."

"Well, after my dad got sick, I decided I wanted to minister rather than teach."

Admittedly, it'd been a while, but my memories of high school were actually good—and powerful. Like it was yesterday, I remembered all the discussion and arguing and learning going on in the most challenging atmosphere I've ever experienced. College had been a total cakewalk after four years of Jesuits. The priests who taught us—they were rare individuals, man. I couldn't imagine that mundane, everyday ministering would really do it for someone who'd been accustomed to working in that sort of high-charged, intellectual atmosphere.

"It's different. But satisfying, Nick. Teaching was for a different time in my life, you know?"

Guess what I was thinking was pretty obvious. "I'm sorry. None of my business."

He snorted. "*Oye*, I'd question it too. I *did* question it. My entire first year out of teaching I wondered if I'd completely lost my mind."

"I can relate to the losing your mind part." My fist tightened around the rosary.

Tico placed both of his hands around my closed fist. "Try it. I'm not saying you'll find any answers—at least not right away. *Mira*, truth is, you might never find any answers. But at least it gives you something to do. Now remember—I expect to get my rosary back." Releasing my hand, he turned and started walking away, pausing only long enough to call back over his shoulder, "It was my father's."

Libby

SEPTEMBER 23

At a casual glance, it appeared he was just leaning up against the vending machine—trying to decide what he wanted. Then I noticed…

B-7.

Again, B-7.

Once, twice, a third time, I watched him press the same two buttons. Nothing impatient, not checking any other combinations, not pressing the return button, retrieving his cash, and starting over. Just B-7, steady and almost rhythmic, his other hand braced against the machine. It was that other hand that gave him away—belied the exterior calm. The fingers curling and uncurling with the same steady rhythm with which he kept pressing B-7.

"I don't think that Mountain Dew is quite ready to be culled from the rest of the herd."

He pressed the buttons a final time before turning to face me.

"Okay then. I can see why you're so hot for the caffeine jolt." A month on and the circles under his eyes had evolved from the dark smudges of a few sleepless nights to deep bruises that marred the otherwise even olive of his skin, giving the impression of a man caught on the losing end of a brawl.

"Come on, though, we can do better than Mountain Dew. That stuff's nasty."

His voice was soft as he replied, "But it's here."

I suppressed a sigh while tensing myself against the familiar clench grabbing hold of my stomach. *Here.* Not just in the hospital, but on the same floor, presumably just a few feet away from his wife's room. He was still beating himself up over the need to forget. Or at least get away, if only for a while.

"Starbucks is barely half a block away."

He looked doubtful—and stubborn. "An hour, Nick. No one, least of all your wife, would begrudge you an hour."

"She doesn't get an hour away from it."

"She sure as hell won't if you're there reminding her twenty-four seven it's what she's living with."

I flinched at the hurt and anger I saw reflected in his eyes, but I didn't look away or back down. He needed to hear this. We all did. How even the patient had to find ways to cope and forget. For Ethan, it had been in writing his columns. For months I'd berated him for working when he should be resting or eating or maybe sitting outside under a damn palm tree and inhaling fresh air until he finally, calmly, and in the way only he could, had pounded through my thick skull what it was he was feeling. He'd written a column about how writing was his salvation. That *I* was his saving grace, but writing allowed him to escape into the realm of himself as a normal man for a while.

It was the first column of his I'd read cold in years, since we often proofed each other's work. But that one he'd sent in without any input from me. So I'd sat there and read it over my morning coffee, just like the rest of South Florida, and, probably like the rest of South Florida, had felt tears gather in the corners of my eyes. Had fought to keep them from falling as I wondered over how insensitive his wife must be that she couldn't see how he needed his work—his own little slice of normality.

Not that it meant I still didn't wrestle with the guilt—except now it was at not understanding exactly what he needed, at not being able to gracefully give it to him without question even once I did know, because I still worried that he was working too hard and wearing himself out. Added, of course, to the guilt I already felt at needing my own time away. Because I was nothing if not thorough.

"Nick…it's an hour." He was shaking his head, yet didn't resist when I grasped his arm and led him away from the vending machine.

"What about Nan?"

"She's not here today."

"Marilyn?"

"She hasn't been going out—wants to stay with Ray."

"But you're not badgering her?"

"It's different."

He stopped then, his gaze following my glance across the nurse's station to a closed door on the opposite side of the floor, then back where he studied my face for a long moment.

"Shit."

I took his arm again, led him toward the elevators. "Don't dwell on it. Like I said, it's different. For everyone."

His mouth was pressed into a thin, hard line, his brows tight over his eyes in a matching line looking like he was about blow. Whatever it was, though, he kept it in—opting instead for quiet. Worked for me. I was happy to do nothing more than walk, taking deep breaths of air tinged with salt from the nearby bay and colored by the exhaust of the traffic streaming past us. Beside me, he walked with his face turned up slightly, as if the feel of sun hitting skin was a foreign sensation—something he hadn't experienced in a while.

Settled in armchairs, we drank coffee and ate muffins while watching the people streaming by on the other side of the window going on about their lives.

"Please tell me Lawrence has shown up."

I turned away from the window. "No."

Marilyn and Ray's son—first class trial attorney and first class asshole. Had never *once* come to see his father during a hospital treatment despite the fact that he worked all of twenty minutes away. Asshole.

Nick was methodically shredding a napkin, long strips of paper falling into his lap. "What's so fucking important he's constantly blowing them off?"

"Big trial coming up. There's always a big trial coming up. Or a client dinner. Lots of witnesses to interview. I honestly don't know what the hell else."

"Little twat."

Nice to know I wasn't the only one calling him names without really knowing him.

"How bad is it for Ray, Libby? Really?"

"I honestly don't know that either." I set the uneaten half of my muffin on the low table between us—chocolate with sawdust aftertaste didn't do much for me. "I haven't seen Marilyn much lately and when I have…I just can't bring myself to ask anything—even in the most oblique of ways. She seems so fragile, like having to face up to the inevitability might just break her. I can't do that to her." I resumed staring out the window as I sipped at my coffee—tried to mask the slight tremor that ran through my hands and made the muscles in my legs tense in response.

"Why do you do it to me, Libby?"

His voice dropped again, to something soft and tinged with only just a hint of anger. More curious.

"Because," I said carefully, "unless I'm wrong, and if I am, please forgive me, you're at a different stage of the game. You don't have an inevitability yet. Not like Marilyn."

Not like me. But I didn't say that, because *I* didn't want to think of it that way. I couldn't. Not anymore than Marilyn could.

I turned in my chair, drawing my legs up under me. "And no one should have to go it alone, Nick. Even if it's what you're accustomed to doing."

"Hey, I've been a team player all my life, Libby. I get what that's about."

Despite the serious nature of the topic, I had to fight to keep from smiling, although I could feel the corners of my mouth twitching. "It's equally hard if you're accustomed to being the one taking charge and making things happen."

Bingo. His eyes widened, jaw dropping just a bit as he stared, then shook his head, rubbing a hand across cheeks that looked as if they hadn't seen a razor in a few days.

"How the hell do you know so much?"

"I don't know that I do." I shrugged and drained what was left of my coffee. "But most of my life has been spent observing. An only kid, mostly hanging around adults. Part of two different worlds yet not fitting in either. Basically, I was this little shadow who just sat back and watched the action around me unfold. I didn't interact with life all that much until Ethan."

And with that, my reprieve was over. Stay away too much longer and I'd begin to feel the bite of the loneliness. Gnawing and insistent and messing with any illusion of control I might have. Standing, I collected our trash, then returned to the counter and picked up a Frappuccino and muffin to go.

"Man, I thought *I* needed the sugar rush."

I smiled up at Nick. "It's for Ethan. The sweetness helps with the aftertaste of the meds."

"Oh." Realization crossed his face. "Do you think I should—"

"No," I shook my head. "Ask her first. Something like this might make her sick if it's not what she wants. It's different for everyone."

A long, explosive breath escaped him. "I think I'm finally starting to understand that."

And in his expression I could see he was getting that it wasn't just different for each patient, either. A baby step. Maybe.

Back at the hospital, I paused in the waiting area, checking him out one last time. He seemed better; the lines of worry smoothed out somewhat, the circles beneath his eyes not quite so bruised and angry, but I wanted to make sure.

"Are you going to be all right?"

"It's a relative state, isn't it?"

I didn't say anything, just waited. Shoving his hands in the pockets of his jeans, he rocked back and forth on the balls of his feet. "I guess. I'll check on Kath, keep her company for a while. Go back to the hotel and get some work done."

And draw back into a shell where he might be too alone with the thoughts in his head. God, did I know him. "I'm probably going to be going back to the hotel after Ethan's done with this." I held up the drink. "I'd love some company for dinner."

One dark eyebrow rose. "Would you now?"

My breath caught in my throat. I tried again. "I think it'd be a good thing if we both had some company for dinner."

A shadow of a smile crossed his face. "That's what I thought, and, yeah, I think you're right. And Libby?"

"Yeah?"

"Can I ask a favor?"

"Sure."

"Can we promise not to bullshit each other? To be straight up?"

I could tell by the sudden, tense set of his shoulders that this was important to him. Insight struck like a lightening bolt—yet another way in which he was like me. He could handle what was thrown at him, so long as he felt he was getting the whole story. No pretense—no beating around the bush.

"Absolutely." I smiled and felt something in me loosen. Something I hadn't even known was holding tight. Followed by surprise, as he leaned in and kissed my cheek in that most quintessential of Cuban gestures.

"¿*Te veo luego?*"

"*Seguro.*" How odd…yet natural. It was as if with that simple act he'd opened up that part of our common background, the conversation that followed flowing automatically in our shared second language. "I'll leave you a message at the desk with my cell number. Just call whenever."

"I will."

Reaching up, I pressed a return kiss to his cheek before heading toward Ethan's room, smiling and feeling…a kind of pleasure, I guess. Something warm and quiet—the kind of thing that had been in exceedingly short supply of late.

Libby

OCTOBER 2

"Damn, Libby, you'd think you'd learn," I muttered to myself. Juggling grocery bags filled with the refrigerated stuff, my purse and my keys, I finally managed to separate my house key and fit it in the lock. "Find the key *first.*"

I pushed open the door, dropping purse and keys on the dining table as I passed by on my way to the kitchen. Needed to get the perishables put away before they, well, *perished*. Even if it was October, it was still stupid hot and sticky and humid—perfect conditions for turning good food into biology experiments in a hurry. And what a waste that would be. Brie, *queso blanco*, and sharp cheddar, baby carrots, hummus, sweet ham, and turkey; finger foods that were my preferred snacks as I worked. Actually, finger foods that generally comprised my food intake most days. By and large, full meals had gone the way of the dodo bird. I'd never really gotten the hang of cooking just for one.

As I unpacked and sorted, I felt a welcoming lick on the back of my knee and another along my ankle.

"Hello, babies." I reached back and absent-mindedly scratched under Sundance's chin while I rubbed Butch's warm belly with my foot. "Okay, that's all you get until I'm done here."

As twin pitiful gazes assaulted me, I reached into the clear glass jar on the counter and pulled out two rawhides—one for Sundance and a slightly smaller one for Butch, who stared reproachfully.

"Butch, get it through your little dachshund head. You are wee. Adorable, but wee." The stare didn't change, but he did deign to stand up on two stubby legs and accept the treat, which he regally carried into the Florida room after his Labrador sister.

"You'll never be able to convince him of that," came Nora's amused observation from behind me.

"You think one of those jumbo rawhides that are three times his size would work?" I asked.

"Probably not."

Because Butch was nothing if not tenacious. Big part of how he'd survived being the cast-off runt of his litter. Even now I could see him sliding his rawhide under Sundance's nose, trying to entice her. Sundance, being an affable sort, took it, leaving Butch to capture his original objective. Crafty little shit. No wonder Ethan loved him so much.

I glanced over my shoulder at Nora. "How is he?"

"Resting right now, but we played cards for a bit. Texas Hold 'Em. He owes me money."

"Oh." I closed my eyes and sighed. A good day. "Maybe he'll be up for some salmon if I poach it for him until it's real soft. Or at least the broth…"

"Salmon?" At Nora's outraged gasp, I opened my eyes. "They're going to skin you alive at Fish Tales. Buying farm-raised salmon at Publix like some tourist considering what you've got available in your backyard."

"Ethan likes salmon. If he'll eat it, it's what I'll buy, even if I have to paddle my ass to Nova Scotia to get it." I shrugged. "I'll go to Fish Tales in the next couple days and get some grouper or maybe shrimp. I've had a taste for red curry lately." And it kept fairly decently.

Her wide mouth curved in the same half smile that I'd inherited. Along with the mouth itself—both in shape and the smartass commentary that tended to come out of it. "Am I invited?"

"You non-vegan this week?"

"For your red curry, yes." Flipping her long, silver-streaked ponytail over her shoulder, she filled the tea kettle at the sink and placed it on the stove. "Especially since I never was able to master a decent curry."

I leaned into the fridge, putting the cold cuts and cheeses away. "Nora, sprinkling curry powder over Hamburger Helper and tofu doesn't even *qualify* as an attempt to master curry." I fought to suppress a shudder at the memory.

Reaching over, I selected two of the hand-thrown and glazed mugs that had been Nora's tenth anniversary gift to us from their rustic wood stand and placed them on the counter. My hand hovered over a third.

"No, I don't think so, Liberty. He was dozing when I left the room."

Nodding, I left the kitchen and went back out to my car to retrieve the rest of the groceries. By the time I returned, Nora had the tea steeping and a crusty, homemade baguette out and on the cutting board.

"Anything else going on with him?"

"No." Even though she was holding them straight in the nun-educated posture she'd never managed to shed, I could still detect the subtle rise and fall of her shoulders as she took a deep breath. "Don't baby him, Libby."

"I don't." I took a deep breath of my own. "But because I don't, I have to ask questions, Nora. I have to know what's going on with him. Otherwise, how can I take care of him?"

I stiffened, as I sensed her coming up behind me, then relaxed as she began stroking my hair—just like when I was a little girl. "*M'ija*, you take good care of him."

My eyes drifted shut, soothed by the simple, comforting gesture. "But is it enough?"

She actually didn't reply—not that I expected her to. She had this habit of not answering questions to which she thought the answers were glaringly obvious. Instead, she steered me to the table and pushed me into a chair. A moment later, a cup of tea and a plate with a slice of bread liberally spread with butter appeared in front of me.

"Have this, then go stretch out for a bit or maybe take the dogs for a walk on the beach."

"But…" So I'm stubborn.

She took the chair opposite mine. After taking a careful sip of the hot tea, she said, "He's going to be resting for a good bit, Libby. *Aproveche.*"

Wait a minute—she seemed awfully certain and rest had been anything but a sure thing for Ethan, especially of late. "Nora, what did you do?"

No answer again. Because the answer was glaringly, *stupidly* obvious given that this was my mother we were talking about. Closing my eyes and rubbing my forehead, I took a deep breath. And another. One more for good measure. "Nora, he can*not* be smoking." I opened my eyes and glared at her. "How *could* you? It's the last thing he needs to be doing."

"I did it because he's been in so much pain, Liberty."

And did she think I didn't know this? Did she think I enjoyed seeing the spasms that took over and hearing the whimpers that escaped in his sleep because he tried so hard to contain them while he was awake? My mouth opened and closed, but all that came out was a weak, "Nora…"

"No one could do more for him than you do. But I also know this is something you wouldn't feel comfortable doing and I do." Her gaze across the table was equal parts defiant and understanding— sort of like she was stuck in some bizarre time warp between the sixteen-year-old who'd run off on a grand adventure and the fifty-two-year-old who'd lived to tell the tale.

"Besides, no one said anything about smoking." One shoulder lifted beneath her orange gauze peasant shirt as she took another leisurely sip of tea.

"Oh my *God*, you made brownies."

Jesus. It'd been years since she pulled a stunt like this. Back when my junior high English teacher gave me that wholly unfair B- on my report on the collected works of Betty Smith. Nora dried my tears, told me to calm down, that she'd take care of it. She did a little baking for the new bachelor teacher in town—he was grateful, probably thinking he was going to score with some free-love hippy. What he actually scored was a naked frolic in the surf with the entire staff of Madison Junior High called out for the event and his tiny little dick immortalized on film from Nora's Polaroid Instamatic. Nothing less than what the Fascist pig deserved. But doing this to Ethan?

"Look, Libby, if it makes you feel any better, I did call Tia Laura and ask her opinion before I did anything."

"You called Tia? *Voluntarily?*"

Espresso-dark eyebrows drew together in a straight line over equally dark eyes. "*Oye*, you don't really think I'd do something like this without advice, do you?"

"Well, no, not necessarily—" But I'd think she'd consult her shaman or the *I Ching* or her horoscope or the mailman. Something I could legitimately berate her over. Not—"*Tia?*" I know I sounded like some sort of demented parrot, but this bordered on surreal that she would call my aunt.

"I'll admit the woman is an uptight pain in the ass, and I wonder about my little brother's obvious affinity for pain given that he's stayed married to her for twenty years, but she's a good doctor."

"And?"

Another shrug as she waved that I should eat my bread. "In between the expected bitching and moaning, she basically gave her blessing."

"Far out," I breathed around a mouthful of warm sourdough.

"She also suggested I spark up and blow smoke for him so that he'd get some immediate relief before the brownie kicked in."

I shook my head slowly. "Far fucking out."

"Indeed." Nora nodded. "I hope you don't mind, but I broke into your Butterfingers stash."

Laughter was good. I was still pissed, but laughter definitely lessened the lingering impulse to strangle her.

After we finished our tea, I left Nora with the cleaning up and went to retrieve my flip-flops from the hall closet. However, the closed door down at the end of the hall beckoned, if only because I just had to see for myself—had to make sure.

The room was dim, blinds pulled against the sharp late-afternoon sun. Near-forgotten memories mingled with the acrid-sweet smoke lingering on the air, teasing my nose and making it itch. And as predictably as Pavlov's drooling dog, an old, familiar irritation tightened my spine. Holy hell, the things the woman had done when I was a kid. And yet...I couldn't deny her intentions were generally in the right place. Like now.

God, he looked almost unbearably peaceful like this, lying on his side, hand curled into a loose fist on the pillow beside his face. Quiet and still, not twitching or grimacing, the lines not as deeply etched. It could probably be chalked up to nothing more than imagination, but the contours—of jaw and brow and cheekbone—even appeared fuller, edging his distinctive bone structure back toward strong and away from the terrifying gaunt appearance that had become the norm. When was the last time I'd seen him look like this without having to resort to pictures?

My fingers traced over those lines and contours, hovering without actually touching. "I love you so much, Ethan," I murmured.

Deep blue eyes blinked slowly. "Hey, gorgeous."

Shit. I dropped to my knees beside the bed. "I didn't mean to wake you."

"S'okay," he slurred. "Not asleep. Flying."

"Man, you are so stoned. How many brownies did you have?"

"Two." His lower lip jutted out slightly. "Wanted another but Nora said no."

"Nora exhibiting restraint?" My eyebrows rose. "Bacchus is weeping."

His chuckling turned into a dry, rasping cough that had me reaching for the water on the nightstand and easing an arm beneath his shoulders to prop him up in one smooth, practiced move.

After a few measured sips from the straw and a couple more coughs, he relaxed back against the pillows with a sigh that rattled only a little. "It didn't hurt."

I slipped my arm free and returned the glass to the table, unable to look at him. The touch of his hand, fingers curling around my wrist, was what finally made me look. "I swear, Libby, it didn't. The meds," he said, the corner of his mouth twitching in its endearingly familiar smirk, "did their job."

When he looked at me that way, so relaxed—so much like my Ethan—I had no choice but to believe him. And to smile in return before dropping my forehead to the mattress. Turning my head slightly, I asked, "You swear?" The skin of his hand warm and dry against my lips.

"Yeah."

"Okay." I sighed before kissing his fingers. "I should let you get more rest then, while you can."

His answer was to slide farther down on his pillows, turning to his side once again. "I want to write some columns. Stockpile again."

I paused, my hand braced on the mattress and halfway to standing. "Think you'll be up to it?"

"Once I quit flying, I think so." Another faint twitch of the corners of his mouth made me smile in response.

"I'll bring the laptop in later then."

No reply at all this time—just his eyes drifting shut, the few lashes that somehow stubbornly survived looking like intermittent pencil strokes drawn across his cheekbones.

It was a good two hours on the beach with the dogs, secure in the knowledge that Ethan was resting, which allowed me to escape feeling like I wasn't there for him. So I took my time, tossing the tennis ball over and over, laughing as Butch took four frantic gallops for every one of Sundance's, trying to beat her to the toy and skidding ass over teakettle when he couldn't put the brakes on fast enough. Enjoyed the deserted stretches, and the heavy scent of salt on the air—took pleasure in curling my toes into damp, thick sand and felt a childlike joy at discovering a near-perfect spiral shell, its graduated shades of pink and peach and coral echoing the coming sunset. Even took the time to give the dogs baths when we returned rather than simply hosing them down, savoring the feel of their fur, sleek with soap, beneath my fingers, and laughing as they both shook themselves fiercely.

"Liberty, you just missed a phone call."

I set Butch down on the floor of the carport and took the towel to Sundance, who'd been patiently waiting her turn. "From who?"

Nora's audible inhale made me jerk my head up—"Nora?"

"Nan."

Before the name had fully left her mouth, I was in the kitchen and reaching for my cell, hitting the autodial.

"Hello, bebe."

"Marilyn?"

"Yes."

Air left my body in one explosive rush as I sagged against the counter. You told yourself over and over you were prepared. Knew it was bound to happen, what the odds were, yet every time it did, it punched you in the gut every bit as hard. Left you reeling and heartsick and railing at the gods.

"How is she?" Stupid fucking question. Asked it every damn time, though.

"As well as can be expected. Her son finally showed up."

Little bastard. "Thank God for small favors."

"No, thank God for Nick."

I straightened. "Nick?"

"*Oui.*" A surprising thread of humor, grim, maybe, but definitely humor, underscored Nan's voice. "Marilyn knew the end was close, was devastated that Lawrence hadn't come yet. Next thing we knew, Nick was dragging the boy practically by his ear into the hospital."

"How on earth…?"

Nan laughed outright at this. "He took me aside and asked the name of the firm Lawrence works for. Told me not to say anything to Marilyn, because he didn't want her getting her hopes up, but I suspect nothing shy of being arrested would have kept him from bringing Lawrence to his parents."

"God, I wish I'd been there to see that."

"It was something, bebe. It offended every sensibility he had that the boy wouldn't come see his father—stand by his mother while Ray slipped away. He's a good one, that Nick."

Yeah. Maybe even more so than I had figured.

"Is he okay?"

"Nick?" Nan's voice held a slight note of surprise. She knew, better than anyone else, that even though I was better about sharing the load, I still tended to hold myself at a remove. A lifetime of conditioning that was a bitch to overcome. And let's face it—a defense mechanism. That I'd already formed something of a bond with Nick? Yeah, definitely merited a bit of surprise. For me, too.

"He's still lost, but coping."

"Story of all our lives." I sighed. "So, what are the details?"

After writing down times and dates and addresses, I hung up the phone and crept down the hall. Easing into the room, I closed the door and leaned against it. I had to wait for my eyes to adjust once again to the shadowy dimness, for my heartbeat to subside enough for me to be able to hear over it, but after a few seconds, there—there it was. I could detect the reassuring rise and fall of the covers—the sounds of movement and breathing. They were faint, but they were still *there*.

God, no…I wasn't ready. I didn't want it to be my turn yet.

Nick

OCTOBER 5

"Nick, relax."

"He's a miserable little shit and I don't trust him."

"Language, bebe."

I looked away from Lawrence and Marilyn making their way down the aisle just long enough to raise my eyebrows at Nan. "You used worse when they ran out of your favorite ice cream last week."

"That was at the cafeteria, this is a funeral. And you're in a house of God. Show some respect. Or at least keep your voice down." There went that wave of the hand that reminded me of my mother. "You'll meet us at the cemetery?"

"Yeah." I tightened my fist. "I won't be long."

With a light touch on my back, Nan slipped from the pew, joining the crowd leaving the church to make their way to the cemetery and later on, the wake. And when I say crowd, I mean *crowd*. Ray and Marilyn were those rare individuals who were everyone's friends—knew the name of every customer who came through their Hialeah butcher shop. The big church had been all but standing room only with more still expected at the cemetery and wake. Even without Lawrence, Marilyn hadn't lacked for emotional support. But it was Lawrence who had mattered to her.

After the last footsteps faded, I opened my hand and stared down at the smooth tiger's eye beads joined together by small silver links. After looking around my house and coming up empty, I'd sucked it up and finally called my mother, asking if she maybe knew where my rosary was. Being my mother, she'd replied, of course *she* knew where my rosary was. Implicit, of course, was that I was a horrible ingrate for not keeping better track of the rosary she'd ordered from the Vatican complete with a blessing from *el Papa* himself and given to me on the occasion of my First Communion.

Late the next day, Fed Ex had dropped off the package; when I opened it, I found my rosary housed in a new carved wooden box, its silver cross so bright, I just *knew* Mami had to have polished the sucker with a toothbrush.

And Tico had said it wasn't about penance. Bullshit. And mentally added another three or four Hail Marys for thinking in those terms.

Hell, I still didn't know why I'd felt compelled to do it. I could've returned Tico's rosary to him—told him I'd bought a new one or found mine. I simply could've returned it without even seeing him, but something about that…it struck me as cowardly. Left me with a sick feeling, imagining lying, even if it was by omission, to Tico. Not just because he was a priest. But because he got it—had some clue what was going on in my head.

The hollow sound of footsteps echoing in that way unique to deserted churches penetrated sometime during my first decade of Hail Marys. By the time I looked up at the end of the series, she was there sitting beside me, her head tilted back as she looked around. In a black suit and with her hair pulled into a loose knot, she was nearly unrecognizable. But even without looking, I'd have known it was Libby. She had an air around her that was easy for me to recognize. Not in a scent sort of way—although she had that too, a light, smoky vanilla that was very her—but more like the immediate area around her was…calm.

"I really like churches, you know? Especially Catholic churches, but the traditional ones. Not the ones that look like the mothership just landed."

I stifled a laugh. "I know what you mean." Not exactly the brick Gothic monsters I'd grown up around, but the stucco and red barrel tile roof of this church did put me in mind of the old mission churches I'd seen on trips to California and Texas. Definitely more traditional vibe than postmodern mothership. I followed her curious gaze past the various stained glass windows, over the altar decorated with its arrangements of white and yellow flowers, and down toward the rosary I had looped around my hand. "Not a big churchgoer?"

"Not with a Cuban hippy mother." She smiled. "I've gone a few times with my grandparents, but I'm a lot more familiar with a sun salutation than this. You?"

"Classic lapsed Catholic. But old habits die hard." I shrugged as I glanced down at my rosary.

Her skin was warm as her fingers brushed against mine, touching one of the smooth tiger's eye beads. "Do you need me to leave you alone?"

"No. It won't take me long." But I wanted to do it because even though my faith was for shit, I wanted to send some good thoughts on with Ray—give some for Marilyn. And to have something to do with my hands that wasn't strangling Lawrence, the arrogant jackass.

Wanted to try to find that quiet place in my head where I wasn't so…on the edge, all the damn time.

"You sure?"

"I'd enjoy the company." I started to bow my head, then froze at the sight of the sun streaming through the stained glass window just behind Libby's head. The intense light made the pale green glass panels in the window exactly match the pale centers of her eyes.

Unexpected. Definitely a little eerie. But oddly, not disconcerting.

"What is it?"

I blinked, half expecting it to be an illusion. It wasn't. "What?"

"You're staring. Tell me I didn't get grease on my shirt. I checked and—"

"Why would you have grease on your shirt?"

She didn't glance up as she smoothed down the front of her shirt, also light green, I noticed. "Got a flat on my way up here. It's why I was late."

I already knew she'd come in late. Nan had said, when she sat down before the service, that Libby had called to say she was running late—that if she didn't make it to the service she'd meet us at the cemetery. At one point during Mass I'd turned and spotted her sitting toward the back of the church, head bowed.

I grasped her wrist. "You don't have grease on your shirt." But she did have a black smear running along the outside of her hand.

Out of sheer instinct, I started to reach for my handkerchief, catching myself only at the last second. A woman who could change her own flat didn't need me playing caretaker. So I settled for pointing at the streak instead, watching as she rummaged around in her bag, muttering under her breath. Finally, I just grasped her wrist again and put my handkerchief in her palm.

She stared at the white cloth. "It'll get stained."

"It'll get washed."

I turned back to the front and picked up where I'd left off on the Rosary. Mostly so I didn't have to look into her face, because that surprised expression? The way her entire being softened and she smiled? Twisted something inside my gut.

Speed-praying my way through the last four decades, I silently recited the Hail, Holy Queen and crossed myself a final time, the silver of the crucifix cool and soothing against my lips despite the faintly bitter aftertaste of polish. Silently, Libby and I made our way out of the church, pausing on the wide front steps.

"Why didn't you call Triple-A?"

"Because I'd probably still be waiting." She tilted her head, her hand coming up to shade her eyes against the afternoon glare. "How's Marilyn doing? I mean, I talked to her for a second after the service, but I couldn't really get much of a read."

Slipping my sunglasses on, I said, "I think more than anything she's relieved it's over, you know?"

"I know she was happy that Ray got to see Lawrence one last time." Her voice was gentle—almost as gentle as her hand on my shoulder.

The gentle tone, coupled with the mention of the little fucker's name, had me tensing, the skin around my eyes going tight and itchy. "You heard."

"Nan told me. Just me, as far as I know." Libby's hand on

my shoulder was warm even through my suit jacket as her fingers tightened slightly. "You did a good thing, Nick."

A good thing? I recalled again how I'd had him bent over his fancy crocodile desk set, pinning him across the back of the neck with a hockey stick as I informed him he was coming to the hospital. Voluntarily or on a stretcher, made no difference to me, but he was coming. And he'd come, and it had brought Marilyn—and hopefully Ray—a measure of comfort. From that standpoint, I guess it was a good thing, but I didn't really want any props for it. Any decent person would've done the same.

"How's Katharine?"

"Fine." A whole new tension took hold. "Fine," I repeated, adding a nod and a smile, hand shoved casually in the pocket of my dress slacks, all the better to conceal the clenching and unclenching of my fist.

Oh, *damn*. The open, concerned expression that had been on her face as she asked the question faded to the same neutral, careful smile and nod with which I'd just tried to bullshit her.

"That's so good to hear, really." And with that, the vet left the rookie absolutely schooled. "We should probably get going if we want to get to the cemetery—or maybe I should just head over to Marilyn's house and help get things ready for the wake. Showing up late to two ceremonies is kind of tacky…"

I caught up with her at the bottom of the stone stairs, grabbing onto her arm like it was a lifeline. "Fine's the last goddamn thing it is, Libby."

Her shoulders rose with the deep breath she took. Curving her hand over mine, she said, "Despite what you might think is evidence to the contrary, I'm really not into causing people undue pain. If you don't want to talk—"

"I do."

After giving my hand a final squeeze, she headed toward the parking lot. "Come on."

I released her arm and followed her toward a silver Volvo station wagon that—practical as she struck me—seemed the most unlikely car for her to be driving. Nice, but bland.

"Won't this be out of your way to bring me back all the way over here?" Since the cemetery and the wake were several miles away in Hialeah.

She just smiled and waved at the passenger seat.

"But—"

"Don't worry about it."

Fine. I wouldn't. Frankly, I was damn tired of worrying.

I didn't say anything else until she slowed, casually guiding the car into a parallel space with an ease that suggested she'd done this a lot.

"The beach?" I glanced out my window at the roiling water and expanse of sand dotted with the few souls braving the threatening weather.

"I think better by the water. It's more peaceful."

Watching her, I believed it. As she removed her jacket and shoes, tossing them into the back seat, her face got calmer, her entire body more relaxed. Same way I'd always felt lacing up my skates—taking a deep lungful of that cold, damp air before stepping on the ice and letting everything else fall away.

I looked up from slipping off my shoes and socks. "What about the cemetery?"

Libby took my jacket and shoes and put them in the back along with hers. "We'll catch up at the wake."

Okay. I'd addressed the most important things. The rest—I'd just go along for the ride. Or walk, as it were, staying just far enough back that the waves couldn't get to my rolled up dress slacks, but close enough for the sand to feel damp and gritty beneath my feet and the occasional faint spray to hit my face. After a while though, I started to wonder what, exactly, we were doing there. Libby wasn't saying anything—she simply walked, holding her skirt down against the occasional wind gust. Every now and again, she'd stop and stare out over the horizon with a blissful, faraway smile as her toes curled into the damp sand.

I didn't know if she was waiting for me to make the first move or waiting for me to give her some indication *I* wanted her to make that move. Maybe I thought since I'd acknowledged my lie—that things weren't fine—that Libby might help me out.

Guess I should've known better.

"She's not the same."

Libby walked closer to the water, allowing the waves to wash over her feet. "I know you're smart enough to realize she wasn't going to remain the same, Nick."

"No—I didn't think that. But I thought at least we'd be the same." I squatted down, dragging my fingers through the sand as I stared out at the murky sky. It was easier to talk facing the incoming storm, somehow. "I mean, I can hardly remember when we haven't been together, Libby."

First week in the dorms at Boston U. I'd spotted a tall, redheaded spitfire and that had been all she wrote, man. I was completely gone. And that was before I'd even spoken word one to her.

"Half my life I've spent with her, and we've gone through so much together. Figured out how to go through things together. To have her cut me out so completely now—"

"You never told me what she has."

"Breast. Found it in her right, but Kath wanted to be proactive and opted for a double mastectomy. It's in her lymph nodes too, it's just...it's fucking awful, Libby. Everyone tries so hard to be positive about it, talk about how young she is, how healthy otherwise. But you know Marco doesn't bullshit...and when *he* uses numbers like less than fifty percent..."

Once again, I noticed just how warm Libby's hands were as they covered mine, prying a huge piece of broken shell from one of them. Her voice was calm as she said, "Last thing you need is stitches."

I lifted one hand and rubbed at the corner of my lip with a knuckle. "Would hardly be the first time."

"No, but now's kind of crappy timing."

"Is there ever any good timing?"

We both knew I wasn't talking about stitches. But she didn't answer the question either. Instead, she led me back up the beach to a faucet where we rinsed our hands, then climbed a set of stairs to a wood pavilion with a bench where we sat, overlooking the beach. "So she's shut you out?"

I rubbed at my lip again, taking comfort in the old habit. Kath had hounded me forever until I broke it, saying it looked unseemly, but right now, I didn't give a shit about unseemly and Libby didn't strike me as the sort of woman who would care.

"I know where you're going with this Libby, and I know I'm a hockey jock and you probably think I'm all sorts of a sexist, walking hormone, but no—it's not that she's losing her hair or that she doesn't have breasts. Okay, I mean, in a way..." I amended myself. "I guess that does have something to do with it."

Jesus. I hadn't even said that to the counselor I'd seen a couple of times. Then again, I tried to control myself around her. Scared so shitless that everything out of my mouth was wrong that I'd wound up saying next to nothing.

"How so, Nick?"

"I want to help her cope. Did all the research, looked for hours at pictures on the net and in the surgeon's offices so I'd be prepared. Read books written by women, by men, by couples. Hell, I even went and consulted doctors on my own so I wouldn't make her feel bad or self-conscious with some of my questions."

Laying it out, all the details, the frustrations, had the rage starting again, hot and acid in my gut. I needed a breather, and Libby, I guess sensing that, didn't press for anything more. Tilting my head back, I kept rubbing at my lip and stared at the clouds as they transformed from light gray blobs to dark, ferocious smears across the sky, bearing down and hemming me in.

"I don't have a fucking clue if anything I've done is the right thing because she's shut down so hard, she won't let me close enough to find out." With conscious effort, I quit rubbing at my lip and forced myself to meet Libby's gaze again.

"At first, I thought it was the surgery. Because she..." My voice faded, unable to form the words.

Libby tried to help me out here. "I think every woman worries about what she's going to look like afterward."

"Actually, I don't think it's so much the looks as—" I took a deep breath and finally said it. "She's lost all feeling there, Libby. At least all pleasurable feeling. First, there was a lot of obvious pain from the surgery, now she's uncomfortable because of the expanders they put in for the reconstruction after she's done with treatment."

At least that's what I *thought* it was, not that she was telling me. But she'd always taken such joy in how they felt. Over the years, I'd learned so many different ways to give her pleasure and now nothing.

"Plastic surgeon told her she could have the reconstructive surgery at the same time as the mastectomy, before beginning treatment. She looked him straight in the eye and said 'Why?' in this completely dead voice."

"Oh God, Nick, I'm so sorry."

Libby shifted to her knees and moved her hand back to my arm. I stared at it as if from a distance—tan and slightly square, the grease stain lighter, but still visible on the outside of her palm. So different from Kath's, long and elegant, able to control a room full of rowdy executives with the subtlest of gestures. Able to control me, as she held one up, cutting me off in midsentence while she said in that same dead voice she'd used with the surgeon, "Just leave me alone, Nick. Please."

But how could I? And she kept retreating, holding up that hand, and saying, "Just leave me alone."

"You know, she hasn't let me see her—what she…looks like—since before the surgery?"

"You haven't seen her at all?"

At my sharp laugh Libby's hand fell away from my arm. "I didn't say I hadn't seen her, just that she hasn't *let* me."

I tugged at the collar of my dress shirt, loosening a couple more buttons as Libby returned her dislodged hand to her lap, back to simply waiting.

"Have I ever told you what I do—for a living?"

She shook her head, shoving a few loose pieces of hair that

were whipping around in the building breeze out of her eyes. "We somehow haven't gotten around to that yet."

No. We hadn't. Last time we'd seen each other, for dinner, our conversation had been light, focusing on movies, the football game that night, the weather, for God's sake. Anything that didn't skirt too close to the personal. For either of us.

I looked up again at the clouds that continued to bear down, dark and oppressive. Thunder rumbled, sounding like it wasn't too far off. If I was smart, I'd say we should go. Get away from the storm—get over to the wake. Say we could continue this some other time with no intention of ever bringing it up again, because even though it was Libby, and we'd promised to play it straight with each other, this was just ripping me apart; and I wasn't sure I could even bring myself to say it. Even to her.

But I'd never claimed to be all that bright. Libby, on the other hand, struck me as pretty intelligent—probably knew I desperately wanted to bail on this. But all she did was spare a calm glance up at the angry sky before looking back at me, brushing those loose pieces of hair out of her face again.

"I'm a pro hockey scout."

"Okay."

With a world of "And that has fuck-all to do with what, exactly?" in that one word.

"Until Kath's diagnosis, I was traveling constantly, always on the lookout for the next Lemieux or Gretzky or Crosby. The next stud."

"Okay."

"I take notes, watch them practice, watch them play. Record them so I can watch on my computer. Sometimes I use my phone— sometimes, a digital cam." I rubbed my lip again. "They're so goddamn small these days, those cameras, you know?"

"Oh, no..." Her eyes widened slightly as the full horror dawned. "Oh...*Nick*."

"Oh, yeah. Reduced to setting up a hidden camera in my bathroom to see my own wife. Like some fucking twisted pervert." My breath was knifing through my chest the way it did when I was skating full out, cold and harsh and just this side of cutting off all my air. The same way I'd felt when I plugged the camera into my computer. I'd been so afraid of what I was going to see that I'd hit the pause button a half dozen times. So ashamed I'd been reduced to this. That I just couldn't let things be. Ashamed that I couldn't delete the recording without ever looking at it and forget I'd ever sunk this low.

"You know the irony?"

She shook her head.

"I couldn't tell at first. It was a few weeks after the surgery, so the drainage bulbs were already gone. Any side views, I really couldn't tell much, but then I got lucky—if you can call it that." I laughed again, but Libby didn't even flinch. "She turned to face the camera, and the big mystery was revealed, and you know what? Not that big a mystery. All I could really see were these two red lines."

Other than that, her chest was smooth and not really visibly smaller than before the surgery. The one thing that threw me was the strange blankness where her nipples had been. She'd stood in front of the mirror, running her hands over her chest, the expression on her face never changing. Then the motion changed. Instead of stroking, she used a finger on each hand to poke directly at the scars.

I'd left marks on my desk from where I dug my nails in, watching as she flinched and that blank expression gave way to a grimace. I'd wanted to run in there, pull her away from that damn mirror, tell her to stop—please, for the love of God, Kath, *stop*. Of course, I couldn't. What I was watching had happened days before, and, frankly, I didn't have a fucking clue what she needed to do for herself. Didn't have a fucking clue what I could do for her.

"She's still beautiful, Libby." A ragged sigh escaped "Different, but it's still her, and I can't tell her."

I dropped my head, my hands locked around the back of my neck as I stared down at the sand-dusted planks of wood. I ran my feet across the rough surface, trying to create friction, pain, *something*.

"You should tell her."

"No, no…" I shook my head back and forth, the tendons in

my neck so tight, it felt like they might snap at any second. "I can't."

"Why?"

"*Porque, la situación se a puesto mas peor todavía*, Libby," I said, inexplicably lapsing into Spanish. Maybe because the words sounded prettier? Because I knew *she*, of all people, would understand no matter how I said it?

"Now with the chemo, she's so sick, and she won't let me hold her head over the toilet or even wipe her face afterward. Won't let me help her pick her hair up from the floor and the pillows and anywhere she sits, because it's all coming out. The only thing she's let me do is hire a nurse." My voice turned bitter. "Someone to help her do all the things I wanted to do for her."

Libby crouched in front of me, her hands resting lightly on my knees—an anchor of sorts.

"It's like she hates me for not being able to understand, but I don't know how to tell her that I do."

"But you don't." She rose and turned to descend the short flight of stairs to the sand where she sat, facing the water.

"There's no way, Nick, that we can understand or know or feel any of what they're going through. We can wish for understanding or pray for it, if that's your particular bag. We might want to take it on ourselves, if only for a day, for an hour, to spare them the pain, but no matter how much we might want to, we *can't*. And they can't help but resent us for wanting to do that for them, because what they're going through—they wouldn't wish on their worst enemy, let alone someone they love."

She stared up at the sky, flinching as a drop landed on her cheek. "He resents the loss of control, having lost his sense of self. That he's been reduced to this one existence where he's defined by this disease, when he's so much more and has been for so long. Especially to me."

For a second, I thought I'd lost her, that she'd totally forgotten my existence and who gave a shit if she had, but then she glanced back over her shoulder, both eyebrows raised. "Sound familiar?"

There was a first—feeling like an absolute asshole at the same time I felt a tremendous kinship. "How long, Libby?"

"Two years, give or take. Started with a small spot on his tongue and a couple of little ones in his throat. Did target specific radiation for a couple of months, all outpatient, got a clean bill of health for the next six months. Afterward, we went to Hawaii to celebrate." She paused and took a deep breath before saying, "And to plan," in such an unbelievably soft voice, the words almost got lost in the wind.

A sick feeling took over in the pit of my stomach, taking everything in there and twisting it in hard knots.

"It'd been just us for over eleven years, you know? Ethan's fourteen years older than I am, but he never made me feel any pressure over it. Said he was happy waiting until I was ready since I was so young when we got married. That he loved it being just the two of us and that mentally, he'd probably always be younger than me anyway, no matter what our birth certificates say." She smiled. "I loved that about him. That carefree, playful attitude. In a way, he was the kid *I* never was. It would've made him such a great dad, you know?"

The knots just kept twisting and turning, getting tighter and more painful.

"We were getting physicals, they found some shadows on one of his lungs and that, as they say, was that. We talked about different options, of course, maybe taking some sperm donations before he started treatment, but he didn't think that would be fair to me—on a lot of levels. I was so unbelievably pissed at him. Felt like he was taking the choice out of my hands. But, much as I hate to admit it, it was his choice as much as mine."

I made my way down the stairs and dropped to the sand beside her. Leaning back on my hands, I stared up at the clouds that were starting to glow with flashes of lightning like they were being lit from the inside while several yards away, the waves rushed in with a rhythmic roar and crash. Just sitting there watching and listening left me with the strangest feeling of closing out extraneous noise and bullshit—as if I was on an observation deck, watching through a window. Which forced me to focus on what was near and immediate: the motion of Libby's hand as she sifted sand through her fingers, that long strand of hair blowing across her face, the sound of my voice—

"That's how we found Kath's, too. We've been together pretty much since college, but only got married earlier this year. We were going to do it all at once—marriage, babies, a real house—all of it. Our parents were so relieved."

No, "Oh, Nick," or "I'm so sorry," or anything else that might have had me snarling and biting. I didn't need sympathy, and God knows, Libby didn't either.

"You know we're allowed to be angry, right?"

"Are we?"

"Oh fuck, Nick, why the hell not? We suffer." Her voice hardened. "Our lives are completely assed over, not just from a practical standpoint, but more importantly, from the emotional. Yet we've got to remain strong because we're the healthy ones."

Healthy ones. What a fucking joke. One that we were both in on and wished like hell we weren't.

Libby
NOVEMBER 1

"*Estás segura que no ay nada—*"

"*Gracias,* Carlos, *pero, no.*"

Oh God, please, no more concern, no more kindnesses...I couldn't—not today. I just couldn't—

"Libby, hey, Nan said you were around today."

Oh *God.* My hands shook as I tried to snap my wallet shut. I pretended not to notice as Carlos reached out and discreetly aligned the flap until the two metal disks clicked together with a tiny snap. I busied myself slipping the black leather clutch into my backpack, gaining a few more seconds—just enough.

"Hi, Nick. How are you?" And pat me on the back for having that come out sounding normal and not choked and strangled.

"Pretty good, actually."

No lie, either. He looked flushed and pleased, bouncing on the soles of his Reeboks, sweat running down the sides of his face and darkening his Florida Panthers T-shirt. So much better than at Ray's funeral, which was the last time I'd seen him. *Why* did he have to look so much better? So...happy?

"How about you?"

"Same old, same old."

Liar.

But he didn't see it, thank goodness. He was either in a really good mood or on a tremendous endorphin rush—maybe both. Whatever. If it kept him on the blind side, better for me.

"You know, I could really use something to drink. Join me?"

Don't do it, Libby. You can't. Not today.

"Um, I don't know…" Well, wasn't that just decisive?

"Come on, please?" He was still bouncing, shaking his arms, probably part of that cool-down thing that jocks did, and looking like an eager twelve-year-old. All of a sudden, I felt ancient.

"I haven't even taken my stuff upstairs—"

"That's cool. I need to go up and grab a quick shower anyway."

Dios mío, he was pushy. But I could've still said no. In the elevator. In my room, as he insisted on bringing my small bag in and setting it on the luggage rack. When he returned less than ten minutes later, back in the elevator, even down in the lobby, I could've still said no. So tell me why the hell I was slouched in a chair across from him in the coffee shop across the street from the hotel?

Because I was powerless, that's why.

"So what's been going on?" Tearing off a corner of the pumpkin scone that had been the first thing I'd seen in the case, I shoved it in my mouth.

I'm sure it was very good.

He took a huge swig from the bottled water he'd bought in addition to his coffee. "Well, I talked to Kath. About wanting to help her—about…" His voice dropped as he added, "Seeing her."

I straightened at that. "You told her?"

"Yeah." Nodding, he drained what was left in his bottle. "Not at first. I wanted to try one more time without resorting to that, but six words into the conversation, I knew she was going to shut down. But damn if I was going to let her."

He took a huge bite of his pastry, a bright, orange-pink blob of guava paste oozing out and clinging to the corner of his mouth. "I followed her around the house for three days, barely giving her space to breathe."

"That was risky as hell."

"Tell me about it. But what else was I going to do? I'd given her space. I'd tried easing into discussion. I'd been as supportive as I knew how. Tried most every damn thing I could think of, except forcing her to actually deal with me. Felt like I didn't have anything else to lose."

"And?"

"She blew a gasket, man. Day three and she'd had enough and just turned on me and let loose." His voice dropped again as he stared into his cup. "Afterward...it was the first time she really let me hold her in nearly four months."

My heart pounded against my chest, and I swallowed hard. Dear God, four months. Poor Nick. Poor Kath, that she hurt so bad she wouldn't let him close. I sent up a silent thanks to the god/goddess *du jour* that, at the very least, Ethan let me hold him. He may have hated my seeing him suffering and withering away, but he let me hold him.

All of a sudden, I realized that Nick was still speaking. "...hasn't gone any further, really, but it's progress, at least. She's still not up for letting me see her, in person, as it were, but at least she knows I've seen her and that I'm not scared and she knows I love her, no matter what. Small steps, you know?" He smiled at me, that happy, relieved smile I'd seen back at the hotel. "And this new cocktail she's on seems to be working a lot better for her. She's not getting quite so sick, not taking so long to recover, so she's been able to work from home, at least part time, and that's also helping her a lot—"

"I have to go."

"Libby?"

My fingers curling into the edges of the table. I shoved my chair back. "I'll see you l-later, Nick—I'm glad things are..."

No, dammit, I wasn't glad. I couldn't be happy...I liked Nick, I really did, but I just couldn't be happy. It was too much—it wasn't fair; it wasn't *fair*.

"Libby!"

I could hear my sneakers pounding against the sidewalk, feel the shift as concrete became asphalt. Horns blared as I ran across Alton Road's four busy lanes. Ignoring the squealing brakes and angry shouts, I strained to reach the parking lot and the safety of my car.

"Let *go*." I broke away from the hard grip, my arm hot and

stinging like when I was a kid and Stacy Alvarez would give me an Indian burn, the little bitch. Stumbling the last few feet, I yanked open the door and dropped into the driver's seat, blindly jabbing for the ignition button.

Finally, I connected, the engine roaring to life, but before I could shift from park, the door flew open. "Libby, for God's sake, what's the matter?"

"Leave me alone! Please, *please*, just leave me alone, Nick."

Where was that voice coming from? That ugly, shrill, painful voice?

"Turn the fucking car off, Libby; you're not driving." His hand latched onto the steering wheel.

"Fuck you." I tried to slam the door, catching his arm, but even though he grunted in pain, his grip held. "I am so goddamn tired of being told what to *do*."

I yanked the gearshift into reverse, the car jerking hard as some instinct drove me to slam on the brakes at the last possible second. Nick stumbled, but his grip never let up on the wheel. "Dammit, Libby, stop."

My head dropped to the steering wheel, my breath whistling through my throat as another scream tried to take over. "Just...leave me alone, please, please, please...leave me alone."

Not a scream, but a whisper that rang just as loud. And he would know I caved.

Powerless. Totally and completely powerless.

"Keep your foot on the brake, Libby, just for a second, okay?"

A breeze blew in as the door opened, making me lift my head. From a remote place way inside myself, I watched as Nick released the wheel and pulled the gearshift into park, angling his body across mine as he did, as if to keep me pinned in place. He didn't need to worry. Wasn't like I was about to try to pull free and take off. The brief rebellion was done.

At the same time, I sure as hell didn't need anyone babying me through this.

"I...I'm fine now."

"Don't, Libby." His voice was flat—nothing soothing or babying about it. "Not with me."

Putting his arm around me, he guided me out of the car and to the side entrance of the hotel, using his key card to let us in. For the first time, something penetrated the fog of my misery as I idly wondered why he would have taken us this way. Front was actually closer. But, *oh*—

Coming in this way, there would be far less likelihood of encountering curious faces or concerned expressions. I sighed and leaned a little closer into Nick, not wanting to see any of that, not wanting anyone to see me.

We got lucky, too, in that no one was waiting for the elevator and no one emerged either, as the doors slid open. No one but Nick to see how bad off I was—see how I was cracking… little fissures breaking across the surface. Now if I could just make it to my room I would be okay. I'd be fine. I could break in peace, then put myself back together.

At least enough to face another day.

"Where's your key?" His voice was a soft croon and oh *God*— there was more cracking, almost audible. If I looked down, would I actually see the spider web of lines crawling across my skin?

I waved vaguely toward the pocket of my jeans, barely feeling it as he reached in and pulled it free.

Pulling away from him, I crossed the threshold and turned, blocking the doorway. I tried to speak, but the words remained stubbornly trapped. Swallowing hard, I tried again, finally managing a quiet, "Thanks, Nick, I—"

He grasped my wrist in a hold as gentle as his voice. "Libby."

Oh *fuck*. If he'd insisted on talking, offered some stupid, "Why don't you tell me all about it, you'll feel better," commentary, I could've made my escape. I knew how to evade that. But just saying my name—making me look up into his eyes where there wasn't concern or even compassion, but…affinity?

A single tear escaped.

"Why do I get the feeling you don't do this real often?"

My knees gave way then—just buckled as a wordless, choking gasp strangled my lungs so I couldn't inhale, couldn't exhale, couldn't do anything but let Nick catch me just before I hit the floor.

We only just made it into the room, Nick, sliding to the floor, his back braced against the closed door as he held me, cradled in his lap. Huge gulping sobs threatened to shatter me from the inside, my chest burning and feeling like it was going to explode as I fought those goddamn tears that continued to threaten. And Nick just sat there holding me, stroking my back, and wiping away the few single tears that escaped.

"Ethan's so…sick. I'm afraid he's getting worse, Nick. No one's saying for sure, but I know…he's getting worse and nothing's helping, but they keep saying maybe this treatment or a new drug and it doesn't matter…it doesn't fucking matter…. He hurts and I can't do anything except what they tell me to do and none of it… none of it helps."

And *that's* when I finally let go, bunching Nick's shirt in my fists, and when that wasn't enough, pounding them against his shoulders. Cotton grew wet beneath tears and sweat and spit as I raged into his chest, repeating, "I can't do *anything,*" until I was hoarse and limp, my breathing as shallow and rapid as my heartbeat.

"You haven't told me much about him." Nick's words ruffled my hair. "I'm sorry."

I didn't move, other than to open my eyes. The sight of me, ragged and drained, staring back from the closet mirror was enough to make me close them again, concentrating on taking even, measured breaths, matching them to the cadence of Nick's heartbeat, slow and steady beneath my cheek.

"Why are you sorry?"

"Because you've been good to me. Listened to all my shit— what I'm going through with Kath—helped me through this crap."

A subtle sense of freedom, of release, washed over me as his hands moved to my hair and removed the elastic from the end of my braid. "None of that could've been easy, not with what you go through," he said as he unwound the long strands, "but you've never turned away from me—even though you probably had every right to."

"It's not a competition. My misery doesn't trump yours" My voice was hoarse, muffled further by his shirt. "Besides, I told you— you remind me of me."

I could feel the slow shake of his head, the drag of his chin against my hair. "No, it's not just that," he said, each word coming out slower and quieter than the last. "You see others. It's how you are."

"I'm no saint, Nick. Please don't make me out to be one."

"Not hardly. But you're human, Libby. Why the hell do you keep yourself on such a short leash? Especially when you're the one who told me we're allowed to be angry?"

"Because allowing yourself to feel it and acting on it are two different things." Tears started pricking at the corners of my eyes, hot and stinging. "And then this is what happens."

Cool air washed over my face as he pushed me back far enough for our eyes to meet. "*No es tan malo*. Not when you're with someone who gets it."

And with that shared glance came a moment of perfect clarity. *You don't have to be so strong around me. You can be strong, and I know you will be, but you don't have to—and neither do I. We won't lie to each other. Deal?*

He pulled me back against him and settled himself more comfortably.

"So—tell me about Ethan."

I took a deep breath, poked at the memories, and realized that for the first time in a long time it didn't hurt to look back.

"He was one of my teachers at Northwestern—honors journalism—and he terrified the absolute crap out of me."

"And turned your crank in a big way," Nick teased.

"Yeah," I laughed, "but I was too naïve and stupid to realize it. So instead, we fought." I laughed again. "Well, *I* fought. I was so scared of him; and when I'm scared, I fight. Astute bastard that he is, he enjoyed jerking my chain at every opportunity. And I knew it and he knew it and he wouldn't stop casting his damn lures, and I couldn't stop myself from taking his bait. But then he went too far."

"What'd he do?"

I shifted uncomfortably. Even all these years later, the memory still left me vaguely queasy. "Assigned me to cover a brutal homicide in a wealthy suburb. Mother of two stabbed to death by the husband's mistress while the kids were upstairs asleep."

"Jesus." My entire upper body lifted along with his sharp inhalation. "Why?"

"He thought I needed to toughen up. It was his opinion that feelings had no business in hard journalism while my counter was that feelings were integral to a good story. He called me a throwback New Age granola. I called him an emotionless asshole who probably enjoyed poking anthills with sticks. So he decided to give me a story so gut-wrenchingly horrible, I'd *have* to separate emotion from fact simply to be able to deal."

"And?"

"And I dealt—just not the way *he* expected me to."

"What'd you do?"

"Packed my bags and left."

"Damn, girl," he muttered as he shifted. God, I had to be getting heavy. There wasn't any reason for me to still be on his lap; I wasn't two, after all. Sliding to the floor beside him, I leaned back against the door with a tired sigh.

"Yeah." I folded my hands in my lap, twisting my rose-gold wedding band on my finger. "Ran back home, tail tucked firmly between my legs, yet utterly secure in the knowledge that hard journalism wasn't for me."

But I'd nevertheless felt compelled to write *my* version of that story, even if I never showed it to a living soul. I'd written about beauty and youth, status and wealth, and how those things didn't automatically preclude desperate acts. About how the threat of losing them could easily exacerbate desperation into evil. Then I took the printed sheets, tucked them into a folder, and hid it away.

"And you and Ethan still wound up together, how?"

"Short version is I couldn't stop writing, so I started a blog—about my dogs initially, then advice on training dogs in general—that newspaper websites across the country started linking to. Maybe not Pulitzer material, but satisfying. And eventually Ethan ran across it."

"And he got in touch to tell you he was proud of you."

"God, you are so optimistic, Nick," I said, patting his knee. "No, he wasn't proud, he was *pissed*. Showed up on my doorstep yelling that even if I couldn't stomach writing hard news, I could at least write women's interest features if I was *that* into my girly feelings, but for fuck's sake, I could do better than how to keep the dog from sniffing the guests' crotches."

"What'd you do?"

I laughed. "Married him."

Of course, there was a lot in between that—even if it happened in less than two weeks. Ethan and I kept fighting until he finally shut me up by kissing me, *then* we finally started talking. About his opinion of my ability as a writer, the attraction that—hey, guess what—we'd both felt. About the teacher/student thing, our age difference, my utter inexperience.

"And him with enough ethics and honor to make Tibetan monks look like they have loose morals by comparison."

This time Nick laughed along with me. God, but it felt good to remember this.

"No, seriously," I managed before a fresh wave of giggles overtook me.

Nick patted my knee. "I believe you, Libby. The way you say it, there's no doubt."

Nope, none at all. My husband, the tough, hard-boiled journalist who'd seen it all, was one of the most sensitive and honorable men I'd ever met. So honorable, he'd wanted to wait for our wedding night. I hadn't. So I'd had to take the initiative the night we'd made love for the first time. God, he'd been terrified. And for once, I hadn't been.

"He was so romantic, Nick. I could hardly believe it. He even asked Nora for permission to marry me."

"That must have been something."

"I would've killed her if she'd laughed, but amazingly, she didn't. She was actually really cool and dignified about it—well, dignified for her. And she adores him."

So many memories. *Good* memories. Why had I fought them for so long? My mind flipped through a photo album's worth of memories. Big things…little things. The everyday life things. Our life as it had been. Not as it was.

"Libby."

"Mm?"

"Libby, you're falling asleep."

I blinked once, then again, the memories receding as my reality returned. As the hotel room took shape around me, I realized my head had somehow wound up resting on Nick's shoulder. "I'm sorry," I mumbled, struggling to sound coherent, but every movement, from blinking to trying to lift my head, felt like I was slogging through molasses. I was so damn tired.

"Nick, no…" Instinct drove me to clutch at his shoulders, my eyes snapping open, then drifting shut against my will as he carried me toward the bed.

"I can—"

"I know you can. But let me help."

I forced my eyes open just for a second—just long enough to meet his gaze.

You don't have to be so strong around me.

"Okay." I dropped my head to his shoulder, the world already fading as I repeated, "Okay."

• • •

I blinked into the dark, breathing deep as I stretched, then relaxed, just like I'd learned during the way too many yoga classes Nora had dragged me to throughout my childhood. I'd already been hovering in that foggy, not-quite-awake place for a while, content to just drift, wrapped in memories of Ethan. Of when the two of us together were as close to perfect as anything I could've imagined.

With another deep breath, I finally rolled to one side, snapping on the light. Just bright enough, it did the trick when it came to diffusing memories and forcibly hauling me back to the reality of the hotel room and my present. Some recollection was good, but the temptation to ignore reality and sink into memory? A little too strong right now. Good things in moderation and all that.

A muffled groan prompted me to sit up, rubbing my eyes to clear out the last vestiges of sleep. My bleary gaze landed on the chair over by the window where Nick was fidgeting, one hand reaching up to rub his neck as the other smothered his yawn.

"You stayed."

His eyes blinked slowly as his gaze found mine. "Didn't feel right leaving. I wanted to make sure you'd be okay."

"But...Kath?"

"I called the hospital—she was sleeping. No point going back."

Crossing my legs under me, I reached for a pillow and hugged it close. "What time is it anyway?" It looked like he'd pulled both layers of the heavy drapes shut, so I couldn't even tell if there was any daylight left or if I'd lost the entire afternoon to my meltdown.

He glanced down at his watch. "Just past seven. You hungry?"

I shook my head and hugged the pillow tighter still as he frowned and sighed.

"Stubborn."

"Um, pot, meet kettle?"

His grin was rueful. "Touché." He stood and stretched. "Well, I guess I'll head out. Maybe call the hospital again. See if Kath's up for a short visit. What about you? Are you going back? We can ride together if you are."

I shook my head. "He—" The word got caught in my throat, making me cough and try again. "Ethan hasn't been doing well after his treatments. He doesn't like...doesn't want—" Helpless to find the right words, I finally settled for, "I'll go first thing in the morning. It's better."

No sympathy or anything soothing from Nick. Just a simple

nod of acknowledgment as he stared down at the paper he was currently scribbling something on. Tossing the pen to the table, he turned to the window, pulling back the drapes to reveal the ink dark of the early November night. November 1st as a matter of fact. *El Dia de los Muertos.* Not a big deal in Cuban culture, but Nora being Nora, she'd of course found deep metaphysical and mystical meaning in the ancient Mesoamerican and Aztec traditions and, as such, had co-opted aspects of the celebrations in her own unique Nora way. Generally, this amounted to an elaborate altar set up in the house and visits to cemeteries and one memorable year, a presentation to the entire elementary school in an effort to increase cultural awareness.

Thank God I was in high school by that point.

Whatever. As a kid, it meant I got to gorge myself on the sugar and chocolate skulls that were traditional *ofriendas*, while as an adult I'd been ever-so-slightly mocking, yet indulgent of her insistent claims that the day was meant as a celebration of life. While still gorging myself on the sugar and chocolate skulls. The last couple of years, though, I hadn't had much patience for it—certainly, not the celebration of life aspect of it. I was too goddamn busy trying to make sure my husband survived.

"What's this?" I looked down at the paper Nick had been scribbling on that he was now holding out to me.

"I'll call in a few, let you know if I'm going to the hospital. Even if I do, I won't be long. She gets tired easier at night it seems."

"Okay." But he still hadn't answered why he'd handed me a list of food items.

"My favorite stuff from room service. I don't think either of us is up to making the effort to go out, so wouldja mind ordering?"

He stared down at me, this combination of glib and cocky that left me unsure whether I wanted to clock him one across that arrogant jaw or hug him. I settled for grumbling, "You are so unbelievably bossy, you know that?"

"Pot, meet kettle." Even laughing, he easily managed to duck the pillow I heaved his direction. At the door he paused. His fingers curled around the handle. "And don't forget the cheesecake. For both of us. You need to eat more."

I looked down at the list, written in a chicken scratch that was even worse than mine, and managed to decipher *dark chocolate* and *cheesecake* down at the bottom.

So maybe not a sugar and chocolate skull, but a suitable offering nevertheless.

Nick

NOVEMBER 16

"Nick, you miserable sonuvabitch, how're you doing?"

I didn't look up from the notes I was typing into my laptop. "I'm not giving you my assessment, Bobby."

"You wound me. I can't just join you—one of my oldest friends—for a drink, maybe a nice meal? My treat."

Now I looked up. He was even managing to look hurt. Pretty impressive for a guy who had a reputation as a shark even among other agents. "I'm one of the only people who'll tolerate your ass, and you must really think this kid is something. You never offer to pay."

"You know, try to do something nice for a friend..." Bobby shook his head as he waved a waitress over. "Yeah, doll, bring me whatever you've got on draft, a Reuben, double slaw, a couple kosher dills, and bring my friend here the biggest plate of ribs you got."

As she left, Bobby took a second to admire her ass, then turned to me. "Hope you don't mind, but you're too fucking scrawny."

"Who are you, my mother?" I took a drink from the sweet tea I'd gotten addicted to traveling throughout the Southeast. No alcohol while doing player assessments. "And only you would order deli in Atlanta."

Smiling and winking at the waitress as she slid a mug in front of him and topped off my tea, he said, "They do it decent down here, and it's the best shot I'll have at anything approaching deli before I get back to New York. Going to Iowa next, then up to Minnesota for fuck's sake. And no, I'm not your mother, but I've known you almost as long. You're off by a good thirty pounds."

"Twenty of which I dropped right after I quit playing."

"Which means you're too fucking scrawny."

"God, but you're a pain in my ass."

"Everyone needs a hobby."

I laughed and pushed my laptop to one side. After waving for a beer of my own, we shot the shit until the food appeared.

I pulled a rib off the rack and bit into it. "By the way, don't think I don't know why you're buttering me up, Bob," I mumbled around a mouthful of spicy-sweet pork. "And I'm still not giving you my assessment until I give it to my bosses first." I sucked the bone clean and pulled another free.

"I'm not worried about it." He shrugged. "Parker's got some serious shit. You know it, I know it—more importantly, your bosses know it, which is why *you're* here checking the kid out. You've got one of the best damn eyes for talent assessment in the organization."

"I'm an eastern region scout, Bobby. I'd most likely be checking him out regardless."

"Not with you out of commission the way you've been lately. If he was just another decently talented schmuck they planned to send to the bush leagues and let him skate his ass off to pay his dues, they would've just sent one of the other guys to check him out. Fuck it," he said, "seeing you here is enough for me. I'll sign him and hope he doesn't turn into a total prick when I get him an unbefuckinglievable deal. How's Kath?"

Normally, I'd be all about deflecting the attention or redirecting the conversation, or just plain bullshitting—I'd gotten spectacular at that skill. But this was Bobby. Who'd known me since college. And yeah, he was an agent and a shark, but he was also a friend. Probably my best friend, which would be terrifying if I didn't know him so damn well and know that an actual heart beat beneath the shark exterior. Besides, for once this question didn't make me want to put my fist through a wall.

"She's doing pretty well, actually."

Bobby's eyebrows shot up toward what was left of his hairline.

"Yeah?" He set down a half-eaten kosher dill and pulled his beer closer.

"Yeah. They've got her on a different schedule with a new cocktail, and it's not just letting her function, but come damn close to feeling human. It's why I'm even here, man. This guy could've been the second coming of Luc Robitaille, but if Kath hadn't been doing better, one of the other guys would've had to check him out."

"Figured things had to be going better seeing as you're out here among the living—*shit*. Sorry, Nick."

Now, *there* was something I hadn't seen often in over fifteen years of friendship with Bobby Horowitz—a genuine blush, red all the way to his ears. I didn't think the guy was even capable of shame after so many years as an agent. I waved it off with a laugh. "Hell, Bobby, you didn't mean anything." And Kath *was* living.

Right now, that's all that mattered.

• • •

I was tired as hell. I had the beginnings of a nasty headache. I was fighting I-95 rush hour traffic.

And I felt tremendous.

The trip had been great. I'd scouted some promising young studs in addition to the big dog who'd been my primary assignment and got to see our team play a couple kick-ass games. Got to hang with players and coaches and talk shop for the better part of three days. Had dinner with Bobby, that asshole. And hell, I wasn't so stupid that I didn't know what the source of the good mood *really* was— Kath was doing better, and, little by little, we were easing back into a routine that could almost pass for normal. Normal enough for me to go on a business trip. Go for our customary dinner out the night before a trip: sushi at her favorite place with her looking as elegant and striking as ever—with a twist. I mean, how many women would have the balls to shave their heads, then wear scarves in the wildest prints and colors, forcing people to look? I know *I* couldn't keep my eyes off her.

Man, she had a pretty skull. Who knew? She'd gotten sick of releasing—that's what her nurse called it, Kath just called it shedding—and decided she was going to take control. The day she shaved it, she'd let me run my hands over the smooth, alien surface. Laughed when she saw the hard-on tenting my shorts and stroked it gently, laughing some more over what she called my previously undiscovered kinks and if she'd known about this before.... And even though it hadn't gone any further than that, it was at least progress—baby steps. Just like I'd told Libby.

God, Libby. I tapped the steering wheel as I waited for a chance to switch lanes. She'd seemed a lot better in the immediate aftermath of her breakdown—like it had been the catharsis she needed—but I was onto her now. Knew she clearly had the fake out down to an art form that put my ass to shame. So for close to two weeks, I'd been wanting to call, but hadn't. Because in a twisted, altruistic sort of way, I didn't want to remind her of her meltdown. She was so fucking independent and strong, and I knew that while she realized that in the long run letting loose the way she had was probably good for her, she was also likely kind of embarrassed by it. I mean, yeah, we were friends, but even so, I got the impression even that wouldn't be enough for Libby to let herself off the hook for losing her shit so completely.

Admittedly, I could've called Nan and asked how Libby was doing. But what ultimately kept me from doing that was that Nan might have asked why. And I just didn't feel right talking about what had gone down between us. Would've felt like...I don't know, a betrayal, I guess. So I was left with hoping I'd run into her when we went back to Miami next week. But if I didn't, I'd ask Nan then. Definitely. Libby didn't need to close herself off that way—not when there were people around to help.

Lost in thought, I pretty much drove the rest of the way home on autopilot, only snapping out of my head as I turned into the driveway of the Mediterranean-style townhouse Kath and I shared. The *pink* Mediterranean-style townhouse. As always, I couldn't help but laugh and think, *Jesus, if the guys back in Jersey could see me now.* But

Kath glommed onto it right away—said it was perfect for the next stage of our lives together. And it had been—at least until the next stage of our lives took this crazy-ass detour. Even so…maybe it was the pink or the red-tile roof or the white shutters, but it did seem homier. More welcoming. A better place to be going through all of this crap.

Short-cutting through the garage into the kitchen, I dropped my bags on the floor and went in search of Kath. Only three days, but it was the longest I'd been away since her diagnosis and while I'd called home every day and I knew she was doing well enough that I hadn't really worried, I'd missed the hell out of her.

"Babe?" I kept the volume fairly low in case she was sleeping.

"Office, Nicky."

I followed her voice into the small, glass-walled room overlooking the courtyard—another thing that had totally sold her on the house. And while I'd sort of grunted and said, "Yeah, it's okay," in a futile attempt to keep the real estate agent from totally raking us over the coals, I had to admit, I really dug the courtyard too. The lush, tropical plant-filled place was like our own private oasis.

While Kath finished with her phone conversation, I stretched out on the couch, kicked off my shoes, and took a swig from the beer I'd snagged on my way through the kitchen.

"So what's it going to take to get them, Jorge?" She stopped and scribbled a note on the pad in front of her. "Oh, you have got to be kidding—they don't do 'sick people parties?' That self-absorbed little twat. How *dare* he? This is for little *kids*, for God's sake. No, no…I'll call their booking agent myself. Lead singer's mother dealt with this last year—very hush, hush, and she's doing better now, but he's such a mama's boy, it totally wrecked him. It was the 'personal issue' they canceled a bunch of dates for on their last tour. No, wasn't rehab. For once. Anyhow, trust me. I will guilt their asses into performing if that's what it comes to."

I studied her bent head, smiling as I sipped my beer. A bright pink scarf today, wild swirls with some blue thrown in. Pucci. Her favorite because the designs were so bold. I'd bought her a new one in Atlanta—all shades of green for my tough Irish girl.

"Sweetheart, I make it my business to know this shit. It's how we organize the best events on the Gold Coast. Look, hang tight. I'll talk to you after I've cornered their agent and made him beg for mercy. *Ciao*."

I grinned as she dropped the phone into the cradle, scribbled some more notes, and tapped on her keyboard, muttering the entire time about selfish little twerps with overindulged senses of entitlement and that she'd make him perform at the benefit if she had to drag his ass there herself.

It was *good* to be home.

"And this is why *you're* the best event planner on the Gold Coast."

She glanced up from writing some more notes on her pad and smiled, her eyes narrowed with the look that indicated she was on the hunt. God, it was good to see that look again—to see her eyes going dark the way they did when she was excited. Growing up in a house full of brown-eyed Cuban girls, I'd always been a complete sucker for light eyes. Every girlfriend from ninth grade on had had blue or green eyes; there'd even been one with a really freaky-light pair of gray eyes, but Kath's weren't light at all. Best way to describe them was navy—a dark, intense blue that seemed even darker against her pale skin. One guy in our dorm had called her an alien freak, with the eyes and the pale skin and the dark red hair. I'd thought she was the most beautiful thing I'd ever seen. Still did.

Leaving her desk, she came over and nudged at my legs until I lifted them far enough for her to slide under. Taking the beer from me, she took a small sip. "Just the Gold Coast?" she asked with a lift of her eyebrows.

"East coast?" I took the beer back, running my tongue along the mouth of the bottle and imagining I could taste her there.

Her eyes following my movements, she smiled. "Well, part of me would love to agree, but taking into account New York and D.C., maybe not."

"So how about we settle for the Southeast, then?"

"I can live with that." We laughed together for a second before

I drained what was left of the beer and turned away to set the bottle on the tile floor, using the motion to mask my sigh. God, not only had it been too long since I'd seen her look so good, it had been too long since I'd heard her sound so good. So like herself. For the first time in a long time, everything felt normal.

I glanced up to find her studying me, her head tilted. "Miss me?"

"You have no idea." Out of sheer habit, I started to reach for her, to pull her on top of me, but at the last second, froze. Her glance moved from my face, to my hand, still hovering between us, and back again. After a long few seconds, she took my hand in hers and lifted it to her lips, kissing the palm before stretching out and lowering herself over me.

"You have no idea," I repeated, wrapping both arms around her. We stayed like that for a while, her breath warm against my neck as I watched the sun set and the room go dark around us until the only light left came from the desk lamp. The entire time I did nothing more than caress her back—small circles between her shoulder blades, delicate lines traced along each side of her spine— all the intimate caresses learned over the years finally blending into smooth deliberate strokes that traveled the length of her back with a few tentative detours over the firm curves of her ass.

Christ, I hadn't been this cautious on our first date. Of course, back then I'd been eighteen, perpetually horny, and trying like hell to get into her pants. Of course, back then, she'd been eighteen, just as horny, and just as anxious to get into my pants, so we had a nice mutual thing going—nothing to be cautious about. This was new territory. I didn't know what she wanted. Didn't know how far she'd let me go. And because I'd never really had to before, didn't know how to ask.

"You asleep?"

I tried to keep my laugh quiet—not break the mood. "I do this in my sleep?" I asked as I rubbed gentle circles in the small of her back.

Her own laugh was light, but in some undefined way, the mood had shifted. "Among other things."

Oh. Well, then. No need to guess what she meant about that. Carefully, I lifted her far enough away so I could ease my legs out from under her and turn to sit up, though I made sure to keep one of her hands in mine, keep her close. Last thing I wanted was for her to feel rejected, because that feeling—it sucked beyond redemption.

"Nicky…"

"No, I'm sorry, Kath. I didn't realize."

Bullshit. Just…bullshit. Of course, I realized. How could I not? Woke up nearly every morning with my dick so hard, I could pound nails through a two-by-four. I'd try to ease away, quick and discreet, before making a break for the bathroom and the shower. Some mornings it was a really, really fucking cold shower. Then there were the days I just couldn't take it anymore and it would be the hottest water I could stand, a lot of Kath's fancy shower gel, and my hand.

Those were the times I had to remind myself—wasn't about me, and I could goddamn well deal. But sitting next to her, so close, physically and emotionally, yet feeling her pull away on both counts, I realized—*again*—this wasn't just about the physical. I missed *her*. I missed what we were together. These little bits and pieces we were getting back—they were good. And at the same time, they were so fucking painful it made my chest burn.

"I just…can't. Not yet."

"How much longer?"

I cringed as soon as the words left my mouth, harsh and raw and as completely selfish as I felt in that second. She slid to the far end of the couch, a cold silence dropping between us as thick as any wall.

"I didn't realize we were on a schedule." Her voice was as cold as the silence had been. Colder maybe.

We're not, it's just—"

"Why can't you be happy with what I can give you for right now, Nick?"

"I *am*—"

Liar.

"No, you're not. You want more. You *always* want more."

"No, Kath…it's not that, it's just—you act like you don't miss me, that you don't miss being together."

She shook her head. "You're unbelievable, Nick. Are you really that anxious to fuck?"

My head spun as her voice went from cold to pleading to angry and all of a sudden, I was angry too. "Yes, Kath, I am!" Jerking my head up I met her startled gaze. Good. She maybe needed to be at least a little startled. "Of course I'm anxious to fuck, to make love, but it's more than that and it's what you don't seem to understand. I want to hold you, whether you're sleeping or puking your guts out. I want to talk to you and laugh with you and not be afraid to touch you or worry that I might go too far. I want to know that you want me to be with you—in whatever way you want. Why don't you get that I want to be part of you again? Be us, again, even if it's different?"

"Why don't you get that I don't want you to?"

I stared at her, my chest throbbing as if I'd been slammed with a hockey puck.

"I'm too fucking busy trying to stay alive to worry about *us*. And what we were? Isn't going to magically come right back just because I'm having a good day or a good week." She lurched to her feet, her hands curled into fists. "Jesus, Nick, get out of your own goddamn head for once in your spoiled life. I'm *trying* to give you what I can, trying to *want* to be with you, but even lying there with you hurts, because I don't have a place on my body that doesn't ache, nowhere that's not altered in some way. Is that what you're so anxious to see? Fine,"

Who knew that fabric tearing was so loud? That buttons popping could sting so hard as they hit skin? Sound so loud as they scattered across a tile floor? I sat, frozen, as she jerked first shirt, then bra, off and stood in front of me, breathing hard, the two lines across her chest a dark, angry pink.

"It hurts, Nick, like you would not believe. They've started pumping saline to expand my skin and it's so cold and I can feel it stretching and it's like nothing I can even begin to describe. I just want to claw out of my body to get away from the sensation."

Even though I felt as if I should, I couldn't look away. God, they *were* bigger. I hadn't noticed at first, but they were definitely larger. How could I have missed that? Why hadn't she said anything before now?

"Or maybe this is what you want to see?" She turned her forearms up exposing the undersides. I breathed hard through my nose, trying to quell the sudden nausea at the sight. She watched my reaction, a faint, mocking smile on her face.

"Isn't that ironic? The way my veins are turning black just like the junkies I've organized countless benefits for? Or wait—how about this?" She pushed her loose-fitting pants down to her ankles and stepped free, flinging her arms wide as she did. "There you go, baby. All of me. Just like you've wanted. All nice and bloated, my skin green, from all the wonder drugs—and oh—you haven't seen this—" She paused, hands on her waist, and hit me with a narrow stare. "Well, not unless you've pulled some more of your hidden camera shenanigans."

Jesus Christ, *no*. Never again. But before I could even shake my head, she'd already pushed her underwear down and kicked them my direction, where they landed at my feet. Numb, I reached down and picked them up. Plain, white cotton—loose, practical—not at all what I was accustomed to seeing her wear.

When had that changed?

My voice was gone—trapped somewhere between my head and my throat, silently yelling at her to please, stop this—it was insane and not necessary. She needed more time, more space—okay, I got that. I was a selfish, stupid prick for not having realized just how much more time and space she needed, but please, please, Katharine, for the love of God, *stop*.

Not that it would have any effect. This was full-bore fury—a rage that made her blow up from a few weeks back look like a kindergartner's tantrum by comparison. Rage that had clearly been wanting out. And I'd started it. This was completely on me. Because I couldn't leave well enough alone.

"Well, lookee there," she said in this foreign, mocking voice as the fingers of one hand stroked a teasing pattern between her legs. "Looks like the 'releasing' wasn't just restricted to my head." She glanced back up, her eyes dark—darker than I'd ever seen them. "Your baldness kink extend to my cunt, Nicky? You like it all bare and smooth? I hear that's how strippers and porn stars keep their pussies. Is that true, sweetheart?"

Hearing words coming out of her mouth that I'd never once heard her use in the nearly twenty years we'd known each other—along with the vicious implications—was what finally freed my voice.

"Kath, please...stop."

"Fuck you, Nick," she shot back in a low, gritty voice. "This is what you wanted. Who you wanted. Or is it?" She leaned down and reached between my legs, squeezing and kneading the mass that had gone soft and nonresponsive. She let loose with a harsh, bitter laugh. "That's what I thought."

She spun away and took off, her feet pounding up the stairs. A few seconds later, the sound of our bedroom door slamming echoed through the house and straight through my chest.

• • •

Stroke...stroke...stroke.

My blades rhythmically cut into the ice, my lungs burning with each cold, damp inhale. That same intense burn streaked down my thighs and across my shoulders as I raised the stick high then brought it down in the smooth, fast sweep perfected over the more than thirty years since my first PeeWee game. Solid and sure, wood hit rubber, sending jarring vibrations up both arms even as my eyes followed the path of the puck landing square in the net.

Over and over, I'd been doing this, for God knows how long.

Long enough that I'd played through a pickup game, welcoming the hits I'd taken, and taking too much joy in the ones I'd dished out. Long enough that after the session was over and the rink closed to the public for the night, I'd stayed and hung with a few of the employees, continuing to practice, to skate, to hit—each other, our sticks, the puck. Especially the puck. And even after the last diehards had called it a night, I'd wanted to keep going. They knew me—it was the big club's practice facility—so the manager just tossed me a set of keys and told me to turn the lights out when I was done.

Not by a fucking long shot, dude.

I kept skating, hitting the puck from every conceivable angle and lobbing wristers that would make a goalie cry. That is, if there'd been a goalie there to try to stop them.

There was no one. No one in net, in the stands, on the bench.

But where else was I going to go?

Not like there was anyone at home, either. Not really. And this, the ice, had been my home away from home since I was six.

Which left me alone, skating down two hundred feet, across eighty-five, up two hundred, across another eighty-five, over and over until I finally dropped. Until my lungs went from burn to pure fire, and my legs went numb—just refused to go any further or hold me up anymore. All I could do then was lay face down, the battered ice digging into my cheek as I breathed in cold, wet air and something—sweat...tears, maybe—rolled off the bridge of my nose and landed on the ice with a near-inaudible hiss.

What the hell else could I do?

Libby

NOVEMBER 24

I stared at Marco, trying to absorb what he was saying. I mean, the man was one of the preeminent oncologists in the goddamn country. He should be using all the big words, the fancy words, right? Not something as mundane as—

"Stable. What's that mean, exactly?"

"Libby—*mi vida*." His mellow hazel eyes blinked behind his half rims as he stroked my arm—long, soothing motions like he was trying to settle a skittish dog. "You know what it means."

"You know, humor me just this once, okay? Pretend I haven't gone through this before and that you have to hold my hand and explain it from scratch."

He rolled his eyes—just a little—and sighed—just a little—but his voice was exceedingly patient as he explained. Again. Because we'd been through this before.

"Stable means things aren't getting any worse."

"And not any better."

"No, but we're going—"

"To try something new," I finished in tandem with him.

His voice went from patient to dry as he asked, "Do you want me to do this, *m'ija*, or should I just let you finish?"

Taking a deep breath, I waved my hand, indicating he should go on.

"We're going to try something new," he repeated. "Alter the combination some, see if it might not kick-start something."

"Or make him even more miserable." I shoved my hands

through my hair, remembering, too late, that it was pulled back in a loose ponytail. Wrestling my fingers free, I yanked the elastic off, and then ran my fingers through again, welcoming the sharp bite of pain from dragging them through the tangled strands.

"It's the risk we take, Libby."

"*We're* not taking shit, Marco. It's all on Ethan." I dropped my head back against the wall, staring up at the fluorescents lining the ceiling. "Is he okay with this?"

"He's willing to try."

Of *course* he was. "You know, I keep trying to decide if he's incredibly brave or incredibly stupid." I shifted my gaze from the ceiling to the closed door of Ethan's room.

"*Yo creo...*" Marco said slowly, "that it's he believes he has something worth fighting for." He reached out, not to stroke my arm again, but to cup my chin, making me feel like I was about six years old. I grabbed on to his hand, amazed, as always, by how dry and warm it was. Doctor's hands. Good hands.

"Marco...*cada vez que esto a pasado*—that he's had one of these stable periods, he's..."

Dammit—it scared me so much, I couldn't quite bring myself to say it out loud. Luckily, Marco knew exactly what I was talking about. Because he *had* been through it before with us. Lowering our hands, he met my gaze head on.

"*Yo se*, Libby. *Te entiendo.* I know you're worried that he's going to take another turn for the worse, but perhaps this time will be different."

"Yeah." Maybe it would. Or maybe he wouldn't just take a turn for the worse but he'd—

"Hang in there, Libby. *Ese hijo de puta* you're married to fights as hard as anyone I've ever known in my life. He's not ready to let go yet."

I wish he would.

I stopped breathing—I swear I did. I couldn't have possibly thought that...*No.* I didn't mean it, I *didn't*—except...

I just didn't want him to hurt anymore. He'd had enough pain for five lifetimes—he didn't deserve this. But I did *not* want him to go. Oh God…no. Not yet. Not yet. I just wanted him to be better, to be Ethan, to be who he'd been.

I wanted *my* Ethan.

And there you had it—the bald, ugly truth.

"It's me who's not ready to let go," I whispered past the band constricting my chest.

Marco didn't sound in the least bit surprised. "He knows that, too, *m'ija*."

My hands clenched into fists against my thighs. "That's not very fair, is it? That kind of demand?"

"He's a grown man, Libby. He knows what he's doing." Shades of Nora in those words. Telling me not to baby him. I pressed my lips tight and squeezed my eyes shut for a brief second, beating the demons back from where they waited at my doorstep.

"Libby, do you want me to write you a scrip for something? Just to take the edge off or help you sleep?"

Okay, I had to pull it together. Couldn't fall apart now. And while something *soothing* was seriously tempting, it wouldn't help. Not in the long run. There wasn't a hell of a lot that would, short of—well…what I wanted wasn't going to happen. Not unless some of that miracle shit decided to come my way. I took a deep breath and forced a smile. "Look that bad, do I?"

All he did was cross his arms and stare.

"I'm okay, Marco. *De verdad*," I added when the eyebrows headed up and his forehead creased. He knew I was bullshitting. And how. This must be what having a normal father was like.

"I'll leave it at the nurse's desk if you change your mind. *Cabezona*." Shaking his head, he leaned in and kissed my forehead before taking off. For a minute, I stayed where I was, watching him talk to the desk nurse, the two of them glancing over with these obviously concerned expressions, before I decided I'd been enough of a sideshow and crossed the hall to Ethan's room.

He turned his head on the pillow, his smile turning to a flinch as Cory, his nurse, opened the line that started the cocktail. After checking the settings, she left us alone with the usual reminders to call her if we needed anything.

After the door swung closed behind her, I said, "I see I'm not late to the party."

Keep it light, Libby. Don't let him see.

"Just tapped the line into the keg, gorgeous," he replied with a wink. He was doing it too. Always doing his best to protect me. "Did you bring the party favors?"

"Fresh from Starbucks." I showed him the bag and drink tray holding his salvation.

"What did I do to deserve you?"

"Insulted my journalistic abilities." I set the drinks and bag on the night table, then pulled a chair close to the side that didn't have the line going in.

"It was simply an honest effort to push you toward your full potential, angel."

"I said it then, I'll say it now—your motivational skills suck."

"Yet you still bring me foofy coffee drinks. How bad can they really be?"

"It's those baby blues," I mock grumbled. "Suckered me with them from day one." I stuck a straw through the opening in the lid of the Java Chip Frappuccino—yes, with whole milk *and* extra whipped cream, as I'd snapped at the size zero barista who'd lifted her pierced eyebrow at me—and put it to his lips.

Taking a long sip, he swallowed and leaned back against the pillows with a sigh. "Oh, that's good. Beats the shit out of corrosive metal aftertaste." He glared at the bag with the skull and crossbones insignia that was the source of the corrosive metal aftertaste, "Thank you for being a sucker for the baby blues." He turned them my way, along with the smile that had also sucker punched me that first day and that still made me go weak in the knees.

Leaning forward, I licked a tiny bit of whipped cream from the curve of his lip, then kissed him. Thank God, that, at least, was the same. No matter how much weight he lost, no matter how much the rest of his body changed, his mouth felt the same—made me feel the same. "Always and always, Ethan," I whispered against his lips.

He lifted his free hand to my neck and pulled me closer, another smile curving his lips as he returned my kiss. "So what else didja bring me?"

One more small kiss, then I eased back and reached into the bag I'd placed next to the tray. "Black and white cookie or a chocolate-chocolate chip cupcake with chocolate frosting?"

Mere formality. I knew which he'd choose.

"Chocolate."

"Sensualist."

His hand captured my wrist as I was swiping my finger across the frosting. "You know it." His gaze locked with mine, he brought my frosting-laden finger to his mouth, sucking off the chocolate blob, his tongue teasing the sensitive skin.

My heart skipped a beat at the familiar touch—at the heat pooling low in my stomach. Maybe Marco was right. Maybe this time would be different.

• • •

An hour later, I eased out into the hallway, closing the door quietly behind myself. He'd had his foofy drink and cupcake, and had even managed to dictate a column before drifting off. I could only hope that the anti-nausea meds, for once in their misbegotten existence, would actually help and he'd get some decent rest. One way or another, I probably had another hour or so to kill before we knew for sure. Wandering in the direction of the waiting area, I stopped dead in the middle of the hallway.

"Nick?"

No response. As I approached, I realized his eyes were closed, even as the rest of his body swayed, fighting even in sleep to stay upright on the sofa.

"Nick?" Softer now, because I didn't want to startle him.

I was the one who wound up startled as he jerked and started hacking and coughing—a horrible, familiar sound that shook me straight to the bone.

"*Por tú madre*, Nick. Hang on." Backing away, I blindly reached toward the water dispenser, and filled a cup, never once taking my gaze from him. Taking a seat beside him, I began rubbing his back, high up between the shoulders, those small soothing circles I was so practiced in. Heat radiated through his knit shirt, making the fine hairs on my arm stand on end. "Jesus, you're burning up. Here."

As the coughing subsided, I held the cup to his lips. "Small sips—you don't want to start again." I tried not to flinch as his hand came to rest over mine, hot and damp.

"Thanks." His voice was hoarse, barely audible.

"Nick, have you seen anyone for this?"

He shook his head.

"Are you insane?"

He made a sound like a barking seal as his hand tightened around mine. "You honestly don't wanna go there, Libby."

Well, then. I studied his bent head as I continued rubbing his back. With my free hand I fished a napkin from my pocket and used it to wipe away the sweat beading along his neck and up beneath the ragged ends of his hair.

So I wouldn't go there—yet. But only because we had other things to take care of first.

"Kath getting her treatment?"

"Yeah." He nodded. "Nurses kicked me out of the room, though, soon as they heard the first hack. Not like she wants me anyway."

Oh man, I could see I was going to have a whole list of things to nail his ass on. Because if he thought I was going to let him keep this all bottled up... "Works both ways," I muttered under my breath.

He jerked his head up, then cringed, as if it had about killed him to do so. "What?"

"You look like shit," I said instead, as I got my first good look at his face and hoped like hell I didn't look as horrified as I felt. Sunken eyes, rimmed in a vicious red, stared dully while beneath the heavy stubble of his beard, the edges of his nose and upper lip were raw and angry, probably from repeated blowing and wiping. Pretty much the works. "What the hell have you been using on your face—sandpaper?"

"Whatever's handy," he said with a shrug that had him cringing again. And yet he hadn't seen anyone? Damn arrogant, know-it-all Cuban man, hockey jock.

"You wait right here and don't you dare move," I ordered as I made certain his hold on the cup was secure.

"Don't wanna."

"Well, you're just going to have to."

He sighed and shifted, squinting up at me. "I mean, I don't want to move, Libby. Don't think I can."

"Even better." I took off for the nurse's desk where I asked that they page Marco. Maybe he was one of the preeminent oncologists in the country, but last time I checked, he was also just a plain old doctor and for now, that's what I needed. Got lucky in that he was nearby, checking on Kath as a matter of fact, so I only had to wait about ten minutes. Ten long, miserable, interminable minutes spent rubbing Nick's back through another vicious coughing fit and making certain he drank more water.

"*Bueno, m'ijo*, Kath mentioned you had a little cold." Marco stood in front of us, shaking his head. "Taken up bullshitting as a hobby?"

"She doesn't know how bad it is. Downed about half a bottle of all-purpose cold shit before we left Boca. Didn't want to be coughing and sneezing the whole way down." He sighed and looked up at Marco. "It's not like you haven't told me over and over how fucked the treatments leave her immune system, so I did my best to keep it away from her."

But…still, he was so sick. Whatever Nick had, it couldn't possibly be something that had just cropped up overnight. Even keeping it away from her, how could she have not realized it was more than a…a…*little cold*? I glanced up at Marco, who clearly got what I was thinking and let me know, with a nearly imperceptible shrug, *I don't know either.*

"*Vamanos,*" he ordered Nick. "*Gracias, m'ija,* for the page," he said to me. "Last thing *este cabrón* needs to be doing is developing pneumonia. As it is, from the sound of it, he might be close."

God, no. I sucked in a sharp breath at Marco's casual diagnosis, a familiar, sick feeling kicking me in the stomach.

"It's not pneumonia." He pushed himself to a standing position, swaying and looking decidedly green.

Marco's brows rose. "*No me digas.*"

"It's not," he insisted. "I've had pneumonia before—it wasn't like this."

"So if you've had it before, then you know you're predisposed to get it again. And that it's not necessarily the same every time. *Vamanos,*" he repeated, putting his hand beneath Nick's elbow and leading him away. As they walked away, Nick looked back over his shoulder with what I'm sure he thought was a really pathetic expression. Well, actually, it really *was* a pathetic expression—maybe not in the "Save me" sort of way he intended, but pathetic in a quiet, heartbreaking way.

Another ninety minutes passed. Time I spent sitting by Ethan's bed with my laptop working on my own column—reassured by the steady rise and fall of his breathing as he continued to sleep. So far, so good. I could only hope that things remained steady and calm, although past experience suggested that was wishful thinking at best. But hey, I was good at wishful thinking. It's what kept me going most days.

At the quiet creak of the door opening, I looked up to find Corrine gesturing that I should join her in the hallway.

"Yeah, what's up?"

"Dr. Aguirre knew you'd want to know how Nick's doing."

"What's the verdict?"

"Nasty upper respiratory infection, but his lungs are clear."

"Well, small favors at least." I sighed and looked into the still deserted waiting area. "Has he left?"

"That's the thing—" I returned my attention to Cory. "Marco

already doused him with cough medicine with codeine—combined
with what Nick took before, he doesn't want him driving. Don't you
both stay at Las Palmas when you're here?"

"Yeah."

"He tried to make noises about not bothering you, but Doc
wasn't having anything of it. Took his keys." She held them up.
"Think you can?"

"Oh, for the love of—" God, but he gave a whole new meaning
to stubborn. I took them from her and shoved them in the pocket
of my jeans. "Yes, of course."

"He's down at the pharmacy waiting for his prescriptions to
be filled."

"Okay, I'll get my stuff and meet him down there." I paused
and glanced back at the closed door behind me, hesitating, even
though I knew Nick was waiting, that he needed me. But Ethan—
my Ethan…

"He'll be fine," Corrine reassured me, before adding, "You
know, when he wakes up, it's likely to be bad anyway."

Yeah, I knew that. And now with this new cocktail, the
uncertainty of not knowing exactly how he'd react—he definitely
wouldn't want me around for that. "But you'll call if he needs
anything or if anything changes?"

"Always, honey." She patted my shoulder. "You're a good
woman, Libby."

"I'm thinking more glutton for punishment." Because on top
of my ever-present worry for Ethan and all the added concerns that
came along with a new course of treatment, I had to also go and
find some other deathly ill person to care for. Clearly, I was out of
my fucking gourd.

But any put-out feelings I might've had went straight out the
window the minute I caught sight of Nick slouched in a chair in the
pharmacy, eyes closed, a crumpled white bag sitting in his lap.

"Let's go."

He blinked owlishly, his eyes puffy and red. "Thought I could
drive myself," he mumbled as I put a hand under his elbow and

helped steady him as we took the escalator up to the glass-walled crosswalk that connected the hospital to the garage.

"Of course, with you able to walk so well and all." All he did was stare blankly, sarcasm clearly lost in the haze of drugs and illness, making me shift my hold to his waist. "Where's your car?"

"Couple rows back. Black Explorer with team plates."

"Okay, wait here." I popped the locks on the Volvo, which was in a handicapped space right by the entrance to the garage, and opened the passenger door. "Anything in particular you want out of your car?"

Silence. He was already leaning back against the headrest, eyes closed, lashes damp and spiky against his cheeks, making him look like a little boy. Shaking my head, I headed off to find his car where I bypassed the hockey sticks—tempting though they were—in favor of the duffel I finally discovered buried under the pads and skates and other assorted hockey jock paraphernalia.

He didn't open his eyes once during the short drive to the hotel. Not even when I slammed on the brakes, trying to avoid becoming one with the typically horrible Miami Beach driver who thought because he was in a Ferrari he could ignore all known driving laws. But when I pulled into a parking space at the hotel and turned off the engine, his eyes slowly opened and he sighed—this unbelievably relieved sound that was as heartbreaking as the look he'd sent me over his shoulder back at the hospital.

"Carlos, Señor Azarias is going to need a second key."

You have to love a professional concierge. Not even so much as a lift of his eyebrow at the unexpected request as we checked in. Just an exquisitely polite and immediate, "Room service, señora?"

"Carlos, that would so rock my world, you have no idea."

"If I may take the liberty—"

"Be my guest," I replied. "Have it sent to Señor Azarias's room, please."

"Charge it there, too," came a sleepy mumble from beside me.

"For God's sake, Nick, shut up. We'll figure that out later."

"Consider it taken care of, señora."

"*Gracias*, Carlos."

I got Nick up to his room and collapsed on the bed before returning downstairs to get our luggage. And again, props to Carlos for being the best of a rare breed, because he'd been kind enough to put us in rooms directly across the hall from each other. Stopping in mine only long enough to drop my suitcase and backpack on the bed, I returned to Nick's room with his duffel, just as room service showed.

I surveyed the cart: soup, a simple egg and cheese *torta*, and in the small bag the server handed me, a couple pints of Häagen-Dazs, one chocolate, one vanilla.

Good concierge. After tipping the server and shoving the ice cream in the freezer compartment of the mini fridge, I turned to Nick, lying in the same position I'd left him. Hadn't even bothered to kick his shoes off. It almost seemed a shame to wake him.

"Nick...dinner's here." He jerked slightly at my touch and turned away. I put my hand to his forehead. Still burning up. Digging into the crumpled paper bag from the hospital pharmacy that he'd tossed on the table, I found the cough medicine, antibiotics, and Marco's scrawled instructions: *Acetaminophen for fever, as needed.*

Well, it was needed—big time—and there wasn't any in the bag. I wondered if that was something else he traveled with, like the ibuprofen, or was I going to have to go make a drugstore run? I stared at the duffel, debating. Given how much I hated anyone poking around in my things, I had a healthy distaste for doing the same, but desperate times and all that jazz.

Kneeling by the duffel, I unzipped it, my breath catching as the interior was revealed. You know, for some reason it had never left me—that image, clear and vivid, of the neatly packed suitcase from our first encounter. The jeans, the folded shirts, the toiletry kit with that fresh, unwrapped toothbrush. I remembered Nick, sinking into the chair, completely pole-axed, saying that Katharine had packed for him—she always packed for him—and seeing his dawning understanding of just how radically his life had changed.

Slowly, I pulled out the clothes, wrinkled from being crammed into the bag, automatically smoothing them out and folding them into a neat pile. Totally random selection—a tuxedo shirt, a couple pairs of sweatpants, a vibrant, green silk kerchief, half wrapped in torn, wrinkled tissue. No underwear, no toiletries, just a near-empty bottle of L'Occitane shower gel down at the bottom of the bag. Chewing the pad of my thumb, I studied the pile, then glanced back over my shoulder at him, still asleep, but curled up and shivering.

Rising, I pulled the half of the bedspread he wasn't lying on over him and quietly left the room. Luckily, there was a Walgreen's a block away, so I was able to go, get what I needed, and make it back inside of a half hour. The *torta* and soup were cold by then, but that's why God invented microwaves.

It took some effort to wake him—so much so I worried he was closer to unconscious than asleep. But just about the point I was starting to consider calling Marco again, he finally struggled to a sitting position, bitching and moaning the entire time.

Good sign.

"Haven't slept all week, now you're waking me up."

"Poor, baby." I dropped a pair of Tylenol into his palm.

"You always this sympathetic?"

I handed him an open bottle of water. "You're catching me on a good day."

Another one of those small, relieved sighs, followed by a quiet, "Good," that had me busying myself fluffing pillows and tucking them behind his back—and to have a few seconds in which to compose myself. Wouldn't do to have him see me getting all emotional. Especially since I couldn't even explain why, exactly, I was so emotional.

Even with the pillows piled behind him, he seemed to have trouble staying steady, so I sat beside him on the bed, letting him lean on me as we ate. Flipping through channels on the TV, I found a basketball game that provided mindless background noise, plus the added benefit of removing any immediate need to talk.

Rising from the bed to place my dishes on the table, I asked, "Do you want some ice cream?"

He shivered. "No, not right now."

Automatically, I leaned down and pressed my lips to his forehead. His skin was still warm, but nowhere near as painfully hot as it'd been. And clearly, that cough medicine was magic, happy stuff on par with Nora's brownies, because he hadn't had anything more than a couple light hacks since we'd left the hospital.

"That's how my mom checks for fever, too."

Startled, I pulled back. "I'm sorry. I didn't even think twice." Then I laughed, realizing—"Must be a Cuban mom thing, since I picked it up from Nora."

"Must be." He smiled and put his empty plate and bowl in my outstretched hand. Now, admittedly, he was a big boy and fever-checking methods aside, I wasn't his mother. At the same time, however, I'd sort of *made* him my responsibility.

"Nick, I hope you don't mind, I unpacked your clothes."

"I smell bad?"

My jaw dropped at the blunt question. "No."

Yes, a little. But that wasn't what I was worried about. A little body odor never killed anyone, and if he only knew what I'd survived throughout a childhood of hot, sweaty summers with back-to-nature types. "But you've been sweating out that fever, and, frankly, you'll probably feel a lot better if you freshen up some—change clothes."

"God—if only it was that easy." He laughed, but it was this harsh sound that drew another cough from deep in his chest and had me handing him his bottle of water.

As he drank, I studied his face—his eyes, in particular. Funny, I wouldn't have ever thought of such dark eyes as being easy to read—Nora's sure weren't—but Nick's were complete windows. Something bad had gone down, and even though a few hours ago I'd been ready to bludgeon the story from him, now I found myself willing to let it go. The details—they just weren't necessary.

We looked at each other, for how long, I don't know. It was as if time became liquid and elastic, a suspended moment between us where the little things—the air conditioner cycling on, the ring of a phone a few rooms away, the faint rattle of his breathing—became the only way by which to mark time. And where the very real, very familiar pain living in his eyes eclipsed all else, leaving us trapped in this hell where the pain had become our entire world.

I was *so* tired of it.

He shook his head, snapping us both out of it, the pain receding, although vestiges of it remained. Like always. "Right—shower."

"Really?" Okay, yeah, he needed to freshen up, but I'd been thinking simpler—sponge bath territory.

"I won't make it a long one, but it's been a few days. Sink and washcloth just isn't gonna do it."

"All right." I handed him a Walgreen's bag. "Here."

Peering inside, he began pulling things out and carefully lining them up on the mattress. Toothpaste. Toothbrush. Deodorant. Razor. Shaving cream. A pack of T-shirts. He looked up, and again the expression in those dark eyes was obvious and readable and left me closing my eyes for a brief moment.

"Thanks."

"I, um, had no clue on your brands, so I guessed. Guessed on the size, too," I said, nodding at the package of boxers that was the last thing he'd pulled from the bag and had resting on his lap.

"No, Libby." He shook his head, his gaze never leaving mine. "Just…thank you."

It was damn hard to find my voice, but I finally managed, "We have a deal, remember?" Managed a smile, too, waving him toward the bathroom. "Go on, take your shower. I'm betting the brief energy burst from dinner isn't going to last long, and when it fades, you're going to crash hard. I'd prefer it not be anywhere you could crack your skull."

From somewhere, even though I know it couldn't have been easy for him, he found a smile too. "I've got a hard head."

"Tell me something I don't know."

Returning the toiletries and briefs to the bag, he rose from the bed, paused by the pile of folded clothes long enough to select a pair of sweatpants, and disappeared into the bathroom. When he emerged less than fifteen minutes later, I saw that I'd been right. He looked like he felt better—and like he was ready to fall over. Good thing I'd already turned the bed down for him. Sliding in between the sheets with a quiet sigh, he caught my wrist in his hand and pulled me down to sit on the bed beside him.

"Stay?" His voice was quiet, his gaze steady on mine.

I bit my lip, my free hand hovering over the one he had on my wrist. Not something I'd planned on—I was just across the hall, after all. Had planned to set my alarm so I could make sure he'd get his meds in the middle of the night—

"Stay, please, Libby," he said again, his voice dropping even further. "I…" His lids lowered, hiding his eyes. "I'm so fucking tired of being alone."

Slowly, I moved my hand to his damp, shaggy hair and began smoothing the waves and cowlicks down, hoping to soothe him to sleep. On one of those slow passes, however, my finger caught on a cowlick, bringing my ministrations to a halt. With my palm resting on his cheek, my gaze found his. He was still awake. Still waiting. Still wanting.

So much.

As I sighed, the hand holding my wrist relaxed, allowing his arm to stretch across my waist as I slid down still on top of the covers. My head on the pillow beside his, I pressed my lips against his forehead.

"Sleep, Nick."

I couldn't, though. I just lay there, drifting occasionally, but mostly just staring into the dark, stroking his hair and neck as he slept, his head on my shoulder, his arm a comforting weight across my waist. After I got him his middle-of-the-night meds, I tried to leave—my brain rationalizing it as he'd sleep more comfortably in the bed by himself, *I* needed to get some rest, blah, blah, *blah*.… But then he latched onto my arm again, more asleep than not, and mumbled, "Please?" in the voice I was beginning to realize I couldn't ignore.

But after I gave him his early morning dose, it was time for me to go. And Nick knew it, too, staring at the watery bars of light filtering past the edges of the drapes before looking back at me with a tired smile. He knew I had to go—to get back to Ethan.

Who'd had a peaceful night, thank God. The morning, however, wasn't quite so calm with him throwing up, although not as violently as usual, which let him joke about it, at least through the first couple rounds. Small favors, because I was exhausted, and I wasn't sure how well I could've dealt if Ethan had had a seriously bad day. He even made it through his second treatment about as well as he had the day before, asking for ice cream to offset the bitter residue from the meds. More small favors, since I could just go down to the cafeteria for that.

However, it also made me think of Nick. We'd never eaten our ice cream last night. Had he eaten any today? Had he eaten anything at all today? But I didn't want to call the hotel in case he was sleeping and, well, because my day—that belonged to Ethan. *Had* to belong to Ethan. I didn't have enough in me to worry about Nick, too. But I did.

And it left me more than a little distracted and irritable, something that didn't escape Ethan's notice.

"What's up, gorgeous?"

"Huh?" I jerked my head up, finding Ethan staring at me.

"I've never known you to just stare at ice cream—even hospital cafeteria ice cream." He nodded at my container where I was, yep, staring and stirring around my rapidly melting cookies and cream.

"It's the latest in exercise and weight loss—stir instead of eat." I tried to shrug it off as I tossed the plastic cup in the trash.

"Libby…"

Yeah, well, so I sucked at faking the man out. "Don't worry, *querido*, I'm just not hungry for it, that's all."

He set his empty cup aside and held his hand out. I took it in mine, and it was so familiar and so good, I tightened my grasp, hanging on for dear life.

"Sweetheart, I'm doing okay. Why don't you go on back to the hotel and get some rest?"

"No." I shook my head and held on harder, pressing my lips to the back of his hand. Lying there, my forehead pressed against his side, I could feel his other hand, the one with the poison flowing into it, come over to rest on my head, stroking gently.

"Libby, I want you to go."

"I don't want to—"

"You're obviously exhausted—you've been out of it all day." His voice was gentle, soothing, and so damn reasonable I wanted to scream. "I'd hate myself if you got sick."

"I never get sick."

"No, you don't. Which would really up the guilt if you did get sick because you're running yourself ragged on my account, and you know how that would piss me off. I much prefer gluttony and sloth with respect to my sins."

Oh, damn him and his rational arguments—and twisted sense of humor. "Ethan, you're doing so well—I just want to stay."

"You're whining, Libby. You don't whine except when you're exhausted. There's no guarantee I'm going to continue to feel okay, and if I do get to feeling worse…"

He wasn't going to want me around anyway.

"All right, *fine*, I give." Sighing, I placed a final kiss on his hand and lifted my head. After collecting all my assorted crap and making sure he really, truly was okay, that he really, truly wanted me to go, and letting the nurses know I was leaving, I leaned in to give him a goodbye kiss.

"All this time and you still don't get it, gorgeous. You're always with me," he whispered against my ear. "It's what gets me through this miserable shit."

I smiled and touched my fingers to his lips. "I love you."

"Ditto, gorgeous."

Back at the hotel, I paused outside Nick's door for several moments, holding the key card and debating. In the end, I turned away and toward my own room. If I hadn't heard from him by dinnertime, I'd check. But dinnertime came and went and I did nothing. After all, maybe it was dinnertime for me, but as exhausted as he'd been? His sleep schedule was probably completely screwed.

So I called the hospital instead, checking on Ethan, my heart sinking as Corrine told me that not long after I'd left he'd gone downhill in a hurry—the vomiting and diarrhea and anxiety all kicking in with a vengeance. It was still going on, and, no, he didn't want me coming down there—absolutely not. He must have known—that sixth sense that came with coping with illness over such a long period of time. It was why he'd been so insistent I leave.

Hanging up the phone, I sat on the bed clutching a pillow to my chest and rocking back and forth, swiping tears from my cheeks. I reached for the phone again—but *no*. Calling Nick now would simply be selfish on my part. Nothing more than me being needy— even if it was under the guise of checking on him.

I decided—if I didn't hear from him by eight. But eight passed with me trying to work on my column and picking at the salad I'd ordered from room service. If he really needed me, he'd call, right? There was no reason for me to bother him. I'd left him my cell number, and he knew I was across the hall. He *knew* he could call me if he needed anything.

So, I'd check at nine thirty, then. And as I stared out the windows at the lights of the Miami skyline across the bay, I could see the bright blue numbers from the digital clock reflecting back at me, ticking past nine thirty…nine forty-five…

It was just past ten when it came. Along with the absolute certainty that the reason I hadn't done anything was because I'd somehow known it would come.

And I'd love to say that knock was completely unexpected. That it was unwelcome.

But my *God*, I'd be lying.

Nick

"Why are you awake?"

"How'd you know?"

"Not sure."

"Mmm." She stretched and resettled herself, her back warm against my chest. "I don't know why I'm awake. But I know I slept great."

Her voice was soft, ever-so-slightly raspy. I really hoped to hell she wasn't getting what I had. In the faint glow the bathroom light provided, I watched as her arm reached out from beneath the covers and grabbed a bottle of water from the nightstand. Uncapping it, she took a drink and then held it over her shoulder, offering.

"Aren't you afraid of getting sick?" But I took the bottle anyway, sucking down several deep gulps.

"Really, Nick?" Her voice was still slightly raspy, even after the water. Maybe it was just the way she sounded first thing in the morning. If it was morning. It was still pretty dark in the room.

"Okay, really fucking stupid question. Sorry." I took another drink and handed the bottle back, feeling the subtle movements of her body against mine as she drained what was left and dropped the empty bottle over the side of the bed. A move that made me smile. Libby being careless—about anything—seemed so out of character.

"No need." With a sigh she turned, shifting to her back, but stayed close. Thank God. She seemed to still need this as much as I did. Whatever *this* was, because hell if I knew.

We both could've drifted back off; by now I'd seen the clock and knew that it was only just past four thirty. I closed my eyes—tried to will my breathing into a steady rhythm. Maybe even succeeded for a few seconds.

"It's all been a lie, Libby." I blinked up at the ceiling, my arm tensing across her waist. "I'm trying so fucking hard to see it her way, to understand as much as I can. And every time I think I'm getting better at it, that I'm actually doing what she wants, it turns out to be some goddamn illusion."

"It's her reality. The way she sees things now. You have to adapt and respect it."

I couldn't see much of her face in the near dark, but I didn't need to. Her voice said it all, dropping into that harsh tone I'd only heard once before—at Ray's funeral when she'd said we were allowed to be angry. Maybe we had to adapt and respect it, but we were allowed to be angry, too. What a fucking tightrope.

"How do you and Ethan make it work?" I was all of a sudden desperate to know because I could see, could tell from what Libby had told me, from that gentle, loving expression on her face every time she said his name that they had whatever it was that Kath and I were missing. They'd figured it out. *I* needed to figure it out before I completely lost my mind.

"Mostly we talk."

Kath and I had talked too. All the time. About the big things, at any rate. Careers. Marriage. Kids. Houses and cars and trips and our future and how fantastic it was all going to be, because we were together. Until cancer came along and became the elephant in the corner that we somehow couldn't seem to talk about. At least not without big, traumatic blow ups. Somehow, I didn't think dramatic scenes were how Libby and Ethan dealt.

"But..." She played with the edges of my sleeve, her fingertips brushing against my bicep. "I can't lie to you, Nick. It's getting harder. He's not...talking as much."

My arm tightened on her waist as her fingers curled into my arm, nails digging into my skin.

"You know, given our beginnings, how he tried to force me to see things he thought were so horrible, to face up to reality, it's ironic how hard he's trying to protect me now. Thinks that by keeping me away from what he imagines is the worst of it, that it somehow makes things easier." Each word was soft, gentle, and so close to the verge of tears that my own throat closed tight in sympathy.

"The one thing that man has never seemed to get is that I see the worst of it every single day, when I see how he fights to keep living. And that it's for me."

That's when I felt the front of my T-shirt start to get damp. This crying though—it wasn't like the first time. That had been violent and harsh—the release of a tremendous load of pent up anger. By contrast, this was just soft, steady and incredibly heartbreaking, with the occasional sniffled, "I'm supposed to be taking care of you."

Oye pero qué mula. And she accused *me* of having a hard head.

"Shh…it's okay. You are taking care of me." Same thing I'd said to her last night. "Letting me do this helps more than you'll ever know." Wasn't just saying it as some placating bullshit either. Holding Libby, being a safe place for her, did something to smooth over all those raw, angry places inside. The ones that had had me skating myself into oblivion every night for the last week. Except somewhere during that week, I'd realized the ice couldn't bring me that kind of solace anymore. But with no other alternative, I'd simply kept skating—kept searching for it.

Now, however…

As Libby had for me, I kissed her forehead, smoothed back her hair. Waited for her to take a deep breath and roll over so that her back was curved into my body, adjusting until she was comfortable and finally fell asleep, her hand resting over mine.

"You are taking care of me, Libby."

• • •

Kath never once questioned why I hadn't gone to see her in the hospital those couple of days, although she surprised me by asking if I felt better. And other than saying, yeah, I did, didn't offer anything more in the way of explanation. I figured if she knew enough to ask how I was feeling, then someone had probably let her in on how sick

I was and that I'd been advised to stay away.

News that probably came as a relief to her.

To me, too, and if that made me a bastard, at least it made me an honest bastard.

The most amazing thing? Those surreal couple of days, being so sick, losing track of time—or rather, having time marked only by when I was with Libby and when I wasn't—accomplished the unimaginable. Finally, after so many months, I was able to deal. I mean, really, honestly cope, not just feel like I was hanging on by a fraying rope. Any time I felt like I was on the edge of losing my shit, I'd back into my office and close the door. There, in the half dark, I would recall the image of Libby handing me the bag of supplies she'd bought, looking like an anxious schoolgirl. Could feel her curved back against me, whispering how this was what she'd missed most, nearly breaking my heart in the process. Any one of the memories from those few days was enough to bring back the sensation of smoothing over the angry, raw places. Allowed me to calm down and give Kath her space.

Which wasn't to say that I still didn't want to help—to be there for Kath. But she didn't want me. Didn't trust me. Every look she sent me made that perfectly clear.

Not such a big surprise then, that the next time we went down to Miami, I found myself desperately hoping Libby would be there.

Definitely not a surprise the relief I felt when I saw the silver Volvo in the parking lot at Las Palmas or when I read the text message on my phone, that said if I wanted to go out to dinner to call her.

And that after I said good night to her and went to my room and showered, I found myself knocking at her door and, God help me, even less of a surprise that I found her waiting.

It should've been shocking how easy it was to fall asleep with Libby in my arms. And it was. Superseding shock, however, was the sense of security, the warmth and comfort that came from holding her, drifting off with her body against mine, my hand on her stomach, hers resting over mine as if to hold it in place. And draped over all of that like a blanket was the sheer relief that it was exactly how I'd remembered and not some messed up byproduct from how sick I'd been.

Weird, then, that I would have any desire to move away from her at any point. But blinking into the dark, having just jerked awake, I tried to figure out how I could do just that. Discreetly slide away— just for a few minutes. Hoping like hell she was still asleep. After all—I reached back behind myself, fumbling for my watch, and squinting until the gently glowing numbers sharpened into focus— it was one in the morning. I knew she was exhausted. We were both perpetually exhausted. Sighing, I dropped the watch back to the nightstand. I really didn't want to move away from her. I just wanted to pull her closer and go back to sleep. Unfortunately, no way that was happening.

"It's okay, Nick."

Every muscle from my gut all the way up felt tight. Hell, even my scalp was tense. "I'm…sorry."

I'm sorry? Jesus.

"It's just a natural reaction."

Yeah. It was. But completely inappropriate. I untangled my legs from hers, slid back just far enough so there was some actual breathing room between our hips. My dick didn't care about appropriate; even as I shifted, it strained at the seams of my briefs, trying to recapture Libby's warmth. Man, I sympathized. I hated moving away, even that little bit.

"I should go take a shower or—something." Probably the shower *and* something.

"Nick." She rolled over, lifting one hand to my cheek. It was still too dark for me to completely make out her features, but that was okay. I didn't need to see her to know she was smiling. Glad one of us found this funny. "Just because it's not as readily obvious, doesn't mean I'm not—"

She stopped short, her head lowering.

"What?"

Her breath was soft on my neck as she sighed, then finally said,

"It doesn't mean I'm not reacting the same…way. I mean, we're human and well—" Her voice lowered further. "It's been *such* a long time."

No. No way. This wasn't going to happen. I would *not* let her feel embarrassed or humiliated by something so basic. *I* wouldn't be embarrassed. And I definitely wouldn't allow this to become a barrier, keeping us from what we both really needed. That strange, unnamable thing that had had me asking her to stay that first night. That had me knocking at her door and her waiting for me each subsequent night we'd been around each other.

No way. Nothing was going to get in the way of that because we both needed it.

"Hey."

"What?"

I put my hands on her cheeks and gently tilted her head up, imagining that even through the dark I was looking into her eyes— that she could see into mine.

"You're right. We're human—and I'm a guy. I'd have to be dead not to react."

The corner of her mouth curved up beneath my thumb. "Definitely not dead," she teased, although her voice was low and breathless and had my groin tightening painfully.

"Libby…" How the hell was it that I'd wound up with my forehead against hers? My mouth so close I could swear I was feeling the brush of her skin against mine.

"You'd better go take that shower."

Yeah. No kidding. A damn cold one because I had this strange feeling that a soapy hand really wasn't going to do a thing to take this new—this completely unexpected—edge off. And if I was completely honest, too, a not completely unwelcome edge, either.

Libby had reopened that part of my nature that was about desire. That loved being close to a woman and engaging in the small physical intimacies that naturally led to emotional closeness and that I'd had to shut down tight because Kath simply couldn't handle it right now. And because the constant rejection—not just of the sexual part of the equation, but of all of it—had come close to driving me insane. Then again, so had shutting it down.

That I could openly admit to desire—without judgment or anger or accusations being tossed at me? That instead of making me feel guilt, Libby had felt safe enough to admit to feeling that same desire?

It was the best gift I could've ever received.

Maybe I wasn't the most intuitive guy around, but I had to think it was because she knew I'd never take advantage. That this wasn't necessarily about the physical. Admittedly, my dick was still hard as a rock, but otherwise, it was enough to have had the acknowledgment—and the trust. No doubt, Libby's unconditional acceptance and understanding left me feeling like a weight had been lifted off my chest, but that beautiful trust? That trust let me feel like a man again.

We hardly slept the rest of that night. We just lay in bed and talked. Neither of us seemed particularly sleepy anymore—or maybe it was just self-preservation kicking in. Besides, I simply liked talking with Libby. As much as the physical closeness, I'd missed the particular intimacy that came from lying in a dark room, sharing anything and everything that came to mind. In the dark, nothing ever seemed too stupid or too off-limits.

She told me some more about Ethan and about growing up with Nora in the Keys, but mostly, she let me talk. I couldn't believe how much I talked. About Kath and our relationship. Its origins. Its tremendous ups and downs, most of the latter having to do with my desire to purse pro hockey and her utter lack of desire to be seen as the arm candy on a jock's arm.

"Pneumonia kicked the career plans in the ass, however. Landed me in the hospital a few times, hanging out in oxygen tents—so I retired. And Kath came back."

Beside me, Libby had tensed. Too late, I realized what would have prompted that reaction.

"Hey, I *am* okay now."

"I know. Sorry."

"Why? Because you care? Don't you ever apologize for that, Libby. Not too many people care the way you do."

There was a long beat of silence between us—so long, I wondered if she'd drifted off to sleep. Wouldn't be a surprise, seeing as it was already past five.

"In general or about you?"

It came out barely above a whisper—almost as if she was testing to see if I was still awake. If I wasn't, it would simply get lost in darkness surrounding us in this hotel room on a long December night, and I knew she'd never ask it again.

"Both." My heart beat faster. Because with that one word I was letting her further in—allowing her to see more of me than almost anyone else in the world ever had.

"She always packed for you, Nick."

"I know." And I understood what Libby was saying and accepted it for the truth that it was.

"She'll come back again."

"Maybe."

Her stomach rose and fell beneath my arm. "Yeah."

That one word made me pull her even closer and squeeze the hand I still held. Libby was an optimist, but she wasn't a fool, and she wasn't a liar.

Thank God.

Libby

"Where are we going?"

"Somewhere."

I tried to tug my hand free from Nick's, tried to dig my heels into the hall carpet, but damn hockey jock that he was, he was strong, and he'd recovered well from his illness. Entirely *too* well, all that energy and good health radiating from him and exhausting me simply with its proximity. It was like wrestling with a Newfoundland.

"Nick, dammit, what's up?"

He stopped and turned so fast, I stumbled, trying not to run into his chest. His free hand catching my upper arm and steadying me, he asked, "Do you trust me?"

"What?" I looked up into his eyes, oddly tempted to brush my fingers along the faint dark circles beneath that were the only leftovers of his illness.

"Do you trust me?" he repeated, both hands now grasping mine, his brows drawn together.

"Of course." Stupid question, I almost added, but caught myself at the deep sigh that met my answer. No. Not stupid question. Not for him.

"There's just something I want to show you—someone I want you to meet."

"But if they call—"

"They'll call your cell and we're not going to be so far we can't come right back, and, honestly Libby, when was the last time they called and told you he wanted you to come back?"

Jerking my hands free, I spun away and stalked back toward my room.

"Libby!"

My hand shaking, I tried to jerk my key card through the slot.

"Libby."

Finally it went, the click and accompanying green light leaving me grateful to the point of tears. Unfortunately, Nick didn't exactly take the hint and went ahead and followed me into my room. Blockheaded, stubborn Cuban...*pendejo*. Didn't he know I really, really wanted to be alone right now?

Of course he did. Would it matter?

Really, really wouldn't.

Damn him.

At least he had the sense not to lay so much as one comforting finger on me.

"Libby, *por favor,* I didn't say it to upset you. I just—" His breath whooshed out in one harsh gust. "Look, I'm sorry, I guess I said it in the worst possible way." He sighed again and shoved both hands through his hair, leaving it sticking up in unruly spikes.

My arms crossed over my stomach, I turned to stare out the window and down at Alton Road, busy as always, especially on this clear, sunny day, cars streaming along on their way to and from the beach or holiday shopping. I kept my gaze focused on the scene outside, refusing to look into the reflection to acknowledge him, not that it mattered. I could sense him coming up behind me, still not touching, at least not directly, although, I felt one hand gently stroking down the length of my braid.

"Were you honestly planning on going back to the hospital?"

My head dropped, exchanging the street view for the painted wood of the windowsill. Bracing one hand on the sill, my fingers worried a tiny paint bubble until it split, a thin layer of eggshell white peeling back beneath the edge of one nail, exposing the pale blue the frame had been painted in some other lifetime.

"No."

"Neither was I."

I knew that. Nan had told me, and I'd seen some of it for myself, how he'd fallen in the habit of lingering for a bit in the waiting room, talking to Marco, to all the duty nurses, assuring himself Kath was okay. He'd call the nurses' station every couple of hours once he left the hospital, check his cell for any messages, but otherwise, he was leaving her alone. He'd confessed it wasn't that much different at home since she had a home nurse taking care of anything she couldn't do herself and that it was the nurse he asked for updates. And he was hurting and relieved and guilty all at the same time to not have to be dealing with the constant tension of interacting with Kath too directly. All he could do, he said, was watch and take his cues from her.

Likened it to walking a tightrope.

"Look, there's somewhere I usually go on the Wednesdays I'm down here, and I want to share it—with you." Then he asked once more, "*Do* you trust me?"

Finally tired of the windowsill and not that crazy to learn how many more layers of paint—how much more evidence of lives that may have passed through this room—might lie beneath the surface, I turned and looked up at him. "You know I do."

His voice softened as he said, "Do you trust that I think we both maybe need to get away from all of this, *aunque sea por un poquito de tiempo?*"

Silence stretched between us—a silence in which all I could think was, *when?*

When had the tables turned? *Dígame,* when had Nick become my particular voice of reason? Had the shift occurred at some point during one of those nights we spent together? When he let me cry into his shoulder and held me and reminded me in so many small ways I was human?

Silently, I took his outstretched hand and let him lead me down to his SUV where he hummed under his breath to the music from the stereo as he drove.

Again I was hit with just how far the tables had turned as I recalled driving to the beach the day of Ray's funeral, not telling

Nick where we were going. Asking for his trust.

"You know, I can practically hear it."

"Excuse me?"

He reached over with one hand and tapped my forehead gently as he eased onto an off-ramp. "You're thinking so hard, I can practically hear the gears grinding."

A laugh—more a puff of breath, actually, something soundless between a laugh and a sigh—escaped before I could stop myself. "Just thinking how much things have changed."

He nodded, one side of his mouth curling in a slight smile that suggested he was maybe getting all the little ironies too, but he didn't actually say anything until he'd parked the car and come around to my side, one hand braced on the open door, the other on the frame above my head, hemming me in, but not unpleasantly so.

"Would I be a complete dickhead if I said I'm kind of glad?"

Brushing my fingertips against the faint bruises under his eyes, I smiled. "No."

A deep breath lifted his chest as he returned my smile. While he busied himself feeding the meter, I wandered toward a wide window, trimmed in acid green tinsel, shaking my head at the elaborate pastel dresses on the mannequins, with their ornate beadwork and ruffles. The rest of the window was crowded with portraits of fresh-faced girls wearing similar gowns and elbow-length gloves, tiaras perched in elaborately curled updos as they posed in impossibly lush tropical settings. My gaze ranged along the street taking in the cigar shops and *mercados* blended seamlessly with Home Depot and Radio Shack and Burger King, into the pastiche that was Little Havana.

I'd been here before of course, for Carnaval with Ethan and Nora. More cultural awareness of *course*—but at least it was my own. During those visits, Calle Ocho had been a riotous, seething mass of humanity complete with killer food and art and music. Today, however, it was just a busy city street on a Wednesday afternoon, albeit a busy city street with a fairly singular character.

"Have you ever been down here before?" Nick stood in front of me, bouncing lightly on the balls of his sneakers, falling back on that jock's exuberance that was endearing or obnoxious, depending on my mood.

"Yeah," I replied and nearly choked on my tongue at the way his face suddenly fell. "But never on a Wednesday afternoon," I finally managed to splutter as his crestfallen expression morphed into a glare. "Come on, Nick, don't be that way. Tell me, what's so special?"

"You'll see." And just like that, the bounce was back as he took my hand and started off at a walk that was just this side of a jog. God, what a pain in the ass. If he was like this at thirty-seven, I could only imagine how he'd been as a little kid, all eagerness and live wire energy.

"Had to park kind of far away, but that's okay, because it's a great day and it gives us a chance to look around and it feels good to walk, doesn't it?"

Digging my heels in for the second time today, I tugged on his hand until he stopped and turned. "Okay, who are you and what have you done with the Nick I know?"

The smile was still there along with something else, an obvious relief that relaxed his features and brought to mind, yet again, an exuberant kid, even with the fine lines radiating from the corners of his eyes and the sunlight picking out the grays scattered through his dark hair. Not even the stubble that was a regular thing for him these days could mask the boyish cast to his face. And all I could think was *hellion*.

"You know this *is* me."

His smile faded slightly as our gazes met—his kind of anxious, if I was reading it correctly.

I squeezed the hand I still held. "You don't say?"

His smile broadened again, the fine lines at the corners of his eyes deepening as he squeezed back. "And just there's something about being down here that...I don't know..." He turned and started with the power walk again. "It just juices me up at the same time it relaxes me."

"You don't say?" But the dry tone was utterly lost on him as he guided me toward an open window, holding up two fingers.

"*Dos, por favor, hermano,*" he said to the man behind the counter before turning his attention to the bakery case. "*Y dos cangrejitos también, si puedes.*"

"Nick, it's not like we don't get café and *pastelitos* on a daily basis."

"Yeah, but it's *different* down here," he insisted, gesturing with his thimble-size paper cup of steaming hot Cuban jet fuel. "And no one ever has the *cangrejitos,*" he mumbled around a huge bite of pastry. "I love these suckers."

I was laughing so hard, I could barely choke down my own coffee and had to take several deep breaths before I could even manage a bite of the sweet pastry filled with the savory ground beef *picadillo.* Still chuckling, I watched as he ordered another coffee and pastry and promptly inhaled both. "Remind me to drive us back, since you're probably going to crash, and hard."

"Nah." Dropping a few bills on the counter and nodding at the man, he draped an arm across my shoulders and led us toward the corner where we actually waited to cross the street, rather than jaywalking, like everyone else and their mother appeared to be doing. "A little sugar and caffeine aren't anywhere near enough to bring me down."

"Yeah, let's see if you're still saying that when you take a header into the mashed potatoes at dinner."

"Nope."

"Of course, you'd say that."

"No, I mean, no mashed potatoes for dinner. More like *yuca con mojo* instead. Or maybe *congrí.* Sound good? I hope so, because we're going to Versailles for dinner. Total Little Havana experience."

Felt like I hadn't stopped laughing since he'd initially pissed me off. Frankly, I couldn't remember the last time I'd laughed this much. "You were that certain I'd come with you that you planned it down to the menu?"

Just then the light changed, and we stepped off the curb and crossed the street. On the other side he stopped and shrugged with a sheepish expression and shy smile. "I hoped."

And there he went—catching me completely off-guard. Again. "All right, so what's next in Nick's Little Havana Experience?" He pointed with his free hand. "That."

"Oh, *cool*. We walked past when we were here for Calle Ocho, but it was so crowded, we didn't have a prayer of getting near, let alone, in."

"You still won't. This is as close as we can get. We're way too young to be allowed entry."

My jaw dropped. "You're kidding."

He waved in the direction of the pavillion. "See for yourself— tell me there's anyone in there who doesn't qualify for AARP."

My smile felt like it was going to split my face as I caught my first glimpse of the tables and players—heard the familiar chorus of furiously clicking dominoes and salsa music and the loud arguing that seemed to be passing for conversation. Pretty much could pass for the annual Santos family reunion, come to think of it. "We're a loud bunch, aren't we?" I observed with a sidelong glance at Nick who stood with a shoulder propped against the tall wrought iron fence that bordered the pavilions.

"Feeling your Cuban half today, Libby?"

"How could I not?" I studied Nick's face—how he continued to relax, the lines of worry smoothing out. "What about you, Jersey boy?"

"It seems more like…what it should be." Grabbing the top of the fence with both hands, he leaned back on his heels, his gaze roaming freely, taking it all in—the palm trees and blue sky and the red-tile roof of the pavilion and the players seated at the tables with their heated games and conversations—before focusing on me again. "At home, we had the sense of family, knew our background, but something about the atmosphere down here—" He stopped with a self-conscious snort. "I'm sure it sounds stupid."

"No." Glancing back over my shoulder into the pavilion then up at him, I said, "I get it. I don't know how I do, but I get it. It makes sense."

He threw back his head and laughed. "Maybe one of these days you can explain it to me, then."

"The minute I figure it out, you'll be the first to know."

We began wandering around the perimeter of the fenced area where I made happy noises over the mosaic walkway with its swirls of tiles in tropical colors bordering a narrower walkway made to look like domino pieces. Before I knew it, I was jumping from domino tile to domino tile, an impromptu sort of hopscotch, laughing and feeling like a carefree little girl, except I'd never ever been this carefree as a girl. For one, I'd always been painfully shy and self-conscious; besides, I'd been too busy trying to look responsible and well, *normal*, to ever allow myself to indulge in this kind of silly, impulsive fun. But something about the atmosphere—about the day—seemed to demand I surrender to little girl impulses. At least this once.

"*Oye* Libby, come here."

I was back against the fence, observing a particularly entertaining exchange between two feisty old men who were so grizzled, they made my seventy-eight-year-old *abuelo* look downright youthful.

Utterly engrossed, I replied, "In a minute." Actually, I was getting kind of worried that if the old guys kept it up, one, if not both of them, was liable to keel over dead.

"*Olvidate, m'ija*, it's liable to go on like that for hours. They're like that every week. But you're welcome to join the pool."

At the new voice, I turned to find Nick settling on a nearby bench next to an older man, handing him a soda before gesturing that I should come over.

"Pool?" I asked as I approached.

The older man nodded, the corners of his mouth twitching. "On who drops first and when."

As the yelling behind me got louder, and the insults more vicious, I looked to Nick for confirmation.

He nodded. "Even they've got bets on which one of them's gonna drop first. Here." He handed me a can of Sprite as I sat down and laughed as I pulled a face at the bendy straw before taking it out and tossing it in the nearby trashcan. After waiting for me to take a long drink, he said, "Libby, this is who I wanted you to meet—Tico Martinez. Tico, this is my friend I keep telling you about, Libby Walker."

"Of course, Libby. *Mucho gusto.*" Tico reached past Nick and offered his hand, warm and dry, his grip gentle, but firm at the same time, reminding me of…of…*something.* As his hooded blue gaze searched my face, the feeling of familiarity intensified, but I couldn't quite place it.

"*Igualmente,*" I replied. "You talk about me?" I said to Nick, as I released Tico's hand and lifted my soda.

He shrugged. "Sure I talk about you. I talk about a lot of stuff with Tico. He's a priest."

Bastard. He had the nerve to sit there and laugh as I struggled between swallowing and choking and sneezing at the bubbles of carbonation making their way up my nose.

"It's okay," he whispered in my ear as he rubbed my back. "I didn't know he was a priest either when I first met him."

"You suck," I whispered back with a sharp elbow to his ribs that only had him laughing harder. "*Gracias,*" I said to Tico who was handing napkins across the big laughing goon.

"Not nice, Nick." Tico's voice was mild, but with a definite stern vibe that had Nick squirming.

"Yeah, I know, but I gotta tell you, it's definitely worth another turn on the Rosary for penance just to have seen that look on her face. I always wondered what kind of expression I copped when you told me you were a priest."

Finally under some semblance of control, I carefully lifted my soda again, making sure to keep my sips small and a wary eye on Nick, in case he was planning on using me for anymore social experiments. And also kind of keeping a wary eye on Tico, too. I'd never really interacted with priests—much. There *had* been one memorable dinner at my grandparents' house, back when I was about five or so, where the special guest had been a priest of the scary, black-suit-and-collar variety insisting I needed to be baptized and Nora responding by offering him "ceremonial incense" in the form of a huge doobie.

No more priests at dinner with my *abuelos* after that.

Tico, with his faded jeans and battered ball cap, seemed more in line with the so-called priests Nora had hung with throughout my childhood, although clearly he wasn't. Which made it difficult to figure out how to deal with him—a vibe he easily picked up on.

"Just call me Tico, *mi vida*. Despite all my years at seminary, I'm not real big on all the titles."

"He used to date girls, too."

My stare shifted from Nick, to Tico, who merely sighed and rolled his eyes, then back to Nick.

"You were never an altar boy, were you?" I groused, stifling the impulse to dump the remains of my Sprite over his head.

With a smirk that could only be described as unholy, he sat straighter. "I was a kick-ass altar boy."

Tico groaned. "*Un poco respeto, m'ijo, por favor.*"

"Sorry, excuse me. A kick-*butt* altar boy." Nick's grin only got bigger. He was getting such a charge out of this, jerking my chain—trying to jerk Tico's even though he probably knew that, as a priest, Tico's chain was too incredibly long and impossible to jerk.

It kept on like that for the next half hour, Nick saying these outrageous things waiting to see how I'd react or how Tico would scold him, laughing and looking impossibly young and I knew he'd been that carefree, not just as a kid, but I got the sense, as an adult, too. Maybe not to such an extreme, but he'd been walking that damn tightrope for so long.

So I egged him on and teased him and pretended to be affronted just to hear that laugh and feel him tug my braid or rest his hand on my shoulder. And in turn, I felt in every word or touch how very much he wanted the same for me—how he wanted me to feel loose and carefree, even though he knew it wasn't an attitude that came naturally to me. It was his gift to me and it made my heart twist a little more with every touch or shared glance.

Finally, Tico stood, saying, "Well, it's that time, but I'm glad you finally brought Libby by to meet me."

His expression turned serious as I stood to say goodbye. "*M'ijita,* Nick's told me a bit about your husband. With your permission, you'll both be in my prayers."

Definitely not a scary black-suit-and-collar priest or one of Nora's holistic nutbar types. Just a decent human being. Taking the hand he held out, I replied, "At this point, I'll take all the help and intervention I can get. We'd be very grateful."

Both of his hands enveloped mine, his steady blue gaze studying my face and, once again, that powerful sense of familiarity washed over me. Then as he leaned in and kissed my forehead, it hit me. Marco. Tico reminded me of Marco. A priest and a doctor—healers both.

"It's my honor. *Dios te bendiga, mi vida.* And come see me again, with or without the *diablito.*"

I grinned as Nick's eyebrows drew together at Tico's assessment of him as a little devil. Well, really, what did he expect?"

"Libby, if you could excuse us—Nick, can I talk to you for a second?"

Nick glanced from Tico to me. "Uh, yeah, sure. If it's okay with you, Libby?"

"Of course, it's okay." But I was confused too, the way Tico was studying Nick with a small smile beneath that hooded blue gaze. Even so, his expression seemed carefully neutral, his general demeanor more subdued than it had been all afternoon.

"I'm just going to watch." I indicated the pavilion where the geezers were, as predicted, still going at it. "Decide who I'm going to put my bet on."

Wandering away, I was careful not to even glance over my shoulder, although the back of my neck prickled with awareness the entire time they stood there, talking. Or rather, Tico talked. Quite a bit, actually. I didn't hear so much as a peep from Nick until I heard him said goodbye. I was afraid, especially after seeing that expression on Tico's face, that Nick might slide into a mood, but he surprised me. He was still so exuberant and cheerful—so the *real* him, as he'd said—that I wound up not giving their exchange another thought until later that night when he knocked on my door, barefoot, in shorts and a T-shirt, his hair damp and messy.

"Why do we even bother going to our separate rooms?" I asked on a laugh, still sort of giddy and high from fresh air and good food and more laughter than I'd experienced in way too long. But Nick wasn't laughing, although he did smile as he dropped to the bed and held out his arms.

"Because I want you to always have the opportunity to say no," he said quietly as I settled in next to him, already familiar enough with the contours of his body that I knew where my head fit best against his shoulder. That I liked being on his left because the steady drum of his heart beneath my ear soothed me; the most basic of lullabies.

"That's not going to happen."

That was it for a while. I was a little surprised, truthfully. As frenetic and loopy and purely happy as our day out had been, I might have thought that we'd try to keep that going as long as possible. But maybe it had been because we were down in Little Havana, which had an identity and magic all its own, and now we were back to the life that had thrown us together in the first place. Back within proximity of the hospital I knew both of us had called as soon as we got back and that I also knew was one reason we did continue the pretense of going to our separate rooms, even if only for a few minutes.

Part of our tacit agreement that outside of any emergencies, when we were together, we'd leave our outside lives, well…outside.

"Can I ask a favor?"

"Sure."

"Can I undo your hair?"

Slowly, my gaze never leaving his, I sat up, then pulled my braid forward and drew off the elastic. He unwound it with great care, gently combing his long fingers through the waist-length mass with the occasional fleeting caress to my neck and scalp.

"You're shivering."

"It feels good."

He pushed it over my shoulder so it fell down my back and pulled me down again. His fingers kept playing through it, occasionally drifting back up to my neck, although it seemed he avoided doing that too much. Good thing. It was a particular erogenous zone of mine.

"You never wear it down."

"I'm lazy. I don't do anything to it—can't even remember the last time I had it cut. Braid's the easiest thing."

And it seemed cruel to walk around the hospital, where so many people were suffering and one of the most obvious signs of their suffering was the loss of hair, with a thick, healthy mass of my own. But I couldn't cut it either, because Ethan—he loved it too. It was one of the few things he still had strength for on occasion—one of our earliest rituals. Brushing my hair.

Time passed in a dreamy haze as Nick continued to stroke my hair, the caresses falling into a steady, hypnotic rhythm.

"Tico warned me to be careful."

"Of?" Although the statement didn't really feel like it was coming out of nowhere. Not with how I was feeling right now. If Tico had picked up on even a hint of this—

"You. He likes you. Probably more than me, I think." His chest vibrated beneath my hand with a soft laugh. "He said I was showing off for you like a horny kid and that you didn't need to be compromised or put into any difficult situations. That you'd had it hard enough already."

"He called you a horny kid? Those exact words?"

"Swear to God."

He sounded so exasperated, I couldn't help but laugh—but it was just a momentary flash of humor, there and gone, before I quietly asked, "How'd he know how hard I've had it, Nick?"

"Because he's a really good priest." He picked up the hand I had resting on his chest, lacing our fingers together. "And because he's been through it too. His dad. He knows what it's about."

"Oh."

"And because I do talk about you a lot—tell him how I worry

about you."

"Oh." Dammit, there went my stomach and my heart turning over and sending pleasure and guilt prickling along my spine in equal doses. "Have you told him about—"

I didn't know how to ask this. I mean, I didn't have much of a clue how this confession thing worked or if Nick had even been seeing Tico in a more formal, confessing any perceived or real sins, sort of way. Or what even constituted a sin, for that matter.

"No." In one sudden motion, he sat up, bringing me along so I wound up facing him, both of my hands in his. "First off, we're not doing anything. We're not going to *do* anything. We're simply two people who've been alone for too damn long." He pressed his lips together tight, not a hint of the smile that had curved his mouth all day anywhere in sight. "In you I've got a gift, Libby, and I'm not going to do anything to jeopardize that, okay? I want you to always feel safe with me."

God, how many times today had he reminded me of a little boy? Honestly, I'd lost count. But I could add one more to the list because sitting across from me, his hands holding mine tight, that dark gaze refusing to let mine go, he brought to mind nothing less than a fierce, earnest little boy, emotion winding him so tight, it was practically vibrating the air around him.

Pulling my hands free, I reached out and smoothed his hair down, those waves and spikes that always caught my fingers. I pushed at his chest until we were both lying down again and stroked his forehead, his jaw, his shoulder and chest and arm, anywhere I could reach, until I felt some of the tension begin to ebb.

"I do feel safe, Nick. How could I feel anything but?"

And with those words felt still more tension leave his body, even as some continued to hover just beneath the surface. That was a different tension, however—a tension that didn't live in him alone and we both knew it. That we acknowledged its existence and its place in allowing us to feel alive would have to be enough.

Libby

JANUARY 3

"Libby."

"Back the hell off, Nora. You're the last person I want to see or speak to right now."

"Liberty."

"And don't use my name like I'm some recalcitrant child to be reasoned with."

"So I'll refrain from saying that that's precisely what you're acting like, since you've so obligingly offered the suggestion yourself."

"Fuck you."

Thank God the onions were so big. I could keep mincing at one for days and still not be done. And the feel of the blade reverberating against the solid maple block was oddly satisfying— especially if I superimposed some choice images over the worn, fine-grained wood. Scooping a mound of onion between the blade and my palm, I tossed it into the gently simmering olive oil, closing my eyes and inhaling deeply of the sweet-sharp steam, and savoring the warm moisture as it soaked into my skin. Although, why the hell I was making chili, of all things—

So what if it had been raining for three days straight and was cool by Keys standards? Wasn't like anyone around here would actually eat this much chili. And you could only make chili in vast amounts—at least, the way I made chili.

Fuck it. I knew why I was making chili. Because it required a lot of prep if you made it purely from scratch the way I did. Not to mention, a lot of chopping—hard, satisfying, imagine-

you-were-burying-the-blade-between-someone's-eyes,   chopping.
Right now, it was a toss-up as to who was at the top of my list, but
since Nora was right here, she'd do.

"*M'ija*—"

"Don't you dare, '*m'ija*' me, Nora, and expect that to do a damn
thing. The pot brownies are one thing—I understand why you felt
you had to step in where I couldn't—but *this*? How could you?"

"Because it's what Ethan wants."

Her voice was infuriatingly calm, cranking my anger that much
more and making me attack the garlic I'd moved on to even more
viciously, twisting the cloves off the head and smashing them
beneath the flat of my blade. With each clove I pulverized, the heel
of my palm stung more, the vibrations rattling all the way up to
my shoulder and neck and making the tightness living there all the
more evident.

"What about me?" Another clove bit the dust. And another.

"This isn't about you, Liberty."

"If that's what you think I mean, then you're *definitely* on
some far out plane of existence." Couldn't mince the garlic until I
separated the smashed cloves from their skins, which meant putting
the knife down, which was probably a good move at this point. "I
know it's not about me, but dammit, Nora, don't you think I should
have at least been consulted?" I kept peeling the skins, staring down
at my fingers as I let the only tendril of jealously I'd ever felt with
respect to my husband trickle out on my next words.

"I mean, I know the two of you have always had this lovely little
club of the Older All-Knowing Ones and that's groovy, really, but
I'd think that after fifteen years and pushing thirty-six, I'd have at
least hit probationary status."

She was either one brave or batshit crazy woman to put her
hand on my back right then. Knife was still within reach, after all.
"He's trying to make this easier on you."

Done with the skins, I picked the knife back up and began
mincing. "And naming you the executor of his estate does this
how, exactly?"

"Liberty, don't play stupid." You'd think Nora pulling out the Mom Voice would be enough to get my attention since she so rarely did it, but too fucking little, too late. I really could not care less what tone of voice she used.

"He's trying to give you one less thing to worry about."

Suddenly reversing my grip on the handle, I drove the knife into the hard maple with enough force that the tip snapped, the blade slipping. "*Fuck.*"

Grabbing a dishtowel, I pressed it against the blood oozing from the cut on my palm and spun around. "It's not going to work. I'm going to worry and I'm going to care and I'm going to stick my nose into every goddamn thing having to do with him because it's my business, and you know why? Because I'm his *wife*, Nora. I know you don't get that, but marriage—*real* marriage—means you do this for each other. For better and for worse, and as worse as this is, I'd rather deal with it myself than have anyone, even you, feel as if they have to deal with it on my behalf for whatever goddamn, space-age reason you've cooked up."

My chest heaving, I exchanged hard stares with her. "Especially if it's in the name of protecting me. Enough, already. Enough."

"Liberty."

We both whirled toward the wide opening leading from the kitchen to the living room. Ethan leaned on his walker, looking tired but determined, and that only pissed me off even more.

"It's not a conspiracy, sweetheart."

"Oh?" I was scared shitless and fighting mad. "So where was my memo? Did it ever occur to you, you stubborn, thickheaded jackass, that I might want a say in all of this? Did it ever even occur to you to *ask* first, how I might feel about this?"

Of *course* it hadn't. I could tell by the look on his face.

"You know, gorgeous—" He eased himself down into a chair at the table, "You still have power of attorney. You can pull the plug whenever you want."

Wouldn't need to, because I was going to break his smug Ethan-neck right where he sat, and he could go meet his Maker with that insufferable smirk on his face. He was pushing my buttons, the asshole, and getting his jollies. Just like he always had. Because in the past it had always worked between us, eased tensions, made me see where I was just taking life a little too seriously. Not this time, though. Not even close. This *was* serious. It was his life and everything he was to me, and if he couldn't see that—

Then, because I wasn't dealing with enough, the silence was broken by an approaching engine—vestiges of my childhood echoing in the low, sonorous growl. And even if I hadn't recognized the sound of that engine, I would've known who it was simply by the way Nora straightened, her mouth curving up into a smile that made her look about sixteen.

Same age she'd been when she first laid eyes on him.

"Hey, where are my girls?"

There he stood—shaking rain from his heavy leather jacket, light-brown hair that these days also had its fair share of silver curling out from beneath the edges of the bandanna covering most of it—my wayward father.

"Hi, Stan," I sighed.

"Stan, *mi amor*, come on in, Libby's making chili." Sweeping past me, Nora threw herself into Stan's arms, giving him a kiss that made me ache even as I got angrier still. I was glad they still had their thing for each other, unconventional though it was. Glad they still had passion between them, even as I swallowed hard over all I'd lost in the last two years. And I was angrier than I'd ever been in my entire life.

"Did you call him?" I demanded from Nora even as I hugged Stan and accepted his kiss.

She didn't need to answer, damn her. That hesitation—the sharp indrawn breath coupled with the exchange of glances with first, Stan, then, more tellingly, Ethan, said it all. Pulling free from Stan's arms, I turned and propped myself on the table, leaning very close to Ethan.

"When were you going to tell me?"

"Jesus, Libby, it's not like that—"

"The hell it isn't, Ethan." My hand curled into a fist against the smooth birch surface of the table. "Naming Nora executor of your estate, having her call Stan—it's all incredibly clear, *querido*, and please don't think me stupid enough to not be able to see it. All I want to know is this—"

I swallowed back the tears clogging my throat and fighting to break free, because, dammit, they weren't going to see me cry. I would *not* give them more ammunition.

"When exactly, Ethan, were you planning on telling me that you'd decided to die?" By that final, hateful word, my voice had become this shrill, ugly thing bouncing off the walls and ringing in my ears.

Didn't bother waiting for an answer, because for all my bravado, really didn't want to hear it. I simply pushed away from the table, whistled for Butch and Sundance, and once outside, while I was clipping leashes to their collars, bent over at the waist and threw up as quietly as I could into the gardenia bushes.

To their credit, no one followed me. There weren't any offers of comfort or rational arguments that might have sent me straight into the abyss. And so I was able to leave in peace—walk calmly down the street to the gas station where I bought a cold drink to deal with the sour residue lingering in my mouth. Worked great to wash away the taste of the bile, but not the bitterness left by the knowledge that my husband and parents had apparently bonded together to plan the next what—few days, weeks, months?—on my behalf.

As I walked the beach, splashing along the water's edge, I knew, deep in my soul, their intentions were good—noble even. That they were, in their own way, trying to make this easier for me. I just resented the hell out of no one thinking I was worth asking about this, and, yeah, I knew just how selfish that was. It was what Ethan wanted, and God knows he'd done what I wanted for so long, fighting and hanging on so much longer than he probably had any right to. He'd *earned* the right to choose how and when to go out. And my wishes—my fears—had to take a back seat.

In my pocket, my phone vibrated its text alert. Pulling it out,

I blinked through the damp, blurry scrim of my vision until the message cleared: *1/6-1/8. You?*

Backing away from the waves, I dropped to the sand, not caring that it was wet and soaking through my jeans. Quickly, I typed out: *Be there 1/7* and hit send.

And hoped it was true.

• • •

It was just a few days, but a more tense, uncomfortable, angry few days I couldn't remember. Not even when Ethan and I were constantly at each other's throats during our teacher/student days had things been so bad between us that we'd forgone the most basic communication. But I couldn't talk to him. Could hardly look at him without feeling a near-crushing sensation of terror and hurt rolled up with that anger. And poor Stan, none of this was his fault and he was being so cool, setting up camp over at Nora's, naturally, but coming over every day and hanging with Ethan, talking to him, even bouncing ideas for his ongoing Great American Novel off my husband's still very active brain. Hell, the likelihood that the man would ever finish the thing were slim to none, but I couldn't deny that as an exercise it perked Ethan up, drawing out the sharp and incisive wit that remained so uniquely his even as his body continued to fail him.

At the same time though, I could barely bring myself to even speak to Stan, because for me his presence only made things worse. By making it clear he was here for the duration, however long it was, he was a living, breathing reminder that my Ethan was preparing to let go.

The night before we were scheduled to head up to Miami—a trip I wasn't even sure we were still making—Ethan finally decided to broach the subject.

"I'm not going to change my mind, Libby."

Amazing how in the dark I could so easily forget how sick he was. His voice was still that same gravelly tenor, still tinged with the slight indefinable accent picked up during an army brat youth spent on bases across the world. Still sounded exactly the same as the day he'd read through the class roster and said, "Liberty? Good God, what the hell were your parents thinking?" It carried, vibrant as ever, through the midnight dark of our bedroom from where he lay in the hospital bed we'd made room for, to our queen-size bed where I still stubbornly stuck to my side and my side only—afraid of what using the whole expanse might represent.

"What exactly aren't you going to change your mind about, Ethan? The executor of your will or dying?"

"The one I have most control over."

The next day, however, he got up as usual, slowly shuffled into the bathroom and showered. Dressed in loose-fitting jeans and a sweatshirt, he sat down at the kitchen table with a tired sigh.

"Never intended to just up and quit on you, gorgeous. Just trying to ease into the inevitable."

Our eyes met over the mug I was pouring coffee into. I'd always loved him for his honesty. He knew that. He also knew that right now, I was as close to hating him as I'd ever been.

I wanted to see Nick.

If I saw him, I knew I'd pour all of this out to him. That he, of all people, would understand how I could be so scared and angry at the same time.

But at the same time, he was the last person I wanted to see, because I wouldn't be able to stop myself from pouring all of this out to him.

I couldn't, I couldn't...I *couldn't*.

This was my gig. He had enough on his plate. So in the tradition of all good cowards, I hid. I hid out in Ethan's room as much as I could, avoiding not just Nick, but everyone, even Nan. Didn't want to see anyone or allow them too close—didn't want anyone to see just how close to the edge I was. I was so far into avoidance mode, that, like a character out of some sad B movie, I even checked that the hallways were clear before I snuck down to Starbucks to get Ethan his fix. Afterward, I sat there watching him doze, my mind wandering between past, present, and trying really hard not to envision the future, until I was jolted from my reverie by the vibration of my phone.

Dinner?

I stared at it for several minutes. Put my phone away. Pulled it back out. Stared at it some more, finally typing, *Not tonight.*

But no sooner had I hit send, than Ethan's eyes fluttered open, struggling to focus. "You need to leave, gorgeous."

"No." Forget it. I was going to stand my ground. "This new cocktail, the last couple of times it hasn't hit you really badly until the second day."

"I can feel it coming on, Libby. Please, sweetheart."

"No."

"Libby, goddammit, you need to go." His eyes were still clear and lucid, not that terrifying, opaque blue that made them look like marbles for all the emotion they'd reflect. "Please, don't make me have to call the nurses."

My breathing, my heart, everything stopped in that moment. "You'd do that?"

"The only thing I've got left to give you is me, when I'm good. After all this time, don't you understand I have to spare you me at my worst as much as possible? So please, Libby, do this. For me."

"After this time, don't *you* understand, there's nothing you can do, no way that you can be, that I won't love you? That I won't see the real you—the good you?" Despite the fact that I felt helpless and furious and ready to scream, I was still able to reach for his hand, bring it to my chest, and hold it gently against my heart.

"I know, gorgeous, I swear I know. But it kills me that this…" he glanced down at his emaciated frame, scrubbed a hand across sunken cheeks, "is what you're left with."

God*damn* him.

Of course I left. Because he asked. And it was for him. No matter how much I wanted to stay, I knew, both intellectually and emotionally, that I'd only be making things worse if I insisted on hanging around, upping his anxiety to unbearable levels. How could

I do that to him and insist I loved him as much as I did?

I couldn't. But I didn't have to feel like some fucking altruistic saint either.

"Libby."

I ignored the knocking. For now it was still soft and relatively polite—easy to ignore. Same way I'd ignored the multiple text messages on my phone, too, as well as the calls and ensuing voice mails. Because, for God's sake, I was going to hold my ground with someone. If not Ethan, than I could damn well hold it with Nick. The only way I could do that, unfortunately, was to not talk to him at all. And forget seeing him. The minute I looked into those dark brown eyes, I'd be gone—and that wasn't any more fair to him than clinging to Ethan was.

"Libby, *te lo juro,* if you don't open this goddamn door, I'm going to go get Carlos to open it or at least give me a key, and don't think I won't be able to do it." I was on the floor, my back to the door and my arms crossed over my head, as if I could somehow physically block his words. "Look, I know you're in there and I *know* something's gone down. Come on, *por favor,* help me out here."

His impatience was this increasingly palpable thing, reaching through the crevices and urging me to unlock the door and let him in.

Really, I might've caved if it hadn't gone silent—if the sense that he was right there hadn't receded—allowing me to breathe again. At least until I heard the warning click and only managed to scramble out of the way an instant before the door swung inward and hit the wall with a dull thud. The bright lights from the hallway flooded the barely lit interior of my room, backlighting him into a dark, ominous shadow.

"What the fuck do you think you're doing shutting me out like this?"

Still sprawled on the floor, I watched the door slowly swing closed, the brief glare from the lights disappearing, and as it did, revealing Nick's expression—anger, as I might have expected, for the repeated blowing off. Fear, which I maybe should have also expected. But I just couldn't...I stared up at him, my chest getting tighter with each harsh breath I tried to suck in. "Nick, not now."

He recoiled as if I'd slapped him, his face tightening into dark, hard lines. "No, dammit. No 'Nick, not now.' I may have to take it from her, but I can't take it from you, too, Libby." Grabbing my arm, he hauled me to my feet, his breath hot on my skin. "What's going on? What's the matter?"

Pressing my lips together, I shook my head.

"What is it?"

I just kept shaking my head, strands of hair flying loose from my braid and whipping across both our faces, as he grabbed both my arms, his fingers digging in almost to the point of pain. "Is it Ethan? Talk to me, Libby, please."

"No."

"*Fuck.*"

God, so much frustration and anguish in that one short word. Echoing everything I was feeling.

Reaching for him, I pulled his face down, sealed my mouth against his, hoping that would quiet him—stop the questions. In the next heartbeat, I recognized it for the complete lie it was as I pushed myself harder against him, wound my fingers tighter in his hair, holding him close when he might have pulled away. But outside of one startled jerk, he didn't pull, but pushed, turning me until I felt the wall against my back and his body, hard and demanding, against my front.

"Libby."

"Nick."

We knew who we were with. That was the last coherent thought I had before he tore my shirt open, buttons scattering as he pushed it down my arms. As soon as my arms were free, I yanked his shirt over his head, letting it drop to the floor while I pulled his head down for another desperate, open-mouthed kiss. His hands moved lower, unbuttoning my jeans and pulling the zipper down while I did the same, both of us shoving material only just as far out of the way as necessary.

"Oh—oh, *God*." Tears flooded behind my closed lids, half at the welcome feel of Nick's body driving into mine, half at the sudden, unexpected pain. *Don't stop.* I mouthed the words silently against his neck, as I clutched at his hips, hoping he'd somehow understand.

Thank God, the pain didn't seem to register or maybe it was my silent begging, urging him to go on, that did. Another shove and he was in me completely, pulling at one of my thighs, freeing it from denim and cotton so he could hike it high around his waist, his grip tight.

"Libby." It's the only thing he seemed capable of saying as his hips began moving, fast and hard, slamming my entire body against the wall while I groped for purchase on the armoire, on the wall behind me, his shoulder…anywhere that seemed to have something I could grab on to so I could fuck him back just as hard as he was fucking me.

"Yes, Nick, please—" Please what? I didn't even know what I was asking, but Nick did. He grabbed both my arms and pulled them around his neck while he wrapped one arm around my waist and braced the other against the wall. His hand cushioned the back of my head as he lowered his to take possession of my mouth again, his tongue surprisingly soft and slow in its explorations. A stark, erotic contrast to the ragged, brutal thrusts and jabs of our lower bodies, each of us fighting for more depth, more contact, more everything.

One last, hard thrust and his body shuddered in mine, hot and alive, sending me into a tailspin even as I fought to hold on—to Nick, to consciousness.

To the reality we'd just created.

Nick

JANUARY 7

She was on the floor, slumped against the wall, one hand resting against her bare stomach. Her bra was still on, but her shirt was a torn mess on the floor, jeans and underwear tangled around one leg, the other bare—and all because of me. My brain was like this compartmentalized thing, registering all these details as I sat on the floor just a few feet away, breathing hard and trying to figure out what the hell just happened.

"Libby."

My God, what have I done? Why did she try to shut me out? Why couldn't I control myself? Why?

Her eyes opened, and my breathing steadied almost immediately. I realized I'd been terrified she was unconscious, but was even more terrified to get close enough to check. The odd centers of her eyes were pale and fierce as her gaze found mine.

"I'm not sorry."

And all I could do was stare.

"God knows I probably should be, but for right now, right this second, Nick, I'm not sorry; and if that makes me a heartless bitch, well then, I'll have to find a way to live with that."

"You're not a bitch." My voice was hoarse, what I was feeling near impossible to define. "And you're definitely not heartless."

She blinked, but her gaze remained steady, never leaving my face. "There are those who would disagree."

"Yeah and they have dick to do with this." I finally moved, sliding forward the few feet that put me within touching range, even though I still kept hands off. "What happened is between you and me, Libby. No one else."

"Yes and no," she said, her gaze shifting to stare past me. I knew what she was thinking—that it also involved Kath and Ethan, however tangentially, because without them we would never have found ourselves in this surreal bitch of a situation. We wouldn't even *know* each other, for God's sake.

Right now, wasn't sure whether to feel unbelievably pissed, unbelievably sad, or unbelievably grateful.

Libby groaned, snapping me out of my head, and *now*, I felt my first real pangs of guilt.

"Stay still." Leaning forward, I put my hand on her shoulder, keeping her down even as she struggled to bring her legs under her. "Dammit, Libby, *stop*."

"I'm fine, Nick."

"No you're not. Jesus Christ, what have I done?" My hand shook as I touched the insides of her thighs where pink-tinged streaks were already drying.

"Really, it's okay."

She'd only ever been with Ethan. He'd been gentle and caring their first time—a man with honor. I *knew* this. And God only knows when they were last able to make love. She'd told me it had been a long time. And now I'd come in like some goddamn battering ram.

"I hurt you."

"Yeah." Again, she fixed her gaze on my face and again those unique eyes practically swallowed me whole. "And don't you dare go feeling bad about it, Nick. I feel…I don't know." Her hands framed my face, her thumbs brushing across my mouth. "Alive. The pain's not a big deal."

Yes, dammit, it was. I stood, yanking my jeans up. Bending down, I took her in my arms and lifted her to the bed. "Do not move."

In the bathroom, I grabbed a washcloth and while waiting for the water to heat up, held onto the edges of the vanity with a white-knuckled grip and tried like hell not to catch sight of myself in the mirror, because if I did, I might be tempted to ram my fist through the son of a bitch staring back at me.

Returning to the bedroom, I sat on the bed and spread a bath towel beneath her.

"Nick, I can do this." She tried to take the cloth, but I grabbed her wrist, pushing her arm down until her hand rested on her stomach again. At least she didn't try to stop me again or insist she could take care of it herself. She got that I needed to do this for her.

I parted her thighs, keeping my gaze focused only on the stains as I ran the washcloth along one leg, then the other, carefully wiping away the streaky residue. My stomach clenched as I wondered again, how much *had* it hurt? But she hadn't stopped, hadn't cried out, hadn't pushed me away. Rather, she'd pulled me closer, held me even tighter.

And cue the clenching stomach once more, this time because I could feel her again—her skin damp with sweat, arms holding me close, her tongue stroking mine. I could feel myself, buried deep inside her—could feel the drag of skin against skin that had been just this side of pain but also felt so fucking good I'd been compelled to drive into her over and over. Could feel her body open to me—grow wet so that each thrust went that much easier, felt that much more welcoming. Folding the washcloth, I pressed gently between her legs, drawing a long sigh from her at the feel of the warm compress. As much like shit as I felt, her reaction still managed to draw a smile. It also prompted my gaze to finally move, following the curves of her body, nude except for the bra—white, practical. Not something designed for seduction. I felt my smile fade.

"How long?"

"Little over a year." Another sigh, a subtle shift of her body that had mine shifting in response. "We've played some, but actually making love just sapped so much of his energy." She glanced away, toward the windows. "I couldn't do that to him."

Slowly, I drew the washcloth away and dropped it over the side of the bed. Then the bath towel.

God, but I was some kind of idiot. It was inevitable. Should have known there was no way we could leave it at that one, frantic, desperate fuck. No way *I* could leave it there. For a lot of reasons. And it *was* between us—only us.

Her sharp indrawn breath made me look up. "Nick."

I dropped another kiss low on the curve of her stomach, that soft spot that for me had always been one of the most feminine, attractive features on a woman. "Shh...I want to." I ran my tongue along the crease of her thigh. "I want to make it good for you, Libby. You deserve that—*you*." I found myself staring into Libby's enraged face, held immobile by her tight grip in my hair.

Her fingers tightened, forcibly jerking my head toward the door. "Get out."

I grabbed her wrists, pulling them free and damn if she didn't take some hair with it. "What's the matter with you?"

"What happened before is one thing. But I'll be damned if I'll be a pity fuck."

"What?" I shook my head like I was trying to shake out what she'd just said. "*Oye*, you're out of your head, woman, if you think this is a pity fuck."

"That's what you just said."

Rising to my knees, I moved forward between her outstretched legs and leaned over, pinning her wrists to the pillow on either side of her head, my face so close to hers, she had no choice but to look at me. "What I *said* was that I wanted to make it good for you. What's so wrong with that?"

Deliberately lowering my voice as I relaxed my grip on her wrists and stroked the length of her arms, I asked again, "What's so wrong with my wanting to make it good for you?"

"You said it's what I deserved." She turned her head on the pillow, but even so, I could see the beginnings of tears in her eyes. "Like it's some sort of consolation prize you feel compelled to hand out."

Lowering my head, I dropped a kiss on her shoulder, moving the strap of her bra aside. "Not consolation prize, Libby." I trailed a line of kisses across her collarbone, between her breasts, down her stomach, between her thighs.

"More…reward. Or solace. And not just for you, but for both of us. Making you feel good…God, I can't imagine much that would be better." My hands resting lightly on her hips, I paused and looked up, finding her staring at me, the expression on her face unreadable.

Then her hands moved in my hair again, her touch far more gentle. Accepting. I closed my eyes and rubbed my cheek against her with a silent prayer of thanks.

"You're wearing too many clothes." She pushed at my jeans and briefs, cool fingers grabbing my hips and trying to bring me closer.

"So are you." I grinned as I kicked my jeans off while I watched her reach behind herself with one hand. Less than two seconds later, the bra was off and landing on top of my clothes on the floor.

"Better?"

"Almost." I urged her up, just far enough so I could reach behind her and slip the elastic off the end of her braid. Quickly, I unwound the thick mass of it, then eased her back against the pillows. "There."

So beautiful.

Not in any conventional sense, but then again, conventional had never really turned my crank. Libby was simply the complete epitome of soft—soft curves, soft skin, soft hair. A soft expression in her eyes, a soft smile as she pulled me down over her body, her arms holding me close. I wanted nothing more than to lose myself in all that softness and by some miracle, she was inviting me to do just that.

As much as I wanted her though—wanted to make this time good for her, I still hesitated. Reaching back for one of her hands, my mouth a breath away from hers, I quietly asked, "Libby, please, are you sure?"

"Nick, really…" My mouth curved against hers in a smile as she kissed me. That was my Libby—cutting straight through my bullshit. It would take nothing less than an act of God or a simple "no" from her to get me to stop, and we both knew it. But she gave me what I needed at the same time.

"Yeah, I am." She arched up, bringing me with her as she settled back against the mattress. Her free hand trailed up my back to my neck, the tips of her fingers tracing a line around my ear and along my jaw. "Very sure."

Slow and careful, I continued easing in, watching her face, making sure that there wasn't any hint of pain. She'd had enough.

It seemed to take forever. Seemed to take no time at all. Finally cradled as far inside her as I could go, I let my head drop to the pillow beside hers. I stayed as still as I possibly could, breathing deep.

"Oh my God, Libby—you feel so good. Do you know that?"

Turning her head, her tongue teased the rim of my ear, her breath warm as she whispered, "What I know is that I'm going to die if you don't stop with this slow crap and fuck me, Nick. I'm not going to break, I swear."

I jerked with a shocked laugh, the vibrations making her shiver beneath me in a way that turned laughter to a groan in a hurry.

Pat me on the back though, because even so, I *still* tried to go slow. Build up to it. I was the more experienced one, right? Should've given me some measure of control. Right. Nice fantasy. Whimpering, Libby arched up hard against me, over and over, her hands grabbing my hips and urging me to go faster and then, when I still didn't quite fall into the rhythm she wanted, she took matters into her own hands, rolling us over in one quick move.

"I won't break," she gasped. At the same time, though, she went completely still, the two of us plastered together shoulders to hips, so close a breath of air couldn't get between us. Lifting her head slightly, she looked down at me, eyes wide, lips parted. I couldn't tell—didn't know—

"Am I hurting you?" Please, God…don't let me be hurting her,

"No." Propping her hands on my shoulders, she leveraged her torso up, shifting her legs until her knees pressed against my sides. Reaching back, she grasped my hands and drew them up until they rested on the pillows beside my head. Just as slowly as she'd raised her body, she lowered herself again, not quite as far as before, remaining suspended just above my chest.

"Nick." Her mouth was so close to mine her lips felt like the lightest caress as she said my name, raising goose bumps over my skin.

"Say it again."

"Nick," she breathed into my mouth. Again and again she repeated my name, as I lifted my hips, meeting each of her thrusts, the extent of what she'd allow me to do since she maintained her hold on my hands, held all of me, inside and out.

The raw sounds of our bodies moving together, the feel of her fingernails digging into the backs of my hands, set something off in me, made me want to give her exactly what she wanted. Made me want exactly what she wanted. That's when I flipped us back over and began moving, slow and deliberate, stretching both hands above her head and holding them there.

"This, Libby?" I whispered against her ear, my tongue teasing the soft hollow behind the lobe, groaning at the shiver that passed through her entire body and vibrated against mine.

"Yes…" Freeing her hands, she drew them down my arms, a slow, sensuous stroke before curling them around my shoulders as she arched up hard, holding me close. "Please, Nick, *yes*."

And God help me, as I wrapped my arms around her and came into her, the last thing I wanted was for her to let me go.

It wasn't until she squeaked, pushing at me that I realized that I'd collapsed on top of her, exhausted and panting.

"Jesus, I'm sorry." I rolled off, but kept her with me, the two of us winding up on our sides, facing each other.

"*Oye*, would you *stop* saying that?"

"Did I hurt you?"

"Would you stop saying that, too?" Shoving her hair from her face, she blew out a long, slow breath, the warm air tickling my throat and chest and, for Christ's sake, making my dick twitch, like it thought it could go again. Right now. Goddamn crazy appendage.

"I'm serious, Libby. That wasn't exactly what I had in mind." Not that it was rough, not like against the wall—but it hadn't exactly been gentle and easy either. I stroked her thighs, moving them apart so I could see the insides, breathing a sigh of relief. No more signs of blood. Made me feel only marginally better.

"As I recall, you said you wanted it to be good." Her mouth against mine, she took my lower lip between her teeth and nibbled before adding, "It was good." Releasing my lip, she lowered her head to catch a drop of sweat that was trickling down my throat, the warm soft drag of her tongue making my body entertain those crazy thoughts again no matter how many signals and warnings I sent it to slow *down*.

"God, woman, what you do to me."

"I do?" Her hands were playing on my chest, walking up my ribs, nails scratching lightly.

"Libby." My turn to cut through her bullshit and she knew it, judging by the small smile that crossed her face as she continued stroking my chest. "You do. And as you can tell, I'd be happy to show you again, but how about after a shower?"

Her smile got a little bigger. "How about *in* the shower?"

And after we'd slept a few hours, in the bed again, this time finally the gentle coming together I wanted to give her, holding both her hands as we kissed and our bodies, now familiar with each other, did this slow, languid dance without any conscious effort on our part. And with each thrust, I lost myself further in her, lost the sense of myself and of her as separate entities until there was only us.

It should've felt perfect. I think it *did* feel perfect. Maybe that's why, holding her close and watching dawn bring a cool gray light into the room, I felt like such utter shit.

Libby

JANUARY 8

Something that seems like a good idea in the dark? That not only is it a good idea but the right thing to do? The only thing you could possibly do?

The light of day has a way of peeling back that handy layer of security and exposing the truth.

And the harsh, light-of-day truth was I was married, I loved my husband, and I'd just spent the night having sex with a married man who loved his wife.

Libby, Libby, Libby. If you're gonna do it, do it right.

Okay, fine. The real truth was that I'd spent the night having *good* sex. Maybe that's what was hardest to deal with. Because I couldn't deny it had been good. Unbelievably good. And so very wrong.

At least I knew that Nick was feeling the same way. He was holding me close, same as all those nights where all we'd done was sleep, but unlike those nights, an unfamiliar tension held his body hostage. A tension that prevented him from curving his body around mine in the way I cherished and needed—so badly—at the end of these increasingly hellish days. So now we'd lost that too.

However, there was no point in torturing either of us, so I let him continue to feign sleep while I crept off to the bathroom. Would've left altogether except, well...my room. Maybe he'd take the chance and leave while I was in the shower. I'd take a really long shower. Let him have plenty of opportunity to take off and not be forced to tell me what a mistake it had been.

Because I got it. I really did.

But of course, having him leave—that would've been way too easy. Cowardly even, and neither of us were necessarily cowards. Wrapped in my robe, I finally left the bathroom and wasn't all that surprised to find him still in the room. At least he'd had the decency to get out of bed and get dressed. He sat slumped in one of the chairs by the windows, the curtains drawn back to reveal the morning, eliminating the last vestiges of that handy, concealing dark. Now, if this was a movie or a book, that window should've revealed a gloomy, rainy day. Something to reflect our moods and the gravity of the situation.

So of course, it was a picture postcard perfect day—the kind of day that had made Miami a winter playground since Henry Flagler had first brought his godforsaken railroad down here. Obscenely bright—the skyline diamond-etched and shining across the calm, deep blue expanse of Biscayne Bay. The gods were having a great time mocking me, weren't they? Because they had to know that from this day on, every time I saw an image of the Miami skyline silhouetted against such an achingly blue sky, I'd remember this day, and, consequently, the night that preceded it.

"We didn't use anything."

I stared at him. He stared out the window. And I laughed. That, at least, made him look away from the window. Made him look pissed, too.

"You know, you'd think that's something we would've thought of after the first time—maybe the second." I dropped onto the edge of the mattress, twisting the sash of my robe around my fingers. "Or the third. Definitely by the fourth time."

"But we didn't." His eyes narrowed, his gaze fixing itself on my face. "What if—"

"I'm on the pill." My voice caught, strangled almost as hard as I was strangling my hand with the damn sash.

"What?"

"I've been on the pill since I was fifteen." I looked up and found him staring at me, his brows drawn together. Right. He knew Ethan had been my first and I'd been twenty-one. So what was a fifteen-year-old virgin doing on the pill? Aside from the fact that I had Nora as a mother. "Irregular periods, and when I get them, they're vicious. The pills keep both under control. One less thing to have to deal with. Do you want to see them?" I sounded brittle and harsh, as if every word might shatter and break into tiny, sharp fragments over our stupid heads.

"God, *no*."

"Wouldn't want you to worry after all."

"Libby…" Now it was his voice sounding strangled. "Talk to me."

Took a second to realize that the laugh bouncing off the walls had come from me again. "That's what you said last night—and look where that got us." He sat there looking wounded and furious and every bit as helpless as I felt.

"At the risk of sounding all *telenovela* and clichéd, what is there to talk about? We—" I caught my breath, nearly choking on my tongue in the process. I had very nearly said "made love." My fingers had gone numb, so I released the sash and rubbed my hands together. "We had sex, Nick." He flinched at the words, but what the hell else was I supposed to call it? "It's been a hellaciously bad few days. I was scared and upset and pissed, and I took advantage of your concern. I just…I needed to be close to…someone."

That was close. I'd almost said, "You, Nick. I had to be close to you." And that kind of guilt he didn't need on top of everything else. Neither did I. Maybe too, I was trying to convince myself that any warm body would've done.

"Wait just a goddamn minute." His fists were clenched on his thighs, the skin around his eyes drawn and tight. "If we're going to be honest and call it what it is, then we're going to be honest enough to both take responsibility. Maybe—" He stopped short and I watched the muscles in his neck tighten and shift as he swallowed. "Maybe you initiated it, but I won't lie and say that I didn't want it. Want…you. Because we both know that would be a lie."

"Does it really matter? What we did, Nick…We *swore* nothing like this would ever happen—"

"No, Libby—*I* swore," he broke in. "I promised you, and I promised myself and—"

"And I'm the one who pushed." I was shaking my head back and forth, twisting my hands in the sheets. "And…and maybe if it had been just the one time, I could've found some way to excuse it or at the very least, forgive myself—but after that first time, it was a conscious choice. We spent the whole *night* making love."

Oh *God.*

"So…not just sex?" His voice was very quiet as our gazes met. I wanted nothing more than to take it back, to look away, to crawl under a rock, but Nick and I—we weren't like that with each other.

"I don't know. Does it really matter?" I scrubbed a hand over my face. "What we call it?"

"I think it does." His gaze was steady on mine, holding on, refusing to allow me to back away or hide. "You can't deny there were feelings involved, Libby. Stuff that takes it beyond just fucking."

A long slow breath hovered between us, pregnant with so many more things that could have been said. That maybe needed to be said. But in the end, I was only able to say one thing.

"No, I can't."

I could admit that. Especially if he could. Took guts to even be having this conversation, considering I'd given him the perfect opportunity to bail and never have to deal with it.

Turning to look back through the windows, he quietly added, "And if I'm brutally honest with myself, I'd also have to admit that while I hate that I hurt you and thought I could stop after the one time, the God's honest truth is, I didn't want to. I wanted you, Libby. Last night, I wanted everything we did."

I sat frozen, staring at his bent head, wanting so badly to go to him and hold him and tell him it would be okay—knowing I couldn't. How the hell was any of this ever going to be okay? What had I done?

"You're my friend, Nick," I said slowly. "Probably the best one I've had outside of Ethan in a long while. But this…" I went back to wrapping the sash just as tight as I could around my hand, a convenient excuse for the pain and the tears clogging my throat. "It can't ever happen again."

His head snapped up. "Of course not, Libby. That's not at all what I was trying to suggest. Of course it can't ever happen again." He stood and walked to the door, each motion stiff and careful. "In one night, I betrayed my wife *and* a friend's trust. And there's not a fucking thing I can do to make it right. For either of you. And to complete the hat trick…" His shoulders dropped as he sighed, his eyes dark and for the first time since I'd met him, unreadable. But he also didn't look away—didn't back down. "Do you remember what you said last night? After the first time?"

Oh yeah I remembered. The same way I remembered the rough feel of the carpet beneath my skin and the throbbing ache between my legs and the slow trickle of wetness down my thighs. I remembered feeling how, for the first time in two years, even if it was only for those few minutes, I hadn't been consumed with misery and worry and sorrow over Ethan.

I remembered the sense of sheer relief. Of…freedom.

I'm not sorry.

"Yeah."

"I'm…I'm not sure I am either." His voice dropped further as he turned the knob. "I just don't fucking know."

I sat there for the longest time after the door clicked shut behind him. Another honorable man. I knew people who thought they were myths.

I knew different.

• • •

I eased in through the partially open door, not wanting to disturb Ethan if he was asleep. Instead, I found him sitting up and watching the door, his expression anxious.

"You're here. Thank God."

My backpack landed at my feet with a dull thud. "*What?*"

"You've never been this late before. I don't know, I thought maybe I pushed you over the edge yesterday…especially after the past few days."

"Shh…" I eased down on the edge of the bed and put the fingers of one hand against his lips, the other stroking his cheek. "I'm sorry I'm late. And that I didn't call."

He untwisted his hands from the sheets and grabbed my wrists. "Libby, I had to do it—"

"I know, Ethan." I drew his head to my shoulder, stroked the satin smoothness of his skull, the curve of his back through his T-shirt, my heart twisting at the almost painful protrusions of each vertebra. Felt it twist again as another back flashed into my mind. Broad, the spine bracketed by smooth muscle, slippery with sweat, the skin giving beneath my fingernails. The memory of which had me holding Ethan that much closer, stroking his head and back as I repeated, "I know, *querido*, I know… It's okay. I love you. I'll always love you."

"Thank God," he sighed, his breath warm against my neck. And I was grateful to the point of tears that I could still hold him and tell him I loved him—that he could hold me back with whatever he had left.

We remained like that for however long it was until his nurse came in to administer his second day's cocktail. While she got him set up, I ran down to Starbucks, picking up Frappuccinos and "something decadent for us to share, gorgeous." I fed him bites of Neapolitan, holding globs of rich pastry cream on my finger for him to suck off, then afterward I carefully settled beside him on the bed so we could browse the net on the laptop. We laughed at all the funny political cartoons and rolled our eyes at the truly wretched headlines and even worse writing on the various news sites until I felt movement beneath the covers. His foot—just the merest twitch, but it was enough.

"Do you need me to go?"

His expression was at first shocked—I had never once ever volunteered before—before he sighed, resting his hand against my cheek. "I wish you didn't have to."

Maybe I was volunteering, but I wouldn't lie to him. We'd been together too long and besides, he'd figure it out for the bull it was inside of two seconds. "Let's be honest, Ethan. I don't have to—and I certainly don't want to. But it's what you need."

"Yeah." His expression morphed further into something so ineffably sad and heartbreaking that all I wanted was to take him in my arms again. But how could I when even resting my hand on his had his skin rippling and twitching beneath mine? He was almost there…to that full-bore agitation where physical proximity—of any sort—was just too much for him to handle. I wondered how long he'd been trying to hold it off.

He surprised me though. When I leaned in to give him a careful kiss goodbye, he pulled me close against him, holding my head to his shoulder as I'd done for him earlier. He didn't say anything, just pressed a gentle kiss to the top of my head as he stroked the length of my back for several long seconds. And as always, I reached out and held tight to this rare, all-too-brief moment where he was just Ethan and I was just Libby and none of this had happened to us yet.

As I drew back, his hand trailed along my cheek. "Such a gorgeous image I'll go to sleep with tonight."

I risked trapping his hand, turning my head to press a quick kiss to his palm. "I'll be here first thing in the morning so we can go home. But call me if you want me to come back before then?" Even though we both knew he wouldn't, he still nodded, allowing me that little bit of fantasy.

For once, I was able to close the door behind myself without that horrible, gut-wrenching sensation that I was abandoning him. Was able to give him space that he needed, and was able do it without giving in to all that helpless rage and despair that left me exhausted. More miraculous was that I was able to do it without feeling the overwhelming guilt I had in the past for needing space as much as he did.

Oddly, I felt no need to sift through the feelings and examine any of them too closely. No desire to try to dissect them and figure out why it was finally possible for me to do this.

Honestly? I was too scared to go probing beneath the surface.

Nick

JANUARY 28

I tried like hell to make sense of everything. Then I'd decide there was no way to make sense of it—best to try to set it aside and move on. Then I'd start over. Because something in me was demanding I make sense of what had happened.

The first time? Easy. Emotional overload. The two of us had been walking the edge, Libby so much longer than me. Clearly something had happened that I still had no clue about, other than it had been a really shitty few days by her own admission—and me, being my usual bullheaded can't-take-no-for-an-answer asshole self, had pushed until she snapped. Except instead of turning away from me, she'd turned *to* me. Combine that with the sort of physical deprivation we'd both been living with and the sexual attraction we'd both acknowledged...

It was like a spark going off too close to an open gas line or some other crappy metaphor.

Second time? That hadn't been bullshit, what I'd said about wanting to make it good for her. She didn't just deserve that—she needed it. We both did. The third and fourth times? Hell, I don't know. That's where the thought process would completely fall to shit, and I went right back to wondering what the hell happened. Those last two times...I had no excuse for. Couldn't define a logical justification. But I wouldn't have given them up for the world. Still wouldn't. And the paradox was driving me insane.

"What the fuck's the matter with you?"

I kept looking into my whisky, staring through it to the wood surface of the bar.

"Yo, bring me a double Balvenie Fourteen, neat," Bobby shouted over the noise to the bartender as he settled himself on the stool next to mine. "You come to town, you don't even call me? I have to find out from one of my agents that they saw you at the game tonight? Force me to come hunt your ass down? Thank God you're such a fucking creature of habit."

"Sorry, Bob." I didn't look up as I lifted the glass and took a drink.

"The hell you are. Because I know you were desperately trying to call me, but this piece of shit, so-called smart phone that my secretary—oh, excuse me, executive assistant—told me is the latest and greatest actually gets crappy reception in the city. Right?"

Bastard. Couldn't help but smile. "When was the last time you actually pulled off naive, Bobby?"

Without missing a beat he replied, "I was sixteen. Convinced Sandy Schwartz I was a virgin too and it would be a beautiful thing if we could lose it together."

"But of course you weren't."

He snorted. "Seduced at fourteen by my little sister's fifteen-year-old babysitter."

"Right." Total bastard. But honest about it. "Seriously, I got in just before the game, went straight to the Garden, then came here. But I should've called."

"Yeah, you should've. Thanks," he said as the bartender placed his drink in front of him, adding, "Start me a tab and put whatever this asshole's had on it, too."

He let me have a couple of minutes while he did his agent's survey of who was in the bar. Not far from Madison Square, it was a popular postgame hangout for players and those hoping to be noticed by said players. Bobby, always with an eye on the bottom line, was checking to see if any of his clients were here and if so, were they doing anything that would potentially land them in lawsuits? Or, more specifically, were they doing anything that might jeopardize his fifteen percent?

From the corner of my eye, I watched him scan the crowd—watching the groupies hitting on players, the players hitting back, the fans and sycophants clustered around, trying and failing to look unimpressed—his sharp gaze not missing a damn thing. So I was more or less ready when he shifted that gaze my way and casually drawled, "So, what the fuck's the matter with you? And I don't mean because you didn't call tonight. You haven't called for weeks."

"Jesus, Bob, every time I see you, you sound more and more like my mother."

"Speaking of which, you going to see the family while you're in town?"

I shook my head and drained my glass. Waving to the bartender for another, I said, "Don't have time. I'm renting a car tomorrow and going up to Vermont to check out some prospects, then to New Hampshire, and then I have to get home."

Besides, if I went over to Jersey, I was afraid my mother would read some big, red "Sinner" across my chest and drag me by the ear to confession, berating me in two languages the entire way. No thanks. I'd even skipped seeing Tico last time I was in Miami, knowing he'd see for sure.

And by the purest of goddamn luck, good or bad, I'd missed seeing Libby by a day according to Nan. God knows I hadn't heard from her directly in the three weeks since that night. Three weeks tonight and I knew that off the top of my head and I missed her more than I could even begin to express—and there was no way in hell I could call her. Even to check on her.

My hands tightened around the empty glass, itching with a near-uncontrollable impulse to fling it at the mirror behind the bar.

"How's Kath?"

I shrugged—tried to prep myself to do the deflection routine, but Bob cut me off.

"And don't try to bullshit me that things are okay and that's why you're even on this trip. You seriously look like hell, Nicky. What's going on?"

For the first time I looked directly at Bobby whose rumpled, slouched-on-the-barstool posture belied the narrow stare he was laying on me. He'd always been an astute fucker, but I figured it was exclusive to business. I'd never really known him to make much use of the skill in terms of interpersonal relations, which was probably why he was on his third wife.

"Health-wise, she's okay, I guess, for the moment. Stable, which means things aren't getting worse at least." Fuck it, it was Bobby. "The rest of it…" I drained my drink as soon as the bartender set it in front me and motioned that he could pour another before he even walked away. "The rest of it is kind of rough. She's dealing with it her way, which amounts to shutting me out."

"Pissing you off?"

"It did." I rolled my filled glass between my palms but didn't raise it. "Not anymore."

"Why not?"

"Got tired of the fighting, Bobby. It wasn't doing us any good."

"Yeah, but Nicky, you're forgetting, I know you."

I kept rolling the glass back and forth, studying the play of light off the surface of the single malt. "What's that supposed to mean?"

"It means as long as I've known you, and that's what—over fifteen years now?—you've never once backed off from anything, not even when you probably should have, until you were forced by circumstances beyond your control. Hell, we both know you should've retired after that first bout with pneumonia, but you're a stubborn ass and kept going until the second go-round nearly killed you, you dumb prick. So whether or not the fighting was doing you any good, I'm not seeing that as a big factor."

"Yeah, but this isn't simply me we're talking about here, Bobby. Didn't you hear me say *us*? Which means Kath, too. And she's the one who has to take precedence."

"And you're not hearing me, my friend. If *you* thought it was ultimately in her best interest to keep pushing, you would. The fighting would be inconsequential. You'd deal with the fallout later."

Leave it to Bobby to ruthlessly dissect me in the space of a couple sentences. And be right about it. Bastard. The whisky burned as effectively the fourth time going down as it had the first. Turning my head away and closing my eyes, I rubbed at my lip—had been doing a lot of that lately. Amazing it wasn't raw and bleeding. The clink of glass made me open my eyes, find that my whisky glass was gone, and in its place a pair of empty glasses with a bottle of Pellegrino between them. I lifted an eyebrow at Bobby who eyeballed me right back.

"You said you're driving to Vermont. Sucks to face all that organic, wholesome, Ben and Jerry shit with a hangover." Lifting the dark green bottle, he filled both glasses with the sparkling water. "Am I right in guessing some serious shit has gone down to take circumstances beyond your control?"

"You could say that."

I turned on my stool to do the same survey of the bar that Bob had, but for different reasons. Jesus, but these people were pretty. The jocks, young and healthy, the wives and girlfriends and groupies beautiful in a shiny, uniform sort of way. How surreal. Everything about my life seemed surreal these days. And how fucking ironic was it that the most surreal situation of all was the one that had felt the most real to me? Probably why I couldn't let it go—why I had to keep turning it over in my mind. It was a way of hanging on to how unbelievably real I'd felt those few hours in the dark.

"I'm not gonna ask what it is, Nicky. But if you ever need to talk—"

Bobby's soft laugh cut through the chatter and music and sound of clinking bottles and glasses.

"What?"

"Well… this is me we're talking about, Nick." He shrugged and lifted his glass of water. "Given my personal history, not to mention the business I'm in, no matter what it is that's happened, I'm in no position to judge, you know? And I worry about you, you stubborn son of a bitch."

I lifted my glass and tapped it against his. "Yeah, I know, Bobby. Thanks."

• • •

"Nick?"

I looked up from the computer screen to find Kath hovering in the partially closed doorway to my office. Pretty rare occurrence these days that I saw her in here, but even I wasn't dumb enough to make a big deal of it. So I kept my response to a fairly mild, "Hey, what's up?" as I paused the game video I'd been studying. As I did, I noticed her gaze follow my movements, eyes narrowing as she took note of the camera attached to the computer. She still hadn't forgiven me for that. Well, she could join the club—I still hadn't either.

"Is everything all right?"

She fidgeted, playing with the doorknob, another thing that wasn't like her. Generally, Kath's style was of the direct-and-to-the-point variety. But again, not dumb enough to say anything, so I just sat back and waited.

"Yeah, everything's okay, just, um, could you come help me with something?"

"Me?" Despite not wanting to make a big deal of it, my eyebrows felt like they were somewhere near the middle of my forehead as I stared at her.

"Yeah—if it's not too much trouble."

"Not at all."

I followed her to the kitchen where, in the much brighter lighting, I could see her pale skin turning pink as she turned toward me, holding out a bottle of Dijon mustard. "Could you...open this for me?"

"Of course." I took the jar, turning away slightly as I opened it. Didn't want her to notice how little effort it took to open the jar she couldn't. Handing it to her, I asked, "Where's Rennie?"

"She had to go to the pharmacy—run some other errands." Kath dipped a knife into the mustard and spread it over the toasted rye bread already on a plate. "She called a few minutes ago to say she'd been held up. Some accident on ninety-five has traffic snarled to hell and back, and she's still half a mile away from the nearest exit."

I smiled as I watched her squeeze mayo from a plastic jar and spread it over the mustard with precise, deliberate motions, the tip of her tongue sticking out. Which made me feel good. So little about my home life these days made me smile.

"Anyhow, I got hungry and even though she left me lunch, I just didn't feel like bean soup. Feel like I'm going to turn into a goddamn legume if I eat more soup."

Shades of the old Kath. "Ham and smoked Gouda?"

A crooked smile curved her mouth. "What else?"

Also felt good to be smiling back—not so worried that the next thing out of my mouth might be the wrong thing. "Nothing else it could be." I watched her place shaved ham and sliced cheese on the bread with the same care and deliberation she gave everything.

"Was your trip okay? I heard you come in late last night."

Wow. Another surprise. I honestly couldn't remember the last time she'd asked about work. "Sorry. I didn't mean to wake you up."

"You didn't. I was still up." She didn't bother looking up, although one shoulder lifted.

Still up because she was probably too uncomfortable to sleep. Something to remember for Marco. "Uh…well, the trip was pretty good. Got a lot done in just a few days—left me with a lot of film to go over." I took a step toward the door. Again, not stupid enough to think she honestly wanted me to go into any huge detail about my life. I'd done her a favor; my guess was she was being polite in return. But at this point, I'd take what I could get.

"Is there anything else you need?" I said it very cautiously and with no expectation of hearing anything other than a "no."

"No."

Not as flat and hard as it could've been, but still a pretty definitive "no." Well, then. I turned to leave but stopped at her quiet, "You want me to leave the stuff out for you?" Because it wasn't just her favorite sandwich, it was mine too. Created years ago during a laughing, late-night rummage through the refrigerator, desperate for something to assuage those raging post-orgasm munchies.

Really, really didn't need to be making a big deal of this. A thought that was followed almost right away by the realization that I really didn't *want* to make a big deal of it. Just didn't have the energy for anything potentially messy. Kath, as always, was going to do what Kath wanted and how she wanted. Maybe once upon a time I understood her motivations without needing to have them spelled out. These days, I was just grateful we were managing to coexist.

Glancing back over my shoulder, I shook my head. "No thanks, babe. I'm good."

Back in my office, I took several deep breaths and leaned my head against the padded back of my chair. That was the closest to—I don't know—herself—that she'd been in months. And even just a few weeks ago I might've taken her up on the sandwich offer, sat with her, taken it as an open invitation to go all eager beaver and start grilling her about every fucking thing that had been going on for the last six months.

And no doubt, would've pissed her right off and given her an excuse to rip me yet another new one for trying to take too much that she wasn't ready to give. That maybe she wouldn't ever be able to give.

Didn't mean I didn't want to. In spite of everything, I still did. I wanted to know what was going on in that head of hers.

But I'd learned my lesson. All I could do was what she wanted, even if that meant leaving her alone. What I really wished—and God I hated myself for being this selfish—was that *I* didn't have to feel so alone.

• • •

I stood in the doorway watching her unpack her bag and arrange things on the bedside table. "Can I get you anything before I go?"

Without looking up she said, "No thanks. I'm fine. You can go."

Of course.

"You'll call?"

Now she spared a glance over her shoulder, expression and

voice both slightly impatient as she said, "Yeah, Nick, of course. It'll probably be day after tomorrow—like always. I'll call when they're ready to release me."

So much for our informal white flag from a few days ago. Honest to God, I was shocked she was still letting me drive her down to Flagler for the treatments, but I think it was a line that even Kath couldn't bring herself to cross—shutting me out to that extent. If she did...I didn't even want to think about going down that road. What consequences it might yield.

As it was, she'd made it clear after my bout with the upper respiratory infection that she was just as relieved to have me stay away while she was getting her treatments. As to where I should go or what I should do with myself, she wasn't quite so helpful. She probably just assumed I was going back home to Boca, going about my life as usual—that is, provided she even gave it any thought.

Maybe it would've been the easier choice, but thing was, I couldn't just bail. What if something happened and I wasn't easily accessible? You want unforgivable? Even if it's probably what she wanted—to have me far enough away where I couldn't interfere— that's where I drew my own line. She'd have to tell me outright that's what she wanted. And there wasn't any sure bet I'd listen. I think she knew that.

So I'd stay just long enough to catch up with Nan and wait to get an update from Marco who was smart enough to know that things were utterly fucked between me and Kath without asking a lot of questions. He always just seemed to know when we checked in and made it a point to make a quick appearance.

"Looks like she's responding well, *m'ijo*. The cell growth appears to have slowed considerably, and she seems to be feeling okay—" He raised his eyebrows over his half rims. A silent question to see what I knew.

"I...I guess." I lifted a shoulder. "Sometimes I hear her at night, pacing." From the guest room next door where I'd be lying, rigid in bed, listening as she moved around in what had once been our bedroom, but now was hers alone. I'd hear her pacing, or moaning in her sleep, or the worst, getting sick—and couldn't do a damn thing about it.

Marco made a note on the chart he held. "I'll make sure to ask about it—tactfully," he added, his eyebrows going up again.

Thank God. I turned and headed back toward the waiting room, nodding at the new people with their lost expressions. People I couldn't handle getting to know. Leaning down, I gave Nan a kiss goodbye.

"You're not staying?"

"I'm going to the hotel—have a lot of work to do." The universal excuse. Somehow, I figured Nan knew that's just what it was, judging by her slow nod and the way her blue eyes studied my face.

"All right, bebe. If you happen to run into her, tell Libby I said hi. We seem to be missing each other a lot lately."

"She's here?"

"Came in this morning. But I don't think she stayed long." She sighed and looked away. "The worse it gets, the less Ethan wants her to see. It's killing her."

Fuck.

Fuck, fuck, *fuck*.

I managed to make it to the walkway before I caved and pulled my phone out. The only other restraint I exhibited was that I sent a text instead of calling outright.

Hey.

By the time I reached the end of the walkway, my phone beeped.

Are you here?

I dialed her number—by the time I had the phone to my ear I could hear her

"Nick?"

"I'm at the hospital, on my way to the hotel. Are you all right?"

"I'm...I...I don't know." Her voice sounded small and young and scared shitless, urging me from walk to a run.

"I'll be there in ten minutes."

"Okay."

No sooner had I pulled from the parking space, my phone beeped its text signal again.

Hitting the brakes, I pulled it from my pocket and glanced down.

Rm 711. Need to see you.

I started to toss it to the console, but for some reason, looked again. The blood rushed through my ears, leaving me dizzy—as if I'd just caught a puck upside the head.

Jesus. I'd read it wrong.

Rm 711. Need you.

Libby

FEBRUARY 5

I'd left the door propped open with the latch, so there wasn't even a knock. One minute I was alone, the next, he was on a knee in front of my chair, his hands resting over mine in my lap.

"Not the smartest idea in the world to leave the door open like that. You never know what kind of asshole might just barge in."

"Sort of what I was counting on." I kept my stare fixed on the window, at the unending sheet of gray beyond because, wouldn't you know it, the day was drizzly and foggy—bay and sky merging together into a murky soup that obscured all but the faintest outlines of the skyline. But I couldn't quite face him—not yet. Because if I looked down and saw pity—it might just break me. I wanted to say what I needed to and then...then I'd look at him and figure out what to do from there.

I took a deep, shaky breath and braced myself.

"When I was with you—not just when we made love, but all the time we spent together—it was—"

"The most normal I've felt in a long time," he finished.

Oh God, he knew. He *knew*. But even so, I still couldn't risk looking away from the window. Because even though he'd figured it out—even though he felt the same way—I still wasn't done.

"I...want that again, Nick." My voice stayed clear and amazingly steady, though each word came out slower than the last. A wrenching, painful, rip-my-soul-out admission. The silent confession to myself had been so goddamn hard. Saying the words out loud—to him—wasn't just an admission of need on my part. It was acknowledgment that a huge part of my life had come to an end and would never again be what it once was. "I…need it. With you."

And then, when I finally looked away from the window and tried to see what might be lurking in his eyes—afraid of what I might find there but needing to know—I couldn't. Because he was lowering his head to my lap with a quiet sigh. His words emerged quiet and slow, but as steady as mine had.

"I do too."

My gaze returned to the window and we stayed like that for a long time.

"It doesn't have to be about sex."

"No, it doesn't. But, Libby, tell me it didn't feel good." The touch of his hand to my face had me turning away from the window to meet his gaze. "And I'm not talking about the sex itself, but the release, the being able to connect so completely with another human on all levels, without reservation. All the way down to your soul." Slowly, he drew his fingers across my lips, leaving a trail of heightened sensation in their wake. "Tell me it didn't leave you feeling as if you could breathe again."

Breathing like I was doing now, our faces close enough that I could practically feel the dark stubble on his face grazing my skin; so close that each breath he exhaled became my next inhalation. So close that it wouldn't take more than a twitch on my part or his for our mouths to meet, to seal the connection between us.

"You said I was your friend."

I nodded. "And friends are there for each other."

"Right." His hands found mine again, palm to palm, fingers sliding together, locking tight, feeling the subtle shift of bone and muscle and sinew. The cool metal of both our wedding bands warming from the contact.

"Let me ask you something, and I want you to really, really think about the answer before you say anything."

Another nod, feeling his breath as a caress from jaw to cheekbone as I did.

"Would you be doing this—at all—if it was anyone but me?"

I didn't have to think about it. "No. Would you—"

He was already shaking his head. "And I know you love Ethan and I love Kath, but the fact is, they don't have enough in them to give us this. And it's a gift we can give to each other—in friendship. *Una benedición*, as my *abuelita* would say."

"Somehow, Nick..." I freed one of my hands and ran it through his hair, feeling the cowlicks and waves trap my fingers. "I'm not thinking this is exactly what your *abuelita* would consider a typical blessing."

His mouth brushed mine in a fleeting caress before he rose, pulling me from the chair in the same motion. Gazing down at me, he copied my gesture, running a hand through my hair, cupping the back of my head in his palm. "She'd probably be pretty firmly of the opinion that there's a reason we were dropped into each other's lives, Libby."

"Sounds like something Nora might say," I said. "Probably after consulting our astrological charts or something."

"Does she know?"

I shook my head. "No one does." None of Nora's damn business, even if she, of all people, might stand a chance of understanding. If I felt so inclined to share. Which I really didn't.

"So it's just ours." The sigh punctuating his comment gave it a sound of relief, and not in a way that suggested he was worried about being found out.

"You like that, don't you?"

"God, yes."

All of a sudden I was having trouble breathing, the fast shallow breaths leaving me mildly lightheaded. Nerves? Anticipation? Guilt? All of the above? Who knew. But before I could get too worked up, Nick, who'd picked up on my agitation, began a soft massage on my scalp that had my eyes closing as he drew my head to his shoulder. The scalp massage was having the effect of turning every muscle in my overtired body to Jell-O, prompting me to slide my arms around his waist and lean more fully against him as he backed up toward the bed.

"Nick." I wanted this. I'd asked him here for this, but paradoxically, I was still terrified. I was absolutely certain what we were doing was okay, at least by the odd standards we'd outlined for ourselves, but a tight knot of emotion still twisted in my stomach. And again, he picked up on my agitation before it had a chance to escalate.

His hands rested lightly on my hips, his expression serious. "You look exhausted. I know I am. Let's just sleep for a while, maybe get something to eat after."

I dropped my gaze to his waist where my fingers were playing with the hem of his T-shirt. "And after that?"

"Whatever you want. If all we do tonight is sleep, then that's fine."

That knot of emotion kept twisting in my stomach but with a more defined purpose, sending warmth out through each limb. I unbuttoned my shirt, after which I slid my sweats down my legs and kicked them off. Wearing nothing but a loose-fitting T-shirt, I slid into the bed and watched as he quickly stripped off his T-shirt and jeans before joining me. But rather than curve himself around my body, he turned me so we were lying face-to-face, his fingers tracing my eyebrows, my jaw, my lips, even the edge of my ear making me shiver.

"Remember what you told me at Ray's funeral—that we're allowed to be angry?"

"Yeah."

"Don't you think if we're allowed anger that we're also allowed peace?"

"Peace?"

Both his hands framed my face, his gaze searching mine as intently as I searched his. "When I'm with you—it's not just normal that I feel, but peaceful, too. Right now—I need some peace in my life. Just...something that's calm and soothing and that I can hold on to when all the rest of my life is falling to shit."

My voice came out hoarse as I said, "You know, you're pretty eloquent for a hockey jock."

He shrugged and slid his hands to my back, drawing me close. "I even read books without pictures."

Laughing together, adding another layer to that little world we were creating, was the last thing I remembered before drifting off.

Libby

Discovery. That's what was different so far, I realized.

That he loved to stay close and keep an arm around me while he slept, I already knew. Also how his body gave off heat like a furnace, but his feet stayed unbelievably cold, so, of course, he'd tangle them up with mine, trying to get them warm.

Strange, what I already knew.

But he had a tiny little mole on his cheek, a dark spot kissing along the shadowy line marking where stubble gave way to smooth skin. And when he was sleeping and really relaxed, one side of his mouth tended to turn up. Hadn't noticed either of those things before.

Which brought to mind the second part of the equation. It wasn't so much simply discovery; it was also the luxury of time. Admittedly, our time was limited, but it *was* ours, with only one possible demand that could take us away from each other. So now, we had the time to discover those things that tension and fear and desire hadn't allowed us last time. I mean, discovery hadn't even been a factor outside of figuring out how our bodies best fit together.

That part, I knew would work just fine. Now it was time for the details. The little things that you studied and burned into your memory banks and kept close enough to be able to summon at will. The stuff that you tended to fixate on and moon over and wonder about in the early stages of a relationship. Except...Nick and I didn't have a relationship—at least nothing you could call conventional. Still—didn't mean I wasn't curious.

"What is it?"

"Hockey?" I lightly traced the thin scar that ran for about an inch from just inside the left corner of his upper lip.

His hand covered mine, his finger rubbing over the scar with a little more force than I'd used before bringing our hands down to his chest. Another detail I'd noticed before—the rubbing—usually when he was upset.

"Yeah." The tip of his tongue came out, touched the scar. "Was screwing around in practice my rookie season, wasn't wearing my helmet, and caught the blade of a stick." His free hand pulled his lip back, one finger tapping the two teeth behind the spot where the scar was. "And like a true hockey jock, these are implants."

"Ouch." I couldn't help but run my tongue over my own teeth, all there, albeit slightly crooked since Nora had deemed braces an unnecessary, bourgeois convention. We'd used the money to go to an ashram for the summer instead.

He shrugged. "It happened so fast, I honestly didn't feel shit—at least not right away. And luckily, the resident who stitched me up was a plastic surgeon wannabe doing a rotation in the ER, so I didn't come out of it so bad."

"Not bad at all." I lowered my head and kissed the corner of his mouth, my tongue following the line of his scar and beyond, up to the tiny little mole on his cheek.

"Does it bother you?"

I drew back and sat up. "Does what bother me? Your scar?"

"God no. You don't seem like the kind of person who's bugged by such superficial crap."

"I'm not." I sighed as his hand shifted to my thigh, stroking gently. "So what then?"

"My being such a bonehead."

"Come again?"

"You know—potential jeopardy to my livelihood…my general health."

"Are you serious?"

He didn't have to say a word. His expression said it all. "You said this happened your rookie season, which meant you were what? Twenty-two?"

His gaze dropped as he nodded, studying the pattern his hand was drawing on my thigh as if he'd be tested on it or something.

"Pretty much everyone's a bonehead when they're twenty-two."

"You were married with a viable career."

"Yeah, but I also didn't have what anyone would call a conventional upbringing. And I was so concerned with not following Nora down the boneheaded path it probably had the net result of making me a huge stick in the mud."

Ha. Probably nothing. Meet the girl voted Most Likely to Become a Prison Matron during her senior class gag awards. Except, I don't think it was so much a gag. Thank God for Ethan. He'd saved me from my own prissy, self-righteousness by making me see it for the armor I'd adopted as a defense mechanism.

"I don't think you're a stick in the mud."

"And I don't think you're a bonehead." I reached out and traced the scar with my thumb, letting it trail across his lower lip. The way he was gazing at me…it seemed as if there was something still on his mind.

"What is it, Nick?"

"I want you to like me, Libby."

Okay. Didn't know what to say to that. "Of course I like you," seemed like the natural response, but it also seemed more than a little ridiculous. Come *on*, he had to know I liked him. So, maybe not the exact response he was looking for.

"How so?"

He grabbed my hand and lowered it to his chest, rubbing his thumb across the knuckles in a light, impossibly gentle movement. "Maybe this sounds stupid, but…I don't want you to think I'm just some idiot who takes unnecessary risks. That I don't think, *tú sabes?*"

"All right," I said slowly, waiting, because the one thing I was getting was that he had to tell me in his own way.

"That's when she left me. I'd convinced her to at least give our relationship a chance, even if it was a long-distance thing, even if she was against my playing hockey as a career, but then I had the accident—" He sighed. "She said it was one thing for me to try to make it as a pro when the odds were against me, but jeopardizing my chances—my future—by being a brainless idiot was more than she could deal with. She wasn't wrong either. I was in the pros, I was kicking ass, having a great time. Last thing on my mind was stuff like long-term consequences of my actions."

Ah—okay. I got it now. "Nick…what we do, what's between us—" I took a breath, considering my next words. "It lasts as long as we need it to. And when the time comes, we walk away, no regrets. That's as much as we need to know in terms of consequences."

"I don't want you to think I haven't considered what might happen." His voice still retained a trace of just-woke-up softness. "I don't want to hurt you."

"Oh, Nick." I cradled his face in my hands, and gently kissed his mouth. "*Mi vida*, you'll never know how much that means to me. But honestly? I don't know how I can possibly be hurt any more than I already have been."

To the tune of having built up a whole new suit of armor and still the hurt found a way in, insidious and mean, striking when I least expected it, the bastard. But rather than stripping it away, Nick had found a way to come crawling into my suit of armor with me, providing another layer against the pain. Again, I kissed him, harder, more completely, sliding my hands from his face, down his neck, to his shoulders as his mouth opened beneath mine.

God, but the man's mouth needed to be registered as a dangerous weapon. One second his tongue was tracing my lips, the next, running along the edges of my teeth, the tip of it even teasing the roof of my mouth in a way that sent corresponding shivers to every other erogenous zone in my body. He trailed a slow, devastating line along the sensitive skin behind my lips, his teeth tugging on my lower lip gently, then biting more sharply as I echoed each gesture.

My lungs burning, I pulled back, sucking in a deep breath and trying to ground myself—just for a second. That feeling of spinning—of falling down Alice's rabbit hole—it was terrifying. And exhilarating. But when he would've pulled me back for another kiss, I shook my head, dropping one against his neck instead.

"Let me," I whispered, waiting until I felt his nod, his hands stroking my back.

Straddling his waist, I began working my way down his body, doing more of that discovery thing, filing the details away. He had an athlete's body—and he didn't. Yeah, he was broad through the chest and shoulders and pretty muscular overall, but it wasn't like he was this walking homage to weight room worship. More like the muscles were so tightly knitted to his frame, they were simply a smooth, integral part of his physique.

Leaning down, I kissed each nipple, teased them with my teeth, which made him gasp and arch his back again, his fingers flexing on my hips like he couldn't decide if he wanted to pull me away or keep me right where I was. Like he had a choice. I took his hands in mine, holding them tight as I kissed my way down his stomach, circled my tongue around and in his navel, wetting the narrow trail of hair leading to and from the small indentation until he was shaking, his thighs tense and trembling.

"Let me," I repeated, more as warning than asking permission. I dragged the waistband of his briefs down over his hips, taking a deep breath of healthy, aroused male, my own desire cranking up another notch. But I could be patient. More discoveries to be made, after all.

"Another hockey memento?" I lightly traced my fingers down the side of his left hip to the top of his thigh.

"Yeah." He arched again, this time more sideways, like he was seeking a more complete touch. I obliged, rubbing my palm over the warm skin, even though by doing so, it obscured my view of the tattoo. Just a few simple, black, curving lines that created a graceful, dark jungle cat.

"Interesting location."

"Considering how many guys I played with had them, my dad knew it was probably a case of 'when' not 'if'—so he just made me promise to get it somewhere it could be covered up."

"Why?"

"So my mom wouldn't have a heart attack."

"Seems a shame," I murmured against his thigh, working my way up to the ink with slow, sweeping strokes of my tongue.

He gasped, one of his hands finding purchase in my hair as I traced the tattoo with my tongue before turning my head to drag a slow, open-mouthed kiss across his lower abdomen to the opposite hip, tiny hairs prickling against my lips.

With my hands, I stroked a long line from his knees all the way up as far as I could reach and back down again. Maybe he wasn't ticklish, but he sure did like this kind of touching, arching and stretching into my hands just like the big, dark cat his tattoo depicted. "Why a cat?"

"Had...a coach say...the way I moved across the rink reminded him of a big cat prowling, waiting to strike."

Oh...my. Now *there* was an image to leave one feeling seriously tingly. Sitting up, I yanked my shirt over my head and tossed it aside, my throat closing and leaving me breathless as I took in the expression on Nick's face. It absolutely froze me, the way his eyes narrowed and his hands reached out and stroked my stomach, cupped my breasts, his thumbs flicking over my nipples, which were just dying for their turn. But not yet.

Shifting my body and lowering my head, I took him in my mouth, just a little at first, and with each breath relaxing and taking more of him in, falling into that near hypnotic state that doing this brought out in me. I moaned when I felt his hands tangle in my hair again, not gentle, like before, but tight, as if he was using his grip to hold himself back.

Scratching the insides of his thighs lightly with my nails, I relished just how close he already was, the heady scent of him filling me and making me dizzy to the point of passing out. I moved faster, until I felt, rather than heard, his groan, low and deep in his chest as he arched up hard, one final time. His hands tightened even more in my hair, sending stars across my vision, even as I kept my gaze on his face, loving the way he looked, lost in his climax. Then, as if he could sense it, his eyes opened and met mine, widening. An instant later, his grip relaxed in my hair, his hands moving to frame my face even as his body continued jerking lightly, like it just didn't want to stop. Or want me to stop.

"*Dios mío, mi vida*...that was...you were...*Dios mío*...how..."

He couldn't even figure out what language he wanted to use. I smiled as I gradually released him.

His hands were back in my hair, stroking gently, as if he was trying to make up for his earlier roughness. Silly man. He didn't have a thing to apologize for, but I wasn't about to stop him. It felt too good.

"You know, just because I've only ever had one lover, Nick, doesn't mean our sex life was vanilla."

"Yeah, Libby, but—" He was still gasping, gulping down huge breaths of air. "Vanilla or not—what you just did—Jesus."

Now I was starting to feel a little self-conscious. Sitting up, I crossed my arms. "What about it?"

Another thing I already knew about him—that he didn't blush. But it didn't mean that he wasn't without his signs that he was embarrassed, the way the tiny muscles around his eyes tended to twitch, and his gaze would slide away, looking for something, anything, else to focus on. Just like it was doing now.

"*Mi vida*, I've—" He stopped, pressed his lips together, shook his head while I felt like I wanted to shake him.

"For God's sake, Nick, *what?*"

The more aggravated I got, the more his embarrassment seemed to fade, the jerk. He relaxed back into the pillows, all tousled hair and sleepy eyes and making me want to throw myself over him every bit as much as I wanted to strangle him. "All I'm saying is, I've been with women who've had a helluva lot more than just one lover, and they didn't give head like you. You...God, you act like you love it."

Maybe he didn't blush, but me? I blushed. And I could feel a raging, full-body flush surging as I shrugged and looked away. "I do."

"Hey." He reached out and pulled me back over his body until we were nose to nose, hip to hip, our legs tangled together. "I'm sorry. I shouldn't have teased. Don't you understand what a gift that is? To not have to lie there feeling like you're on the receiving end of some big favor? You were so beautiful to watch, Libby."

His voice dropped as he spoke, one hand sliding down between us. "You owned me, Libby. Totally and completely."

Amazing how everything could tighten and turn liquid all at the same time. From the smallest of gestures, the simplest of words. Something else I'd missed...so much.

Little orgasms trembled within as he stroked, taunting with their promise of the larger release that had begun building as I made love to him.

"How, Libby?"

His voice was a low, sensuous rumble against my ear, and all I could do was sigh and dig my fingers into his shoulders, but it was enough of an answer for him. "How have you survived?" His breath was a warm caress against my skin before he pulled back, his gaze dark and heated and sending yet another tremor coursing through me, one more step up the intensity scale.

"Don't know," I finally managed to say. "Damn vibrator's only ever good to take the edge off. Not like this." I stretched, groping for purchase on his sweaty shoulders.

"Vibrator?"

"Mm..." I nodded, moving my hands to his hair. Much easier to grab onto even if it was sweaty too. "Nora decided I needed one."

His hand stopped moving. "Your mother gave you a vibrator?"

"This *is* Nora we're talking about." I sighed. "About six months ago, she told me I was being impossibly crabby and maybe it would help."

Silence. Utter silence, then the son of a bitch started laughing.

"Stop it, Nick, it's not funny!" I tried to smack him, but even laughing like a damn loon he still managed to catch my hand and hold it against his chest, heaving with his gasping laughter, like it had been forever since he'd laughed like that and the more he laughed, the more it vibrated along my arm and the more I started feeling it. And no matter how much I wanted to be annoyed with him, I couldn't help but love how joyful he looked and really, it was absurd. So goddamn absurd, and then I was laughing, just as hard as he was, the two of us giggling and wiping tears from our faces.

Until all of a sudden…it wasn't about laughing anymore.

Nick

"Libby?"

Silently, she slid from the bed and disappeared into the bathroom while I sat there wondering, *What the hell?* One minute, we're laughing, I'm feeling better than I have in months—the next, the joy was gone. And I wasn't sure how or why.

Maybe I should leave her alone—but this was Libby. I couldn't. She had to know I couldn't. And the fact that the bathroom door was cracked open, that it wasn't closed and locked? Yeah, she knew. She'd just needed a few seconds of space, for whatever reason.

"Can I come in?"

More silence. But it also didn't have that "Fuck off, asshole" vibe, so I figured her silence pretty much equaled an invitation. Pushing the door further open, I found her sitting on the edge of the tub, her arms crossed over her midsection.

Kneeling in front of her, I uncrossed her arms and took her hands in mine. "Libby, *qué es?*"

She wouldn't look at me and it was killing me. Especially when a single tear slid down her cheek to the corner of her mouth where it disappeared.

Another tear, down the opposite cheek, but losing the chance to make it to her mouth as I reached up and caught it with the tip of my tongue, tasting Libby in the salty drop. Imagining I could taste the rage I felt holding her body tense.

"I just realized again how goddamn tired I am of everyone taking care of me. Nora, Ethan, even Stan, for God's sake…" Her gaze rose, meeting mine. "Did I tell you he showed up?"

I leaned back, shaking my head as I tried to remember…Stan,

Stan…Oh *Jesus.* "Your *father?*"

Her nod turned to a hard shake of the head as she looked past me. "Yeah. Stan. Playing at being daddy for once in his misbegotten existence." She sighed, still staring off into the distance. "Poor Stan—that's so unfair to him. He can't help how he is, and I know he loves me. I know they all love me, but *damn* them. They all think I'm so fragile—can't handle the big, bad world without someone running interference."

"Fuck them."

I rose, grabbing her upper arms and pulling her up along with me. Gently winding one hand in her hair, I pulled her head back until I could look into her eyes.

"And fuck everything else, Libby. "I struggled with each word, not sure why I was so angry—just knowing that I was. "Inside these walls, *this* is our world. And the outside world and anything that's ever happened out there can go straight to hell."

I spun her away from me and pressed her up against the bathroom counter, the two of us facing the mirror while I trapped her from behind with my body. "Look at us, Libby," I whispered against her ear. "This is us—in *our* world. Anything beyond that door—it has no place here. It just doesn't exist when we're together."

No hospitals, no cancer…no spouses, because I was just now starting to realize how jealous I was—and hell if I knew why. I had no right to that jealousy. There was no goddamn way I could ever claim it. But in this world she'd only ever been mine, and I'd only ever been hers. Yeah, it was a fantasy, but it was a fantasy we needed.

I watched her face in the mirror—marveled the range of emotions that crossed it. Her tears and her smile—*God*, that smile. Watched as she reached an arm up and hooked it around my neck, turning her head so she could kiss me. Turning in my arms, she pulled back far enough to meet my gaze, the connection, without the barrier of the mirror between us, feeling that much more real and tangible, and I could see she got it. She got what I meant. And I could see she felt it, too.

"Nick." Her voice was soft but nevertheless intense.

I kissed her neck, her mouth, as she relaxed against me and allowed me to scoop her up in my arms and let the fantasy take over.

• • •

We were back in bed after a shower. I was leaning up against the headboard with Libby draped over me, her head on my shoulder, one arm across my waist, as I stroked her damp hair. For the longest time we stayed like that, quiet, just staring out the window at the reflections the high rises cast on the nighttime waters of the bay.

"*Me gusta.*"

"*¿Qué?*" I replied, although I had a good idea what she meant.

"*La idea que este mundo es solamente de nosotros.*" As she continued in Spanish, I felt another layer of intimacy wrapping around us that had nothing to do with sex and everything to do with just us—as we were. One more thing that was uniquely ours—the shared background. The ability to move freely between our two languages, being able to use just the right words to express exactly what we were feeling. It was something I'd never had with another lover. Something I knew she didn't have with Ethan. That made me tuck her closer against my side and brush a kiss against her mouth.

I picked up a long piece of hair, held it toward the light from the one lamp we'd left on, checking out all the different shades of brown, even a sort of silver-brown that reminded me of the trees in winter back in Jersey. Like her eyes, her hair at first appeared to be just an ordinary brown, then you realized there was a lot more there. Just like Libby. On the surface, ordinary.

Like hell.

"*Es igual para mí también,* Libby. I like it, too, and…" I dropped her hair and returned my gaze to the window, trying to look beyond the dark.

"And?"

I closed my eyes at the warmth of her cheek rubbing against my shoulder, her hand stroking my side. Taking a deep breath, I finally admitted, "*No te puedo mentir*—it scares me. It scares the hell out of me, just how much I like it."

Libby

MARCH 10

My eyes snapped open, my thighs clenched and shaking around the hand I had trapped between them, sheet twisted in my other fist as I tried to figure out…where…what…

"Libby?"

I blinked, struggling to adjust to the dark. Tried to steady my breathing as I realized—

My room…my bed…

"Libby, are you okay?"

Oh *God.*

Like a shot, I was up, swinging my legs over the side of the bed, the tile floor cold and hard against the sole of one foot, Sundance's solid back warm against the other. The contrast was enough to shock the rest of the sleep out of me—what little was left.

As details of the dream I'd just woken from trickled through the filter of sleep and into my conscious mind, a sharp stab of guilt twisted its way through my stomach, hard and painful. I was in our bedroom, our *bed*, for God's sake. Yet I couldn't deny…even as my stomach continued to twist, leaving me vaguely nauseous, there was also a deep heat coiling through every muscle of my body, tempting me to sink back into the mattress and back into the dream's seductive embrace. God, I didn't know it was possible to feel guiltier—but there it was.

"Libby?"

"Yeah, Ethan. I'm fine. Are you all right?"

"Yeah, gorgeous, I'm good—Just heard you."

"Heard what?" *Ay Dios mío*, please, *please*, God…

"I dunno, exactly." His voice sounded slurred and sleepy and, God forgive me, sent still more heat through me. "Sounded like you were having a bad dream."

Praying my legs would hold me, I stood and crossed the short distance to his bed, Sundance padding alongside. "I'm okay. No bad dreams." Except the ones where I was losing him, but that wasn't a sleeping dream, unfortunately.

"Can I comfort you anyway? Reassure you there're no monsters under the bed?"

I could almost hear the smile in that soft, drawled comment. Could even see it, as my eyes adjusted to the dark. "What if I already know there aren't any monsters?"

I rested my hand against his cheek, stroking skin that was unnaturally smooth and soft and tried like hell not to think of Nick—his face heavily shadowed with stubble, rough and abrasive and so unbelievably erotic. Once upon a time, Ethan's beard had been every bit as heavy and a rare source of contention between us. He'd hated shaving, I hated how it scratched.

What I wouldn't give to feel that…just one more time.

And just what kind of lowdown specimen was I that in one breath I could be aroused by the sound of my husband's voice and the next by the memory of my lover's skin. A memory that in turn, spurred a memory of my husband's touch?

And let's not forget the part where I had been awakened from an erotic dream starring said lover.

There simply weren't words.

"What if I'm the one who needs comforting?"

My breath caught, my hand stilling against his cheek. "Ethan, are you really okay?"

The sheets made a soft sound as he shifted in the bed, making Butch grumble and leap down from his post at the end of the bed to Sundance's abandoned cushion where he flopped with an indignant huff.

"I'm really okay, gorgeous. At least as okay as this fucking disease and a dose of Nora's brownies allows." His hand reached out and caught mine as it slid from his cheek. "But I miss you. I miss you next to me, your breath on my skin, your legs rubbing against mine. I hate that I'm here in this stupid goddamn bed and you're across the room in *our* bed, alone. It's so unfair." His voice was low, lacking the humor that usually laced it; instead it was raw with a pain that for once had nothing to do with the cancer eating him alive.

My eyes were hot and stinging, but I wouldn't let the tears fall. "But it hurts you so much."

"I'm okay," he repeated. "For the time being." His laugh was short. "Libby…we won't have too many more opportunities to just…be."

Goddamn him and that honesty. I wouldn't—couldn't—turn away. Argue rationale or cite reasons why it was the last thing we should be doing. Especially if—

Don't go there.

Lifting the covers, I slid in next to him, but still kept to the edge of the bed…inexplicably afraid in a way I'd never been before. Until he reached for me, putting a hand on my waist and urging me close and closer still, until our foreheads touched. He sighed, his hand shifting lower to rest on my hip.

"You feel so unbelievable—so right. Did I ever tell you that enough?"

And with those words, my fears disappeared—shoved into insignificance by Ethan's need. And my own. I edged closer, exploring the vastly changed contours of his body, caution and fear over causing him pain giving way to desperation. I wrapped myself around him with abandon, sinking into the blessed familiarity that was my husband's embrace—that had always been the other half of my soul and without which I'd felt so incomplete for so long.

His mouth covered mine as he eased up the hem of my sleep shirt, his hands gentle as they cupped first one breast then the other—less so as his long fingers played over my nipples, hardening them almost to the point of pain and making me whimper into his deep kiss. I broke away from him only long enough to pull the shirt off along with my underwear, before taking his face in my hands, returning his kiss with all the feeling I'd been bottling up. At the same time, however, a small piece of me held itself at a remove, maintaining distance. I didn't want to hurt him—didn't want to destroy this moment—

"Liberty, stop it." He sucked hard on my lower lip, the small, sharp pain focusing my attention, His hands grabbed my wrists in a surprisingly strong grip. "Don't you dare hold back from me," he whispered against my mouth.

Breathing hard, but for the first time in a long while not sounding harsh or labored, he eased me back on the mattress, settling me in the curve of his body, one hand beginning to play over my body with the skill developed over years of practice and experimentation, familiar and, *God*, so welcome. Stroking small circles over my abdomen, his fingers gradually ventured between my legs, as he lowered his head to my breasts.

"Ethan, please…" I wanted to beg him to stop, because I didn't want him to wear himself out. Wanted to beg him to never stop… never leave me.

"Relax, Libby. Just go with me." His hand stroked back down between my legs, his fingers teasing over every sensitive spot I owned, rubbing with just enough pressure that I was seeing stars, trapped in that amazing place between too much and not enough. And just as it began to edge past too much, he shifted, sliding his fingers high inside as his palm started rubbing hard circles on the outside and that's when it because too much, not enough, just enough, everything, all at the same time.

"*Ethan.*"

I lost myself completely then, clutching his neck, his shoulders the way I always had—pulling his mouth to mine and sinking into the pleasure even as I strained for more.

"There, gorgeous…that's it…" He continued stroking and rubbing, bringing me up and over the edge once again—this one more gentle, not as earth-shattering, simply a warm, comforting aftermath. "I love seeing you like this." He drew me closer still, one hand stroking my hair, the other still trapped between my thighs as my muscles continued to twitch, holding tight, almost as if they were in search of still more. Definitely reluctant to let go.

"Promise me, Libby." His voice was a slow, soft whisper, but delivered right against my ear where I could be sure to hear, where there could be no mistake as to what he was saying.

"Promise what, Ethan?"

"Don't ever let yourself lose that again."

My body was finally started to ease back, relaxing from the incredible ride my husband had taken it on. "Lose what?"

"The way you look right now. God, how I've loved seeing it again."

"Okay, *mi amor*." I was still floating along in the aftermath of my climax, slightly foggy and not quite sure of what he meant other than he loved my pleasure—but then, he always had. Had taken great joy in teaching me how much pleasure could be found in giving sensual fulfillment as in receiving.

"No, Libby." His hand rested over mine, hot and damp, stilling the motion of my fingers at his waistband. "This was for you."

"But—"

"Don't worry—I got what I needed, gorgeous." In the dark he gazed at me, his hand rising to trail along my jaw, rubbing his damp thumb against my lip, before kissing me, slow and soft and deep. "I just wanted to bring that look to your face one more time."

There was the reference to that look again. And deep down, even though I wouldn't allow myself to acknowledge it, I understood what he meant.

"I love you Ethan Walker. Always."

"I've never once doubted it, Libby."

Libby

MARCH 14

The worst part, in some ways, was coming to grips with the fact that I felt as if I was cheating on two men. The guilt had been neatly compartmentalized where Nick was concerned. In the world we'd defined for ourselves, within the four walls of any given room at Las Palmas, we were doing for each other what our spouses could no longer do for us. Beyond that, we were nothing more than friends. But somehow, in invading my dreams, Nick had broken beyond the barriers of our self-contained world; and in once again bringing me the joy he so often had in the past, Ethan had reestablished, in a fleeting, searing moment, his mark on my body and always, on my heart.

Convoluted way of saying my worlds had collided with a big, painful bang.

I knew Nick had seen it. We'd passed each other in the hospital corridor as I walked in with Ethan and even though our gazes only met for the merest instant as we exchanged casual hellos, there had nevertheless been *something* in that split-second exchange. Something that left the tiny hairs on the back of my neck prickling with heightened awareness. Glancing over my shoulder, I wasn't that surprised to find Nick still staring after me, the line of his shoulders tense even as he leaned in toward Nan, nodding and smiling at whatever she was saying.

And felt fresh shards of guilt poke holes in my carefully constructed defense.

This was ridiculous. There was only one man I was cheating on—

Only one man? *Only?*

What the hell was the matter with me? How had this become justifiable?

I didn't even know if it was. I'd just somehow reached a point where I couldn't function as effectively in my everyday world without the release my world with Nick provided

As was his habit, he'd texted me his room number so when I arrived at Las Palmas, I didn't bother with luggage or the front desk or *anything*—just headed straight for the elevators. My breath coming short and fast, I ran down the hall where I barely touched my knuckles to the door before it swung open and he pulled me in, his mouth covering mine and swallowing words that weren't important.

I pulled away, holding tight to his hair, searching his face, his gaze. "In here you're mine. I'm yours."

We tore at our clothes, mouths and hands roaming and stroking, driving each other close to the edge—so close but still holding back, tacitly understanding that we wanted to go over together. Then the strangest thing happened—as the last piece of clothing fell away, as he lowered me to the bed and I welcomed the heavy weight of his body over mine, the tone changed. Urgency slowed to the rhythm of a sensual dance accompanied by deep breaths and soft words—eased by sweat and heat and his tears, hot against my neck as he drew my entire body flush against his, shaking with an almost violent intensity. Frightened, I held him, stroked the strong, vulnerable curve of his back and cradled his head close. And even after his body had settled, he wouldn't release me—or let me release him, rolling us carefully to our sides, staying deep inside my body.

"Nick?"

He wouldn't look at me, keeping his head down, gaze fixed, it seemed, on where our bodies remained joined. He stroked a hand up my thigh—skimmed the backs of his fingers across my abdomen and up along the curve of one breast where he paused, as if taking measure of my heartbeat. With a shaky breath, I drew his head to my shoulder and stroked his hair, waiting.

"Katharine might be in remission."

Another breach—the outside world reminding us what we had

was so fragile…so temporary.

"Marco's running some more tests. Just to be sure. But…"

As his voice trailed away, I recalled the tense line of his shoulders, the quick, haunted meeting of our gazes back at the hospital. It wasn't so much what he'd seen in me. It's what he'd already known. What I knew now.

"It's over, Nick."

Even as inside I screamed, *No… no… not yet—don't take him away too. Please no, it's too soon.*

You'd think this was when I'd pull away, put some distance between us, start reestablishing that line we should have never, *never* crossed. But we had crossed it and still—even riddled with guilt and with the fear of letting him go choking off air and leaving me feeling as if I wouldn't ever be able to breathe again—I couldn't bring myself to regret it.

And even though I'd always known in my deepest heart I'd be the one to break it off—had prepared myself by envisioning the scenario—it had never been like this. In what I'd imagined, it had been me suffering Ethan's loss and having to send Nick away because the scales would have tipped—our unorthodox arrangement no longer fair to either of us. But to have it happen this way? Even though it had always been every bit as likely a possibility as any other? No, no…this was too fast, too brutal. I simply couldn't.

Wrapping my arms around him, holding him tight within me, I whispered, "I don't want it to be over—not yet."

"Me neither, Libby. *No sé que voy—*"

"*Una noche más,*" I continued in a soft croon, almost a lullaby as I rocked him in my arms. "Just one more night, and then we'll have to walk away because that's what we promised."

"Stop." His voice was raw and anguished and just about broke my heart.

"Nick, you love Katharine."

"I do, but…" Both his hands moved to my face, tilting my head back so he could take my mouth with his. Perhaps we didn't have the familiarity borne of years of togetherness that Ethan and I had, but the passion Nick and I shared was never too far from the surface—a seductive drug I just couldn't get enough of.

"Libby…*mi vida.*"

No. It would be too easy to succumb, but we *couldn't.*

"I'm no one's substitute, Nick. I don't deserve that and neither do you." I wouldn't release him from my hold, wouldn't allow him to feel rejected, but he needed to hear this. "And neither does Katharine." His chest jerked with his sharp breath as he tried to pull back, but I held on even harder. "If you didn't love her, you wouldn't be feeling so torn up about this, Nick—which is why you have to take this second chance. Without me in the way—there as some sort of fail-safe."

My voice dropped. "I know I would."

So hard to say, but God, yes. As much as I cared for Nick and didn't want to let him go—as much as what he'd done for me had effectively saved my life—if I had the chance he was being handed, I'd take it like a greedy toddler being offered a cookie, shoving it in my mouth and swallowing it whole.

I knew he'd go.

He knew there'd never really been any question, despite the momentary doubt.

But we could give each other this gift of one last night.

Deep into that night, in a fathomless dark where all we could rely on was touch and scent and sound, he moved in me again, slow and quiet, both hands holding mine.

"I've only ever told one woman I love her."

"Let's keep it that way."

• • •

As dawn bled around the edges of the curtains, I pretended to be asleep. He pretended not to know I was awake.

No goodbyes.

No looking back.

Just the quiet click of a door as it closed.

Nick

MARCH 15

Walking away, hearing that door close behind me—

Knowing I was, in effect, leaving her to close in on herself once again, but also knowing I had no other choice?

Hardest thing I've ever done in my entire life.

Libby

APRIL 2

In the end, it was at home and it was quiet.

A long, shuddering breath—like a sigh of relief—and he was gone.

It was simultaneously the saddest and happiest moment of my life.

Nick

APRIL 10

"So, bebe, planning on lurking over here all afternoon?"

"Pretty much." I stared through the dark lenses of my sunglasses at the group gathered on the beach about a quarter mile down from where I sat. "She doesn't know I'm here, does she?"

Nan slid onto the picnic bench beside me, sliding a beer across the table to me. "She doesn't know much other than how much she misses Ethan and how much she hurts. It was very quick at the end. In spite of how much he'd been deteriorating, I think it caught her by surprise."

I nodded as I watched Libby laugh at something someone was saying—heard the whole group burst into laughter. Clearly, one of those memorials where funny stories were exchanged, maybe even a few dirty jokes—where the good times were remembered. This was the kind of send-off I wanted—beer, joking, warmth— remembering me as a good guy. It's all anyone could ever ask from a life, right?

Her body continued shaking, but something in her body language changed—a subtle shift, her shoulders tightening, hair that, for once, was loose, falling forward to expose the curve of her neck. She wasn't laughing anymore. But before I could act on the half-assed impulse that would've had me down the beach and taking her away from whatever was hurting her, she was turning to the dark-haired woman next to her as a man in jeans and a tie-dyed T-shirt put his arms around both of them. Her parents. Had to be.

As the knot of the three of them got tighter, the noise from the rest of the crowd died down, as if carried off on the breeze that had just started picking up. Glancing up, I watched the sun slide behind a cloud and nodded my own agreement. Yeah, that was better—it was good to have sun for the remembrances, but something a little dimmer for the goodbyes. Had a gut feeling we were getting close to those.

"I think she'd probably like seeing you."

"No." Jesus, but my voice sounded flat and harsh—even to me. "I...I don't think so."

"Oh." Followed a few seconds later by, "I did wonder."

For the first time, I looked at Nan—at the knowing and sympathy in eyes that didn't have the barrier of tinted lenses blocking them. "Did you?"

Her smile was sad and her soft, accented voice didn't have an ounce of judgment in it as she answered, "If it makes you feel any better, I didn't know for certain until right now."

Damn. I had to wonder who else might've figured it out. I knew Nan would be the last to do or say anything, but if anyone else had figured it out—I didn't want any potential hurt coming down on Libby. She'd had enough.

"Nick." She waited until I met her gaze again before going on. "You don't honestly think you're the first it's ever happened to, do you, bebe?"

"Yes. No. Hell, I don't know."

"Trust me—you're not."

I stared down at my beer before lifting it and taking a long drink. "It's never happened to me before. Or her."

I watched as Libby pulled away from her parents and wiped at her face, back to laughing again at the giant snowy white handkerchief her dad pulled from the pocket of his faded jeans and offered her. God, but I wanted to be there. Wiping her tears with the white handkerchief with its faint grease stain that had never come completely out and that I carried with me all the time now. I wanted to lend support and kick the shit out of any hint of badness that tried to touch her.

And let's repeat it—last goddamn thing I had any right to be doing.

"It's not just some ordinary affair, Nick. You understand that, right?"

"Wasn't." I tossed the empty beer bottle toward the battered drum that served as a trashcan, closing my eyes at the crash of glass shattering against metal. "*Wasn't* some ordinary affair. With Kath in remission and now, Ethan…gone, Libby and I—" I swallowed hard. "It's over."

"I understand that—and I understand why. But Nick, don't discount what it was. Or what it did." She stood, then reached out and cupped my chin, tilting my face up so I could meet her gaze. "It would have been so much harder. For both of you. And honestly?" She glanced briefly at the group on the beach before meeting my gaze once more. "Without you, I don't know how she would have made it these last months. You brought her peace. And now, she can say goodbye with a smile on her face."

She bent down and brushed a kiss against my cheek. *"Bonne chance, mon ami."*

As Nan rejoined the group, Libby picked up a metal urn and walked with her parents to the water's edge. She paused there and kissed each of them before slogging out into the choppy surf on her own, far enough for the water to hit the tops of her thighs, sending spray across her shirt. Finally, she stopped, unscrewed the lid and, bracing her body, waved her arm in a huge, sweeping arc that sent a shower of fine, gray ash up into the wind and over the water. After pressing a kiss to the urn, she drew her arm back and flung it as hard as she could into the ocean, watching until the waves flooded it and sent it sinking.

And as she turned and made her way back to the shore, shoving her damp hair back from her face, I could see it. There was a whole lot of sad and hurt and loss in it, but Nan was right.

She was smiling.

• • •

"Forgive me, Father, for I have sinned."

"Nick?"

I sat on the pew, vision blurred as I stared hard at nothing in particular, rosary and the white handkerchief clenched in one hand, the other curled around the back of the pew in front of me. I should have gone home after I snuck away from Ethan's memorial. *Should* have. Should have returned to Kath, who was relaxing, regaining her strength, secure in the knowledge that it had all worked out. That all the pain had been worth it and that things were going to be better. At least for her health.

But instead of going home, I'd come here. For the first time since we'd met, I was on Tico's turf. No more of the neutral territory of Domino Park where he was just Tico and I was just Nick, a couple of guys with shared backgrounds and experiences. No, right now, I needed to be somewhere where the control fell completely in someone else's hands, because me? I had control for shit.

"*M'ijo...*"

Without looking up, I repeated, "Forgive me, Father, for I have sinned." It came out as little more than a whisper, but to my ears, it sounded like it echoed throughout the huge, empty church. My hand clenched tighter around the rosary and handkerchief. "Forgive me..." And as my voice cracked and Tico rested his hand on the back of my neck, I let go and for the second time in my adult life— for the second time in less than a month—I broke down and cried like a baby. Harsh, painful sobs that didn't make any sound but made my chest burn and feel like it was going to split right in half, like when I'd had pneumonia, fighting for every breath in that damn oxygen tent. Except worse.

"God, Tico... *¿qué hice?* What have I done to her? What have I done to both of them?"

Tico remained silent, his hand on my neck, waiting until the near-violent shudders settled to the occasional spasm and finally... nothing. I just didn't have anything else left.

"Forgive me, Father, for I have sinned."

Slowly, I lifted my head to find Tico, both hands folded in his lap, staring up at the cross above the altar. Releasing a deep breath, he turned to face me. "It was you I worried for, as much as Libby. And I should have said that to you. I shouldn't have held back. I should have let you know how frightened I was for you both, but I hoped if you knew I was worried for her in particular, knowing how protective you felt of her..." He sighed again. "Please forgive my sin of arrogance, *m'ijo*."

"You knew what would happen, didn't you?"

"I prayed it wouldn't." He turned to stare at the cross again. "But you were like two wounded animals finding solace in each other against the rest of the world. I suppose the real surprise is that it hadn't happened sooner."

My chest ached with renewed pain. "It was so hard—being alone. I missed Kath so much and Libby understood, because she was missing Ethan just as much—if not more. And I was so damn angry at all of it and so was she."

Nothing I hadn't already admitted to him in various ways during our long afternoon talks, but with a lot more layers of meaning, I guess. I loosened my fist, allowing the rosary to slide to the seat beside me as I spread the handkerchief over my thigh and smoothed it out. "And now, Kath's in remission and Libby—she's so strong, Tico. Sent me away. She knows I have to take this second chance. See if Kath wants it."

"She's your wife and it's your obligation." The words came out clipped and harsh. Then, in a softer voice, "And obviously, Libby understands that."

A short choked sound that I think was supposed to be a laugh escaped my throat. "And you think I don't? Believe me, Tico, I do." The hand I had resting on the back of the pew tightened, the action pushing my wedding band into the skin of my finger. "For better, for worse, in sickness and in health. I meant those promises, and even though I didn't say them in front of a priest, I did say them in front of my family and friends and above all, I said them to Kath and God knows, I *meant* them."

The words echoed around the sanctuary, then faded away into

a long beat of silence.

"I wondered if you'd ever acknowledge that."

"What?"

"That you did make those promises in front of God."

My fingers tightened even more, knuckles turning white. "Do *not* go Jesuit on me right now, Tico—arguing semantics. I can't handle it."

"It's not about arguing semantics, Nick. It's about being honest. Libby was…a moment. A special one and perhaps one that was necessary. The man in me understands that. But above all, I'm a priest, and I consider you not simply a friend but someone I counsel, and as such, I have to remind you that it's Kath you committed your life to in front of your friends and your family—and God."

"Libby was more than a moment," I countered. No way I'd allow her to be reduced to just a moment. "But—she'd be agreeing with you." My hand cramped and aching, I finally released the pew. "And you can save the rest of your arguments, because I do too. In spite of everything that's happened—in spite of what I've done—I love my wife. I always have. So I've got no choice but to see if there's anything left worth salvaging."

"There's always something worth salvaging when there's love involved, *m'ijo.*"

My head jerked up. "Is that the priest talking now or the man?"

"Both." He shrugged, his eyes narrowing as his gaze wandered around the sanctuary. "No matter how dark it seems, I have to continue to have faith, Nick, otherwise, I've got no business wearing this." He brushed his fingers against the collar that I noticed for the first time. Realized, with a faint sense of surprise, it was the first time I'd ever seen him wearing it. "Lesson learned the hard way with my dad."

I nodded and we both fell silent for a few minutes, letting the oddly noisy quiet of an empty church surround us. Abuelita had always said that it was the sounds of a congregation of spirits providing company and support for those in need. Being a smartass, know-it-all little shit, I'd laughed, and being my grandmother, she hadn't said a word, like she'd known I'd have to come to my own conclusions someday. Right now, I was hoping she was right. And that those comforting spirits weren't restricted to just churches.

"Libby's husband—*se murió.*"

"*Yo se.*" His gaze met mine again. "I saw the obituary, sent her an e-mail with my condolences, and she called me. Told me about the memorial and asked if I was free to come, but I told her I couldn't."

"Why?" I asked, remembering another day, another memorial, another church—Libby's face, so damn radiant in the moment I offered her the handkerchief I currently handled as gently as if it was a baby. As if it was her.

"I had other obligations I had to attend to—I was needed here. She understood, told me I was welcome to visit at any time. That *she'd* welcome it." His hand stroked the back of my head, like he was settling a skittish animal. "And now...well, I understand why else I was compelled to say no. *Pero no te preocupe.* I'm going to go see her in a few days."

Staring down, I nodded again, my thumb skimming the faded grayish streaks staining the white cotton. "Would you tell her—"

What? Tell her how I felt? How scared I was? How much I missed her, not just her body and the intense physical pleasure we'd found in each other, but *her.* Talking to her in our fractured mix of Spanish and English, laughing with her, wiping away the tears that she let so few see.

"Tell her—" Again I stopped, still searching for the right words as I folded the handkerchief once, then twice, then watched as Tico placed my rosary in the soft cotton and folded it over one more time.

"Nick...no. It has to stay finished, *mi niño.* For her peace of mind." I looked up, seeing all the sadness and sorrow I was feeling reflected in his eyes. "And yours. To make this work, it has to stay finished. Completely."

"I know." Copying Tico's earlier gesture, I lifted my gaze to the cross, trying so hard to draw the peace he so clearly did from the act, from this place, and feeling...empty.

The Miami Herald

OPINIONS:
SAYING GOODBYE

ETHAN WALKER
LIBBY SANTOS WALKER

APRIL 17

This has been a hell of a column to write, knowing it's my last one—and not much of one at that because, sorry, folks, I just don't have a lot left in me. But I guess you know that by now. Thing is, though, I'm not leaving you completely in the lurch. I'm using this final opportunity to introduce my successor, and I can't even begin to tell you how happy it makes me that it's one of the most talented writers I've ever had the good fortune to work with. She's also the most remarkable woman, and I've been a lucky bastard in that I've been able to share the last fifteen years with her as my wife. Now, before you start screaming nepotism, let me assure you—she's earned this. She didn't even know I was going to do this, and once she finds out, if she can figure out a way to bring me back from the grave in order to berate my sorry self, trust me, she will. And after you read this, if you don't think she's earned it, feel free to join her in bringing me back from the grave. Keep in mind, too—she was only twenty when she wrote this. Fifteen years later, she's just that much better.

So, I give you your new columnist, Libby Santos Walker, and as for myself, I'm going to borrow the immortal words of a far better journalist than I in bidding you all, good night, and good luck.

• • •

What happens when beauty and youth, status and wealth, don't automatically preclude desperate acts? Is it perhaps because of those things—the threat of losing them—that desperation exacerbates into evil?

Those were the questions I found myself asking as I observed my first ever crime scene...

Nick

I glanced over again at the paper lying on the passenger seat, even though I practically had the whole thing memorized. Still, those words, "beauty and youth, status and wealth," jumped out from the page and twisted like a knife in my gut, *again*. Same as they had when I first read them yesterday over breakfast, my hand shaking so damn much, coffee had spilled over the edge of my mug and trickled down my hand. I'd barely noticed the heat and slight, stinging pain because in that moment, I was no longer in my kitchen, but leaning against a door at Las Palmas, cradling Libby and listening to her tell me about Ethan—how they'd met, how he'd scared her, how she'd run away and, most of all, how much she loved him, because I'd finally gotten my head far enough out of my ass to think to ask her about him. To ask her how she *felt*.

I was listening to her tell me about writing the article he'd assigned and hiding it away, never intending to let it see the light of day. But somehow, Ethan had found it or maybe she'd finally shown him—a final gift that he'd turned around and made into a gift for her.

Would be completely in keeping with how perfect they'd been for each other and how fucking unfair it was that their life together had been cut short. And now, here *I* was, sitting in her driveway, staring at the small white house with the bright blue door. The house where she and Ethan had built their life together and where she was going to have to keep going, alone.

Hell, it wasn't that I didn't think Tico was right. He was. In order for her peace of mind and mine—in order for me to see if Kath and I had anything left—it had to stay finished with Libby.

Thing was, though, we hadn't finished a damn thing. I'd walked away that morning because that's what she wanted. What we'd both needed at that moment, because it was so raw and hurt so damn much and we couldn't be around each other another minute without that pain blindsiding us both. But, I'd felt unsettled as hell ever since, a feeling that had only grown after Nan called me to tell me that Ethan had died. I understood then that somewhere in the back of my mind I'd intended for us to have a real goodbye. Not in the making love sense—we'd had that. But Libby and I needed to actually say goodbye—and a few other things.

At least, I did.

So explain to me why now, after a more than three hour drive, I'd been sitting in my car for the last twenty minutes too fucking terrified to travel the final twenty feet to her door?

The decision was taken out of my hands as she rounded the corner at the back of her house, barefoot, in shorts and a T-shirt and, as always, her hair pulled back in a braid, attention focused on the two dogs who walked alongside. She'd spent hours telling me about them—Butch and Sundance—her best friends outside of Ethan.

And me.

My throat closed as I recalled the shy admission made late one night.

God*damn*. I really didn't want to have to say goodbye.

"Hi, Libby."

She froze, hand on the wall-mounted spigot, and slowly turned her head. As I approached the fence, Butch moved in front of her, growling, while Sundance continued to sit beside her, looking from Libby to me and back to Libby again with a curious expression, although her tail wagged.

"Butch, back off."

The growling died down, but the little shit held his ground until Libby spoke again, saying, "Butch, heel," in a voice that backed him right off, but only just far enough to flank her other side, staring me down the whole time. Good for him.

"He's not going to rip my balls off if I come too close, is he?"

One side of her mouth twitched as she glanced down at the fierce little bastard. "He's not even all bark, no bite. More like all bluster, aren't you, baby?" She bent down and picked him up, nuzzling his head with her cheek while with her free hand she reached down and scratched Sundance's head, making sure the big dog got her fair share of attention.

With Butch in her arms and looking downright blissful, I felt safe enough to close those last few feet, although I stopped with my hand on the gate latch. I locked gazes with her, unable to say a damn word. Then again, not as if we really needed them.

After a long silence, she said, "Let me get their leashes. We'll go for a walk on the beach."

Because that's where she thought best.

A minute later she reappeared through the front door.

"You want to take Sundance? She's good with new people."

"Sure." I reached out and took the leash, dropping down to a knee to meet the big dog face-to-face. "Hey, girl, how are you doing?" I grinned as Sundance licked the hand I held out then rubbed against it, making happy noises. Much as I loved them, I hadn't been around dogs since I was a kid—hadn't had the time for one. Now I couldn't help but wonder if maybe that wasn't another one of those things I needed to do—slow down and make time for simple things like owning a dog. Not stress so much about the big things.

I'd had enough of big things for a while.

Shifting slightly, I turned to Butch but looked up at Libby.

She smiled. "You did fine with Sundance, just do the same with him. He really is a sweetheart."

I nodded and turned back to the little dog. "Are we cool?" I asked, holding my hand out, but not so close that he could take an easy chunk out of me. After glancing up at Libby, he approached and gave a tentative sniff, a lick, and a slight wag of the tail before backing up and lying down next to her, dropping his head between his paws.

"He misses Ethan."

Clearly, not the only one. This close, I could see the dark circles beneath her eyes and the lines radiating out from the corners that hadn't been quite so obvious before. Could see the gold chain around her neck with the two matching bands hanging from it, the smaller ring resting just inside the larger one. And maybe most telling, there was just this overall air of sadness around her. I knew her. I knew she was happy Ethan wasn't in pain anymore. And I knew she'd take the loss a thousand times over to spare him that pain, but it didn't diminish the fact that she missed him.

Silently, we walked the few blocks from her house to the beach where she kicked off her flip-flops and left them under a bench. Following her lead, I toed off my sneakers and left them beside her shoes. Even though it was a Thursday, it was a sunny, bright day and there were plenty of people on the beach, so we kept the dogs on their leads, but walked close enough to the water that they could splash through the waves as they came ashore. The cool water felt good against my overheated skin—tempting me to dive straight in and go as far below as I could and not break the surface until I could figure out how the hell to initiate this conversation.

I'd probably drown before I could figure it out. But as she had so many times before, Libby saved my ass.

"Why are you here, Nick?"

I pulled the paper from where I'd shoved it into the back pocket of my shorts, folded into thirds, the dual bylines visible.

"How are you doing?"

She stopped, staring out across the water. "I thought I was doing okay—until that." She nodded at the paper I held. "Editor called me day before yesterday, told me it was going to run, and formally offered the column. Told me that, yeah, Ethan had strong-armed him into running the piece, but after he read it, he didn't need to be strong-armed anymore and it was mine—on my own merits—if I wanted it."

"Nationally syndicated op-ed. Big move."

She nodded. "Not anything I really aspired to. I've been happy with my pet blog, but it's...nice." A small smile crossed her face, "Validation that my girly writing has potential appeal across a wide spectrum. I mean, hell, if I could win over Ethan—" Taking a deep breath, she stared out toward the horizon where a cruise ship slowly drifted by.

"You won him over a long time ago, Libby."

"I know. But this...I never wanted this. Didn't need this to know..." Her voice trailed off as her head dropped and her braid fell forward over her shoulder, leaving the curve of her neck exposed and vulnerable, and it was all I could do not to go to her. To rest my hand on the soft skin and stroke the muscles beneath that I knew would be tense and tell her it would all be okay, because I had even less right to do that than I ever had before.

"Are you going to take it?"

"I don't know. It's a way to hold on to a little piece of him— and probably a lot healthier than sleeping with one of his old shirts. But I have to be absolutely certain I can do justice to his readers. I wouldn't expect any less—neither would he." A short laugh escaped as she added, "Actually, he'd be pissed as hell if he thought I was shortchanging them, so I'd better be damn sure before I take this on."

Standing, she turned and started walking again, her voice drifting back on the wind. "Why are you really here, Nick?"

I stood there, stunned, although not like I really should've been. Pure Libby, cutting through my bullshit in one short question.

"I'm sorry."

She stopped, which gave me the chance to catch up to her and repeat what I'd driven over three hours to say. "I'm so fucking sorry, Libby."

Slowly, she turned, shoving her sunglasses to the top of her head, the expression in her eyes sad, even though the corners creased slightly. A smile, I think.

"You've never needed to apologize, Nick."

"Yeah, I did—do—need to apologize." The words came out in a rush, anxious to get out, to make sure she understood. "You were right when you said you didn't deserve to be anyone's substitute. Maybe it was only for a split second, but that's exactly what I wanted. The easy way out. Right at that second, knowing I was going to lose you and not sure if I was ever going to get Kath back, I wanted you to be everything I'd had with her and that's unfair as hell to you, because you're *not* her. And it's insulting to both of you, and I'm a miserable son of a bitch for considering it for even a split second."

"Nick...*Dios mío,* ease up on yourself, please. It *was* just for a split second. I understood that then. It's okay."

"No, it's not," I insisted, shaking my head and blowing out an impatient breath. "Don't you get it? I want what I had with you *and* what I had with Kath, too. I want both...I want—"

Her hand on my chest stopped me cold. I stood there, throat closing, struggling to breathe, as if I'd physically been punched.

"It's okay to want, Nick." Her hand slid up my chest to my cheek, her thumb brushing against my mouth, the light touch making me hurt in more ways than I could even begin to describe. "I want more than anything for Ethan to be back and to be whole and be with me, yet at the same time, I want what you and I had, too. It doesn't make sense, because those two things couldn't possibly coexist, but at its most basic, it's what I want." Her hand left my face to flip her sunglasses down over her eyes—not quite fast enough to hide the tears catching on her lashes.

"We just have to know what we can't have."

We walked for a while longer, not talking, not touching, except for the occasional brush of our hands until we finally retraced our steps to the bench where we'd left our shoes and the final few blocks to her house. After she let the dogs into the backyard and filled their water bowls, she returned to where I was waiting by my SUV.

"I had to say goodbye, too, Libby. Really say goodbye."

Thank God, she didn't argue or disagree or say a damn thing. Just stood there, trembling slightly as I pulled her sunglasses off, set them on the hood of the truck, and drew her close. "*Una vez más,*" I whispered as I pulled her closer still, until barely a breath remained between us.

Just like all those times we'd made love, she kept her eyes open, watching as I pulled her braid forward and loosened it. I ran my fingers through her thick, beautiful hair and wound it in my fist as I drew her that last breath closer. "One last time," I repeated and that's when her eyes finally closed, her hands gentle on my face as she drew my head down.

A split second before our lips touched, I felt her breath brush across my skin, heard her soft, "Nick," that took me back to the dark rooms of the world we'd created for ourselves; and for those few seconds, I let myself be transported back—let myself remember the feel of her body around mine. Let myself believe it was all real again.

"Look at me." My voice was rough as I pulled away, tilted her head back, and waited for her eyes to open. "I love you. A piece of my heart and my soul are always going to belong to you, Liberty Walker. Maybe you thought that keeping me from saying it before meant it didn't exist or that it would make it hurt less, but sorry—doesn't work that way." I pulled her even closer—so close, she had to be feeling how hard my heart was beating against my chest. "Simple fact is, *mi amor*, a part of me is going to love you always, even if I have to let you go."

The words I'd been holding in for over a month finally said, I rested my cheek against her hair and closed my eyes, breathing in the smoky vanilla scent of her. "I am going to miss you so damn much, Libby." Without opening my eyes, I found her mouth one last time with mine, tracing her lips with my tongue until she opened. Her hands curled into my shoulders as she leaned further into me and deepened the kiss, her tongue stroking mine in a mindless, desperate caress before she pulled free.

Before I could open my eyes, I heard a soft, "I'll always love you, too," followed a few seconds later by the slam of her front door.

Opening my eyes, I stared at the bright blue door.

"Bye, Libby."

Libby

"Who was that?"

I heard the words but didn't really hear them. Physically, I was inside my house, sagging against the solid bulk of my front door—mentally, I was outside, still hanging on to Nick. Feeling and smelling and tasting him, like I'd never imagined I ever would again—except in those damn dreams. Ethan occupied my waking hours, my daydreams, even those groggy, gray-edged mindscapes somewhere between sleeping and waking. But once full sleep took over, Nick would move on in. Between the two of them, they were having a field day making me absolutely insane.

I really didn't need anymore help.

"Liberty, *te pregunté*, who was that?"

Really didn't need anymore help. And all I could do was stand there and shake, swiping at my wet cheeks with one hand while I hung on for dear life to the chain around my neck with the other. God*damn* both of them.

Goddamn Nora and her shit timing. I couldn't deal with her right now. I really couldn't.

"What are you doing here?"

"I made some fresh bread—sourdough. Because I know no matter what you say, you're not eating, and then the dogs wanted in, and I didn't see you out back, then I looked out the front window and, Libby, who—"

"Nora, leave it," I broke in, finally pushing myself away from the door and heading into the kitchen where the smell of fresh bread almost, *almost* managed to eradicate the faint hint of Nick's cologne that lingered on my skin. Almost.

231

"You're shoving your tongue down some man's throat right there in your driveway and you want me to leave it?"

I reached up into a cabinet and pulled out a glass, then rooted in the fridge for the bottle stowed in the back. Because God knows I needed it. "Don't be such a prude. Since when have you ever cared what anyone thought?"

"Who said anything about caring what anyone thinks? Libby, who is that man and how could you do this to Ethan?"

The filled glass toppled and rolled off the counter, cold wine and shards of crystal stinging the tops of my feet as the glass shattered. "Ethan's *dead*, Nora." I slammed the bottle on the counter, half surprised it didn't shatter as well. "I can't do anything to him because he's dead, and he's not coming back."

And damn her for making me say it out loud because until that second, I hadn't said the actual words. I'd say he was gone, I'd say he lost his battle, I'd come up with any reference, clichéd or oblique or what*ever*, that didn't actually involve my associating the word *dead* with Ethan, and now, Nora had forced me to say it and with the words, my heart broke all over again. Destroyed that last thin wall of protection—that final bit of fantasy. That maybe, by some miracle, my Ethan—*my* Ethan—would come back.

My fist closed tight around our rings, I stepped past her and went down the hall to our bedroom, returned to the way it had looked for so many years. Before the nightmare. In here, I could pretend none of it had happened. I could lie in bed—his shirt on the pillow beside me—conjure up the feel of his body in bed next to mine, and that's how I'd drift off to sleep. After I was asleep, however…*Nick*. My fingers curled around the edges of the mattress as I tried to will away the feel of his body against mine, because I just couldn't handle the overload right now. I was too close to the edge—

"Libby, *mi vida*, who is he? What are you doing with him?"

I gaped at her standing in the doorway, all flowing peasant skirt and Birkies and the T-shirt that clung to a figure that hadn't changed in years, still slightly round and Earth mother and incredibly sexy to the many men who'd flitted in and out of her life.

"It's not any more of your business who he is or what I'm doing with him than any of your male friends were my business while I was growing up. Or have you conveniently forgotten that? 'Who was that?' I'd ask, and you'd wave your hand and say, 'No one you need to worry about, *mi cariñita*. Just a…distraction.'" I waved my hand dismissively, just the way I'd seen her do time and again, usually accompanied by a toss of her head and flirtatious laugh.

Dead silence dropped between us, the lack of sound only broken as both dogs edged into the room. Sundance curled up at my feet while Butch jumped onto the bed, his little body pressing in close against mine, tense and shaking.

"Right," she finally said. "You would have begrudged me friendship."

"Friendship." I laughed. Then laughed again, just because the concept, as applied to Nora, was simply that fucking funny. "Well, if that's the case, then the man you saw out there is my friend. A *good* friend."

Her breath audibly caught. For once in my life, I had shocked Nora. But give the woman props—if nothing else, she knew how to roll with the punches. And deliver them.

"You were always so damn sanctimonious, Libby, sitting in judgment when you didn't know shit about my life. Didn't *want* to know about my life, so I did what I thought you wanted and spared you the details, and now you throw that back in my face."

"I could say the same for you, Nora. Sanctimonious in your own free-spirited, organic hippy sort of way. Judging my choices, cutting them down because they didn't jibe with your lofty ideals."

"I never said a thing—"

"You didn't *have* to. It practically vibrated off of you, this distinct *aura*, if you want it in your native tongue. All disappointed and shit that I wasn't out writing fiery, save-the-world columns for some radical underground publication or website."

"Says *who*? That's ridiculous—not to mention unfair. I respected that you had the freedom to make your own choices, same as I did."

"Whatever." I sighed. "Needless to say, I gave up trying to please you and live up to your expectations a long time ago, Nora."

"I have *never* been disappointed in you until this minute, Libby. *Dios mío*, cheating on your husband? When he was so sick? Because, clearly, if you're such good *friends*," she said with a raised eyebrow emphasizing the word as much as her acid tone, "he's not someone you just met yesterday."

"Of all the things for you to be disappointed in me about." I snorted. "So much for the free-love 'tude."

"Have you ever seen any man in my bed or even my bedroom other than your father?"

Oh she wasn't serious? "Just because I didn't see it, doesn't mean it didn't happen, Nora. *Distractions*, remember? Those are easy enough to take care of on the sly away from the curious eyes of the kiddies. Even in the commune. I mean, what do you think the older kids talked to us about?"

Her face, her neck, even the skin of her upper arms beneath the sleeves of her shirt all gradually turned a bright mottled red as she very slowly said, "I have never cheated on my husband." Punctuating each word with a short pause, as if speaking to a tiny child who couldn't quite grasp the meaning of the words. But I wasn't a child and I was tired of this.

"Tough to do when you don't actually have one."

"I *do*," she said, each word even more slow and distinct than before. "And yes, I've also had friends, male friends, because who gives a shit the gender when you're offered friendship—but *te lo juro* on whatever holy text you want to use, I have never had a remotely romantic relationship or even slept with another man in my life other than your father who, piece of paper or not, I consider to be my husband. And those men—those friends—*were* distractions, because I missed your father so much, I couldn't stand it, but never once was I tempted to stray, even though the offers were definitely there. I simply knew that whatever fun we might have couldn't even begin to measure up to what I have with Stan. He's been it for me since I was sixteen, and do you think *that* knowledge was easy to live with?"

As I stared, open-mouthed, she left the doorway and started pacing, her agitated movements causing both dogs to move in closer to me, Sundance quaking and Butch, whining low in his throat They weren't used to this. None of us were.

"You think I didn't know how you mocked and scorned me for taking a path less traveled? That I didn't give you a more traditional upbringing? You think that was easy to live with?"

"You always made it seem that way."

"It wasn't, but it's what I needed to do. I figured out early on there was no way I could ever live the predetermined life of a nice Cuban woman. Or any kind of average life, for that matter. It wasn't me, and I thought if I gave you any gift at all as a parent, it would be the freedom of choice. Of not being expected to follow any path other than your own. If you had wanted to be a nice Cuban woman, believe me, I might have wondered why, but it would've been completely cool with me." She stopped dead in front of me, fury turning her eyes almost black. "And you have the nerve to sit there, all moral and passing judgment on me, and yet for all that you've paid lip service to tradition and vows and to how much you loved your husband—" she spat the word like it didn't hold any meaning where I was concerned. "That you betrayed him like this."

The word "betray" hung between us like a brilliant crystal— shimmering, multifaceted blue, exactly the color of Ethan's eyes— and all of a sudden, I understood.

"He knew."

"¿Qué?"

Once again, my hand closed around the bands hanging from their chain. My talismans. "God, he knew. Ethan knew." I looked up at Nora and smiled, even though she was looking at me in what looked like a combination of fury and thinking I was finally losing my mind. But for the first time in months, I felt like I wasn't. "And what's more, he approved. I had his blessing to love another man."

Nora's eyes drew together in a dark straight line, clearly furious all over again. "Ah, seguro...Here they come. The convenient justifications."

I threaded the tip of my ring finger through both bands, holding them together with my thumb, strangely at peace. "Nope. No justifications, and I certainly don't need to discuss with you what my husband and I shared in the privacy of our bed. But trust me, Nora. Ethan knew about Nick and knew I loved him and was happy for it."

"Don't ever let yourself lose that again…the way you look right now. God, I've loved seeing it again."

A sensuous rumble, I heard Ethan's voice almost as if he were right beside me, whispering in my ear the way he had the last time we made love. And his words hadn't been merely about the sexual release. I'd known it then, but hadn't allowed myself to acknowledge it—both that I loved Nick and that Ethan knew about him and had been happy I'd found someone to love.

But…oh *God*. That's why he finally let go. He thought… "Oh, Ethan," I sighed. "I'm so glad you didn't know."

"You just said he did know. Now you're saying he didn't. *Bueno*, which is it, *m'ija?*"

I looked up at Nora who didn't look as furious anymore, but still suspicious as hell with a nice side of accusatory. "Again, not that it's any of your damn business, Nora, but Ethan didn't know that Nick wasn't—" I stopped. Chose my words carefully, even though I really didn't give much of a damn what Nora thought of me at this point. "Wasn't free to stay with me. What you saw, Nora—that was goodbye."

A beat, then another, as I watched a kaleidoscope of expressions cross my mother's face. "Jesus, Mary, and Joseph, Liberty, he's married too?"

Wasn't going to bother to answer the obvious. I just held my rings and sent up a silent prayer of thanks to whoever might be listening that it wasn't something Ethan and I had ever spoken of explicitly, because, hey—it was Ethan. If he'd wanted to talk about it, there's nothing that could have stopped him from getting all the pertinent details. Pain in the ass. Part of what had made him such a brilliant journalist. Part of what made him so completely Ethan. God, but I missed him.

"*Qué coño tú estaba pensando, jodiendo con un hombre casado.* And what the hell was *he* thinking, the son of a bitch, taking advantage of a woman in your situation—"

"Nora." Releasing my rings, I held my hand up like a traffic cop. "I'm going to ask you to stop right there. You just accused me of not knowing or understanding anything about your life when I was growing up, and I'll concede that you're right and believe me, I'm sorrier than you'll ever know. However, grant me the same courtesy here of accepting that you don't know or understand anything about this part of my life." I dropped my hand to my lap and took a deep breath. "Let's just say that *thinking* isn't something you do a whole lot of when your entire life is going to shit. And that's the last I'm going to say about it—to you or anyone else."

She didn't look like she wanted it to be the last I said, but while I could fault Nora on a lot, she had always pretty much known how far she could push with respect to my personal boundaries. However, while she might not have been a nice Cuban woman, she was still a Cuban *mother* down to the marrow of her bones, which meant she'd likely save it for another day. For right now, though, she'd probably let it go.

"Hey, where are my girls?"

Especially now. Looked like I'd be doing some emotional propping up myself, even if all I wanted to do was crawl under the covers and not come out for the next month—or year.

"We're here, *mi amor.*"

I managed a weak smile as Stan appeared in the doorway behind Nora, resting his chin on the top of her head, the pale silver-brown of the goatee he'd cultivated during his stay contrasting with, yet complementing the dark brown of Nora's hair. "Hey Stan, you getting ready to hit the road?" Because he'd been here since, what?—the beginning of January? Four and a half months had to be a record for the man. His ass was probably itching to get back on the Indian and out on the open road.

"You didn't tell her?"

"Tell me what?"

"We were…distracted."

"Tell me what?"

"Distracted by what?"

"Later, *mi vida*."

"Tell me *what?*"

I watched Nora's shoulders rise with a deep breath, prepping to answer, but it was Stan who spoke. "I'm staying, Libby-girl."

I blinked. "For how much longer?"

He smiled, looking all proud and relieved, and for the first time ever in my memory, like an actual father. Or as much as a long-haired, barefoot middle-aged man wearing ragged cutoffs and a battered Roy Orbison T-shirt could manage. "For good, baby. Your old man's put his time in on the road. I've been a stubborn old ass, but even I can acknowledge it's time to hang it up, you know? It's past time I was here for you, and I want to be here with your mom. Want us to be together for good."

Butch squirmed against the hold I hadn't realized had grown so tight. Loosening my arms and scratching behind his ears in apology, I studied first Stan, who was looking dazed, like he still couldn't believe it, but happier than I'd ever seen him, then Nora, who had a faint smile on her face, her eyes closed as if in prayer, and I couldn't help but wonder—how often had she prayed or chanted or *whatever* for this moment? And that it had taken *this?* That Ethan had to die?

No. It just wasn't fair.

"But…what are you going to do?" And while it was Stan I was staring at, it was Nora who answered, the two of them already working in tandem like two perfect cogs of a wheel.

"All that time spent working in coffeehouses has given your father a pretty good idea of how to run one. And God knows I've got enough connections down here—we're going to open a café, make it kind of an artist's retreat—have book readings and open mic nights and poetry slams. Have live music—display local artists.

Make it a community hangout."

"Of course you are." I didn't mean to sound sarcastic or like I was blowing off their dream. I really didn't. Actually, to my ears I sounded sort of…matter of fact. Maybe stunned. In a stupid sort of way, because I just couldn't come up with anything else to say. But before Nora could nail me again for being an insensitive little brat, Stan spoke up.

"And I'm going to work on my book again, Libby. Really work on it."

"Of course you are."

Stan, thankfully, seemed to get that I was in genuine shock and didn't take it personally. Leaving Nora's side, he sat beside me, taking my hand in his. "Ethan was amazing with me these last few months, Libby. He encouraged and critiqued and tore my ass apart in ways that no one has since I was a snot-nosed English major. In ways that let me know he was really taking me seriously and that he thought I had the chops to do this. Made me really feel it was time to settle down and actually *do* something about the thing and not have it continue to be this amorphous, some-day-in-the-future pipe dream. One of the last things he said to me—that it was one thing to have the dream, but you had to have real balls to act on it."

God, Ethan. Yet another gift. I had no idea how the wily bastard did it, but he did. I know he did. A gift for me and maybe more importantly, for Nora because he'd loved her too. I hope she realized it.

"So yeah, I'll be sticking around."

"Of *course* you are."

Nearly forty years of independence and go where the wind blows attitude and now, he was going to turn into Father Knows Best—he and Nora setting up a happy little love nest. If Nora started wearing pearls and he started calling me "Kitten" I was *so* gone. As it stood, I was seriously verging on the edge of hysteria here. Just too much drama for one afternoon, with Nora and Stan and acknowledging that Ethan really was dead and wasn't coming back. That he'd known about Nick.

Nick…here—then gone.

Two losses, one day. Just…too much.

Stan's steady, entirely too kind gaze conveyed he understood just how close to the edge I was riding, even if he didn't completely understand all the reasons why.

"You look beat. We'll talk some more later. We'll have plenty of time to talk more." Smoothing my hair back from my face, he pressed a kiss against my temple—smoothed my hair again. "Your hair looks pretty like this baby girl. You should wear it down more often."

A final stroke down the length of it and then he was rejoining Nora in the doorway where she leaned into him, her arm going around his waist. Looking over her shoulder she said, "We'll clean up in the kitchen and lock up behind ourselves, Liberty. Your father's right. You look tired. Should try to rest."

Her voice was mild and those dark, dark eyes, difficult as ever to read, didn't give me a hint as to how she was really feeling. It didn't really matter. I suspected that with Stan in the picture for good, she'd hash it out with him, and he'd make her see reason or at least get her to lay off. Anyone who'd lived in as many places and interacted with people from as many walks of life as he had—God only knows the stories he'd heard. The things he'd seen. I mean, a barista was just one step removed from a bartender, right?

Curling up on my side, I felt for Ethan's shirt beneath my pillow, gently stroked the edge of a sleeve as I watched Nora and Stan walk down the hall, arm in arm, the late-afternoon shadows making their bodies meld into one dark, beautiful abstract form.

And as I caught a faint whiff of Nick's cologne on the loose hair drifting over my cheek, I allowed one final tear to escape.

Nick

JUNE 2

I liked that my home office had big windows. These days, I liked even better that they faced east, instead of west, like the ones in the sunroom. Meant that once the sun crossed past my windows on its way to yet another glorious sunset, my view was usually shades of blue and gray, shadows crowding the corners, even as the light hung on, usually past eight at night this time of year. Unless of course, it was raining. Also pretty common for this time of year and pretty much just as welcome as the shadows.

And what the hell was I doing there, sitting in shadows? I should be doing something, right? Anything, to try to fix the rathole insanity that passed for my life. I'd come home that day in April, full of every good intention in the world—to try to honor what Libby and I had had by making things right with Kath and bitch of it was, I couldn't. It's like I was frozen. Still so filled with Libby and the lingering sense of what might have been that was so damn tempting—and dangerous.

"You need time to mourn, *m'ijo*."

That's what Tico had said, last time I saw him, a couple of weeks back. Once I confessed, on our usual park bench in Little Havana, that I'd had to see Libby one last time to say goodbye—once he'd been assured that the battle had been fought and won and I was as at peace with my choices as I'd ever be—that's what he'd said.

"Mourn what? I'm the one who's got everything."

"Do you?"

Damn enigmatic Jesuit.

It's not that I didn't know what he meant, but it was all about context. Bet he knew that too.

Since Tico's advice hadn't been half bad in the past, and not having any better ideas myself, I took him at his word. Made a deliberate effort to retreat into myself, into a quiet place where I wasn't always moving, always on the run, mentally or physically, in some desperate effort to exhaust myself and not be able to think too hard. I forced myself to stop and take the time to mourn—and ask myself the hard questions. And after weeks of introspection that could put a monk to shame, all I could come up with was that the answers weren't going to be easy to come by. That it was going to take time.

Freakin' Tico. Lay money he knew that too.

But I missed her so damn much. Didn't even have her column with which to hold on to her, because since Ethan's final column, there hadn't been anything else. She must have decided she wasn't up to it, which pissed me off and was the one thing that nearly had me calling. Didn't she know how talented she was? And it wasn't just that *I* needed to hear her voice again, even if it was in print or onscreen or *whatever*. A lot of people needed to hear her. That unique brand of girly wisdom, as she'd put it, that was as much practical as it was compassionate and influenced by her nutty, unorthodox upbringing, whether she ever actually admitted it or not.

"Nick—may I?"

I twisted around on the sofa, finding Kath standing just inside the door, a folder in one hand.

"Yeah, sure." I gestured for her to join me on the sofa. "Always, Kath."

"Well, you've been in here a lot, lately—working, I guess?" Settling herself on the opposite end of the couch, she ran her fingers around her ear, as if pushing back hair that would most likely be long enough to push back in a few more months. As it was, she already had a full head, buzz-cut length, and a dark reddish-brown that was different, but still suited her, making her eyes look that much bluer.

"Working. Thinking, too." Not that long ago, I wouldn't have admitted that. Not to her—figuring she wouldn't care one way or another. But that was one of those issues I'd been working out. That situation had to change. I had to be more open with Kath. Not bludgeon-her-over-the-head-with-information open, but just let her in on what was going on in my head. Leave opportunity for her to ask.

She spread her hand over the folder that was now on her lap. "There's a coincidence. I've been thinking too and I..." She stopped and shrugged. "I kind of wanted your opinion on something. If you've got the time?"

"Of course, Kath. Why wouldn't I?" Especially since this was probably the first time in nearly a year that she'd asked for my opinion on anything.

"Well...if you were working...I hate to bother you." Her fingers played around her ear again, as if she was desperate to have her long hair back, to twist a strand between her fingers as she wrestled for words in a way that was utterly foreign. "And it's not like I should expect you to drop everything at my whim, especially with...well, the way we've...that I..."

"You should expect my attention." Slowly, I slid across the sofa, stopping with a good foot between us so I wouldn't crowd her and carefully slid one hand under hers on the folder, ready to pull back if she flinched or even so much as narrowed her eyes. "Anytime you want, Kath."

It was just for a brief second, but I felt her fingers close around mine, just enough pressure to let me know it was on purpose. And she didn't draw away, but rather, used her free hand to pull the folder out from beneath our hands.

"What'd you want to ask about, babe?"

The muscles in her throat worked and her mouth moved but it's like she couldn't quite bring herself to say it. So I tried to make it easier for her—took the folder that clearly had something to do with what she wanted to ask, and put it on the cushion between us.

Opening it, I studied the contents with the same attention to detail I used on game tapes.

"I…I've been thinking about it for a while, Nicky. That maybe it's time."

I looked from the folder to her face. "You don't have to do this, Kath. Honest to God, you don't."

"I know I don't, but I think I want to."

Thinking she wanted to wasn't good enough. "Make damn sure you want to, babe. You shouldn't go through this unless it's something you really want." I looked back down at the series of before and after pictures of various breast reconstructions. She hadn't said a word about it since that last brutal fight when she'd told me how it felt having the saline pumped into her body and stretching her skin, how she'd just wanted to crawl out of herself. And she'd been in so much pain, physical and otherwise, that I'd prayed she wouldn't go any further with it, especially when it would involve more surgery and more pain.

"Just so that we're clear, I certainly don't need or expect you to do it."

"I know, Nick." Her gaze was focused on our hands, her voice soft, and with each word, sounding more unsure—so not like her. "But *I* need to do it, I think. I want to feel pretty again. Feel whole."

It wasn't that, though. She could do that with a wig and makeup or just by getting healthy again. We both knew that. But by telling me she wanted to make this kind of a physical commitment…

She was done just existing. She wanted to live.

I lifted my free hand to her cheek and brushed my fingertips against her pale skin with the hints of pink returning to the cheeks. My heartbeat sped up as she closed her eyes and leaned into the touch.

"Let me know how I can help?" With feeling pretty, with advice, with any damn thing, I added silently and hoped she could hear and understand how I meant it.

Her eyes opened and she smiled. "Double Ds?"

"'Scuse me?"

Her grin got broader, exposing the two small dimples that had returned as she regained weight. Gradually, everything was coming back. Maybe different, like her hair, but coming back.

She pulled her hand free from mine and gestured at her chest. "Should I go for the porn star boobs? I mean, if I've got the chance..."

I laughed out loud in a way I hadn't done since—

No. I couldn't think of that now. That had been time out of time, and I needed to let it go and move forward with Katharine. My wife. And hopefully, my friend once again. "You know, once upon a time, I might've jumped at that chance, but that's when I was young and ignorant."

"Oh?"

"I've heard some of the guys on the team talking about making it with super-enhanced chicks."

Her eyebrows rose. "Yeah?"

"Like bouncing off an icy trampoline."

After we both quit laughing, I took her hand in mine again—again, being careful to keep my hold loose, giving her the opportunity to pull away at any time. "Whatever you want, Kath. Seriously."

"I'll think on it some more." Pulling her hand free, she closed the folder. "In the meantime, do you want to go out for some dinner?"

Another mental sigh of relief. Not only did she want to keep on living, it seemed as if she wanted to do it with me. And for the first time in a long time, I started to feel like maybe, just maybe, I was making the right decisions. "That'd be nice. Sushi?"

"Are you going out of town?" Since once upon a time it had been our usual before-a-trip ritual.

I shook my head. "No, but as it happens, there's actually something I wanted to talk to you about, too—ask your opinion. Although I'm pretty sure I know what I want to do, I still want your input and, besides, I'm just in the mood for sushi. Sound good?"

"Sounds wonderful." Pausing by the door, she turned back. "Nicky?"

"Yeah?"

"Thank you, baby."

I nodded and waited for her to close the door behind her before I pulled out my phone. Pulling up a contact and dialing, I waited for it to ring its customary three times before it was picked up.

"You miserable sonuvabitch, you're actually alive."

I laughed. "Yes, you smartass. and it's not like I didn't just talk to you last week. Jesus, Bob, you're still worse than my mother." I settled more comfortably into the sofa and listened to him continue to bitch for another minute before I broke in. "Bobby—shut up a second."

"What?"

"Listen, how would you feel about having a legit opportunity to chew my ass out? On a regular basis, even?"

"Are you fucking serious?"

"You've been after me to do this for what? The last two years?"

"Three years, four months, and I'll have to check with my secretary—excuse me, *executive assistant*—but I think, twelve days."

"Smartass." I laughed again, then shook my head, not quite believing I was actually doing this but completely certain over how right it felt. "I must be out of my mind, but yeah, I'm serious. I need to talk to Kath about it before I give you a final answer, but…yeah."

His voice got softer, all the sarcasm and joking gone. "I think it'll be a good thing, Nicky."

"Yeah, me too."

Libby

JUNE 10

Three phone calls, a few thousand e-mails, and a trip to Hawaii could work wonders in changing a girl's mind.

The three phone calls had been from Ethan's editor—now my editor. The first one had been to warn me about the column running and to formally offer me the job of taking over for Ethan. The second one had come after I'd regretfully turned him down, and he'd said that Ethan had told him that's what I'd do and to give me a couple of weeks.

Honest to God, it was almost enough to drive me to one of Nora's shaman/priest/*santero* friends to try to communicate with the inveterate pain in the ass. Jerking my chain from beyond the grave—now there was a gift.

The third phone call came a week later and, thankfully, wasn't prompted by Ethan in any way, shape, or form. This was simply Toby, my about-to-be-editor, begging me to allow him to forward the e-mails they'd been receiving for Ethan—and me.

Fine. I wouldn't even have to look at them, right? But then, they started streaming into my inbox—one thousand two thousand…I stopped looking at the counter after three thousand, because I was seriously freaking out by that point. Toby, as wily a bastard as my husband had ever been, personally forwarded a few that had been sent directly to him. Predictably, they expressed sorrow over Ethan's death, but more unpredictably, at least to me, many asked when my next column would run.

You can bet I checked their provenance to make sure, because, honestly, there wasn't much I wouldn't put past Ethan.

Once I was assured the e-mails were legit, I told Toby to give me two weeks. Two weeks and I'd be his—editorially speaking, that is.

The first week I spent in Hawaii. Maybe it was a little on the self-flagellation side, deliberately returning to this beautiful, magical place where Ethan and I had gone to celebrate his first recovery—to plan and dream and revel in each other and how much we were in love and how happy—but strangely, it didn't have the feeling of punishment. Not at all. I was able to spend hours walking along a beach and splashing in water and thinking, and something in the thick sea and fruit-scented air, the powdery sand, and endless, impossibly blue Pacific—so different from my moody Atlantic—served as a balm.

I said my goodbyes to Ethan there.

As for Nick…my goodbyes for him were a little more complex. I'd said them with that final kiss, but hadn't really let go. But that was the other thing Hawaii gave me. The knowledge that maybe I wouldn't be able to—at least, not for a while. Maybe not for a long while. And that realization actually lessened the constant hurt that was Nick. He could live in his place in my mind and in my heart—not at the surface, but not completely gone either and that was okay, too.

The second week, I spent just sorting through the letters, reading them, making notes, every once in a while crying. Most of them were so sweet—condolences, encouragement, sympathy, stories of people who'd gone through the same thing, be it the loss of a spouse or the cancer or both.

There was one from a little girl:

Dear Miss Libby,

I am very sorry that your husband went to heaven because of cancer. I hope he's found my gramma. She makes really good cookies. She'll take care of him.

If Ethan had found Gramma, he was probably teaching her how to play Texas Hold 'Em.

Then there was this one:

Libby,
> *So sorry for your loss. It must be hard on such a young woman.*
> *But I saw your picture. You're pretty hot—a chick like you shouldn't*
> *go without for too long, so when you're ready to date again—*

Yeah, I deleted it after that point. Whackjob.
Then this caught my eye:

Dear Libby,
> *How did you cope?*

That was it.

Dear Libby,
> *How did you cope?*

Six words, and for the first time in a long time I felt it. The creative buzz thrumming through my veins, my fingers practically itching as they rested on the keyboard. Sitting at the table in my sunny kitchen, mug of coffee beside me, Butch in my lap, Sundance under my feet, and Joni Mitchell on the stereo, I found myself smiling. I was smiling because I knew what I was going to write and I was...

Happy.

Opening a blank document, I quickly typed:

How Did You Cope?
by Libby Walker

Then, I sat, hands poised, staring at the pristine expanse for another endless moment, knowing this was it—point of no return. Because the minute I started typing, it was the beginning, everything that had happened to this point...the past.

My fingers practically started on their own, slow at first, then gradually faster as the words flowed like it was something that had been restrained for the longest time and was anxious to break free.

How did you cope?

That was the entirety of a letter I received today. One of many, many thousands of letters full of sympathy and condolences and similar tales of loss, and to all of you who read my husband's words and had them touch you to such an extent that you felt compelled to write, I thank you. But then there was this one simple e-mail, just that one question, not even a signature. And thing is, the answer was immediate. It was right there and I knew it, like I know my name and the feel of my dog's fur against my bare feet and the beauty of a Florida Keys sunset. I knew it, because in the last several years—this last year, in particular—it's grown to be as intrinsic a part of my nature as everything else I mentioned. And although it's almost beautiful in its simplicity, it was a lesson that was painfully hard in the learning.

I know going in, this is going to sound unbelievably selfish, but I suspect that anyone who's gone through this will understand. You see, the thing that became most important, that ultimately saved me, was finding a unique space for myself. Carving out a place for myself where the cancer didn't exist, where things were normal, where I was simply Libby with no other identity or agenda.

I coped by finding a space where I could just…breathe.

Acknowledgments

This book has had such a remarkable journey that to acknowledge everyone who's had a hand in bringing it to this stage would yield text almost as long as the book itself. So, in the interests of keeping it brief:

Thank you, first and foremost, to my most remarkable agent, Adrienne Rosado, who was always game for another go with this manuscript. She is also a fine whisky connoisseur and most excellent talker-off-ledges—all good things for an agent to be.

Thanks to my very patient editor, Randall Klein, who took this book and with his enthusiasm, made me see how it could be made even better.

To Sarah, Hannah, Brielle, and the rest of the team at Diversion—thank you, thank you, thank you, for helping to make this dream a reality.

To my WriterGirls, y'all are the bread to my butter. Love you beyond all redemption.

To my Facebook and Twitter families—you guys take a very isolating job and make me feel as if I work in the world's most social office with the biggest water cooler ever.

To my family—Lewis, Nate, and Abby—you're my everything. Never ever forget that.

Finally (and this may sound odd) I need to acknowledge singer Josh Groban. It was his interpretation of "Broken Vow" so very many years ago that planted the seeds for this story that would not let go. At all. For that I either owe him a huge debt of thanks or to shower endless curses upon his head. I settle for thanks.

CPSIA information can be obtained at www.ICGtesting.com
Printed in the USA
BVOW08s0217220515

401411BV00001B/10/P

9 781626 817012